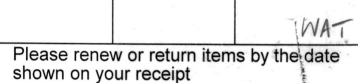

D0508954

BY LINDSEY PIPER

Dragon Kings series:

Silent Warrior (e-novella)
Caged Warrior
Blood Warrior
Hunted Warrior

HUNTED WARRIOR

LINDSEY PIPER

THE DRAGON KINGS
BOOK THREE

PIATKUS

First published in the United States in 2015 by Pocket Books,
A Division of Simon & Schuster, Inc., New York
First published in Great Britain in 2015 by Piatkus

1 3 5 7 9 10 8 6 4 2

A CIP catalogue record for this book
is available from the British Library.

ISBN 978-0-349-40305-2

Printed and bound in Great Britain by
Clays Ltd, St Ives plc

Papers used by Piatkus are from well-managed forests
and other responsible sources.

MIX
Paper from
responsible sources
FSC® C104740

Piatkus
An imprint of
Little, Brown Book Group
Carmelite House
50 Victoria Embankment
London EC4Y 0DZ

An Hachette UK Company
www.hachette.co.uk

www.piatkus.co.uk

To NCW and RM.
We made it.

ACKNOWLEDGMENTS

I am forever grateful to the following people for making this book possible: Lauren McKenna, Elana Cohen, Kevan Lyon, Cathleen DeLong, Tria Braun, Sarah Maudlin, Mary and Janet, Fedora Chen, Sarah Frantz Lyons, Ericka Brooks, Dave Schilz, the Group That Shall Not Be Named, Dennis and Kathleen Stone, and Keven, Juliette, and Ilsa Lofty. From confidante to life raft to compassionate professional, you've been there for me. I thank you.

HUNTED
WARRIOR

✗ CHAPTER ✗
ONE

They called her the Pet, but she didn't think of herself as a creature in need of protection, care, or condescension. She'd left that life behind. Neither was she a captive, as she picked her way through the ruins of a crumbling rock labyrinth on the island of Crete. How she'd come to be there was a story she didn't dare contemplate for fear of going mad. There was no rhyme, no reason, no guide other than the future she saw in bits and patches.

The sun was fierce and gorgeously freeing on the back of her neck. She was a Dragon King, and Dragon Kings loved fire. Most wouldn't admit how much the cold sunk under their skin and sapped their sense of near-invincibility. Maybe that was for the best. The would-be gods didn't realize that all empires ended, even those blessed with access to what humans would consider supernatural.

Turning to stare into the blinding white-yellow glare, she didn't bother to shade her eyes. Her second sight— the gift from the Dragon that gave her the ability to see the future—was always with her, no matter its unpredictability. A man sought her.

A man who hid his violence behind titles and lineage.

Time was slippery like moss on a riverbank. Time was slippery on her fingertips. Time was running out.

She continued her cautious journey through the abandoned ruins of ancient kings. The ground was strewn with pieces of the crumbled labyrinth. Once-high walls had been reduced by countless rains and droughts, decades and centuries, until all that remained were bleached waist-high spikes and jagged edges. There was nothing to grab should she fall—not without impaling her hand. Dragon Kings healed rapidly, but some damage was too much for even their advanced physiology to repair.

Archaeologists had long ago dubbed the site of little historic worth. Its condition was so deteriorated that they could gather little new information about the Minoans of Crete. How blinded they were. Humans suffered the hubris of a society that believed itself the most advanced to ever walk the earth. Any thought as to the Dragon Kings' existence was disregarded as fairy tales of Valkyries and Olympians and countless messiahs.

The woman called the Pet knew differently. All the myths were true. What was once, would be again.

The Chasm isn't fixed.

Why her predictions of the future had led her to Crete as a means of stopping the Dragon Kings' slow extinction was beyond her. She had to trust. She'd always needed to trust, when little in her life stood as an example of why to believe. Maybe her real gift from the Great Dragon wasn't the ability to see the future but to have faith in what she couldn't explain.

The labyrinth was waist-high, yes, but it was still a tangle of dead ends, wrong turns, and twenty-foot pits. When she realized a mistake, she couldn't climb over the wall and continue on. Her hands would be shredded. So, as with all mazes, she doubled back and kept the details firmly in mind. The conventional wisdom was that if one chose a direction and stuck with it—all left turns, always, no matter what—the heart of the geometric puzzle would be revealed.

Those three-story pits barring certain passages made that impossible.

And time . . . Yes, time was slippery. She needed to hurry, because the man was coming.

Yet she couldn't even describe what she sought. A gift for Cadmin. That's all she knew.

She drew on powers as both soothsayer and true believer to remind herself of her journey's importance. Cadmin was the closest she'd ever known to having a baby of her own, although the fetal child had developed in another woman's womb.

"It took some time to find you," came a voice at her back. "But you knew I'd never give up."

The Pet turned and met the steady, distant glare of Malnefoley of Tigony, the Honorable Giva. With that title, he should've been the unquestioned leader of their people. His leadership was a listing ship, however—the derisive nickname the Usurper attested to as much— barely righting itself in time to escape the swell of each new wave. It wouldn't survive much longer.

"I escaped," she said. "I didn't attempt to hide."

"I'm taking you back to Greece." He flicked his eyes across the irregular half walls. He stood some two hundred meters away, just beyond the outermost wall that marked the border of the labyrinth. Given time and patience, he could climb across three lanes to apprehend her physically, but he had a gift far more crippling and violent than hers.

Electricity was his plaything.

"I don't want to go back to Greece." She pushed at the sleeves of her thin purple blouse, which contrasted with her militaristic cargo pants and heavy boots. She was a lover of contrast. In revealing bare skin, she also revealed parallel incisions across her left biceps that had healed to papery scars. "There's work to be done. For all Five Clans."

"You were Dr. Aster's companion for how many years? You commit blasphemy when speaking of the Five Clans."

"I *was* his companion. Now I'm not." She nodded to the parallel scars. "These are the reminders I gave myself as proof of my freedom and loyalty to our kind."

The intensity of Malnefoley's expression increased a hundredfold when he narrowed his eyes. His lips tightened. She could see his anger, even feel it, despite the distance and obstacles between them. He looked like an emperor whose displeasure would result in countless deaths.

Did others see him as she did? Were they so awed or bitter as to miss the signs? Or was fear what caused so many to whisper "Usurper" behind his back, rather than challenge him outright?

"You'll forgive me if I don't believe a brainwashed servant."

"I didn't serve him," she said, snarling.

You wouldn't understand. No one would.

In some warped way, her relationship with Dr. Heath Aster, heir to the human Aster cartel, was that of a victim coming to love her torturer. He had hurt her. He'd also left her in isolation for months at a time. She'd been twelve years old on the first day of her imprisonment. After decades of such treatment, she'd craved his attention, no matter how painful, because being alone was far more devastating. Affection was a strange emotion to feel for the man her logical mind knew was her abuser, her dismantler, her maker.

"You aided in the perpetuation of his crimes," the Giva said. "You helped him keep hundreds of Dragon Kings imprisoned as the victims of his sick experiments."

She exhaled. Her shoulders slumped, which was a surprise. Had she really expected anything different from the Giva? "Your mind won't be changed by anything I say."

Without looking at him again, she resumed her slow, careful push through the ruins, searching, not knowing what her eyes—her *soul*—needed to find.

"You can't walk away from me." His voice was no louder now, but more commanding. He possessed some trick of supreme confidence. It radiated from him like the pulse of heat from a raging furnace.

"I can if you don't know the way to follow," she said.

The hair on the backs of her arms and neck lifted—such susceptible little pores, awakened by the smallest wash of fear. The Giva, however, was no slight threat. The Tigony were like turbine engines. They pulled bits of electricity out of the air, down to the barest hint of static, then whirled and intensified them into storms worthy of the mighty Zeus throwing lightning bolts. The Pet briefly wondered if Malnefoley was descended from the Tigony man who must have inspired timeless Greek myths of Mount Olympus.

"You'll come back with me," he said, his voice darkly ominous. "Now."

She turned a corner, then another, looking back only briefly.

He was the revered, hated, distrusted, *undeniable* Malnefoley of Tigony.

He should've looked ridiculous wearing an Armani suit in the middle of an abandoned archaeological site. Yet, tall and imposing, his body was built for well-tailored clothing. Electricity snapped from his fingers and arced like a heavenly rainbow across his aristocratic features. The sun was merciless, but it cast shadows as it dipped toward the west. The Giva banished shadow. He was completely illuminated. Blue eyes were bluer. Cheekbones were more dramatic. Blond hair was transformed into filaments of gold.

He bore his considerable power as if it were feather-light.

Surrounded by the snapping proof of his clan's magnificence, he adopted a grim, humorless smile. "Don't make me repeat myself. And don't give me reason to lose my temper."

"You won't hurt me. I spent enough months detained in your Tigony fortress to know that. You're too convinced of my worth."

Her heartbeat was a metronome that kept time with all the subtlety of a sledgehammer, pounding a frightened tempo in her chest. She had survived so much, and she would survive the Giva in all his tempestuous conceit. But surviving was wearisome.

Rest was a word from another language.

Cadmin was waiting for her. Somewhere. The Pet could only pick her way through the rubble and wait for the worst to happen, let it pass through her, and move on. That had been her life. That would always be her life. She gave herself a moment to absorb the sadness and pain, then reduced it down and down and down until she could breathe.

When it came, the bolt of electricity stole her vision, obliterated her ability to hear, and seemed to peel back layer after layer of skin. In the moment between strike and agony, she was glad she couldn't see her half-bared arms, for fear of finding exposed bone rather than healthy flesh.

But the agony would not be denied. Her heart's metronome stopped its clicking smash. She blinked three times and fell to the rocky ground.

The crackle and fire in Mal's veins was like having indulged in the strongest spirits. No, even stronger. Lava replaced blood. He was made of lightning and his pulse boomed like thunder. The release of a single bolt of concentrated energy was practical; it did the trick. But it was also a tease. A woman sliding slim, feminine hands between his thighs, massaging, urging, then jerking away—that would've been less frustrating. When he let his gift build and build, it was such a temptation to let it *all* go.

Yet he had taught himself restraint a very long time ago. He was cautious in his use of violence, no matter the resentment that simmered deep in his bones. His temper, if left unchecked, could level cities. He knew firsthand.

As the head of the Council that served and oversaw the governments of the Five Clans, he was the consummate politician. In truth, he was a warrior forced to live a lie. He was no politician, not in his heart and his blackest soul.

That didn't mean he was prone to giving in to the urge to solve disputes with force. His temper was ever-present, but it was a constant reminder of his younger, deadlier self. It was a part of him he constantly needed to restrain, for the sake of the Dragon Kings.

Dr. Aster's Pet, however, was an exception.

Unlike members of Clan Pendray with their berserker furies, the Tigony were a refined people. Mal knew his gift's potential down to the slightest variable. To deliver his electric punch, he had taken into account an estimation of the woman's weight and physical condition, and even the ambient temperature. The result was a strike strong enough to knock her out for no more than two minutes, without lasting damage.

Then he breathed. He put his fleeting, petulant anger away. For two decades, he'd been the Honorable Giva, even when behaving like a calm, neutral leader had constricted him like a full-body straightjacket. That entailed rational thought, smooth negotiations, and measured discussion—the training he'd received from his parents, the heads of the Tigony royal house. For years, he'd kept his powers close like a gambler holding a straight flush.

The Pet was far too canny for his liking. He needed

her back in the Tigony stronghold. And he needed her to start talking. That meant finding her in that tangled labyrinth. She'd dropped to the ground following his blast, behind the rugged half walls of the ruins.

Five days before, she'd escaped the stronghold of Clan Tigony, high in the mountains of Greece. He didn't know how. None of his guards—loyal and tested—knew how. It was as if she'd transformed into air, swished through ventilation shafts, and caught the first breeze south to Crete. Yet she told the truth: A woman who feared getting caught would've made a better point of hiding. When he asked humans about an unusual, plain-speaking, coltish young woman with wild raven-black hair, the answers had been quick and sure.

She had served Dr. Aster as his devoted companion—so devoted that no one referred to her as anything other than the Pet. She must know the madman's secrets, including how he was able to help Dragon Kings conceive. A woman connected to the highest echelon of the Aster cartel was invaluable.

Why was she here? What scheme was she enacting? Something on behalf of the Asters?

That didn't ring true. If she wanted to remain with the insane doctor, she would've escaped with the man when Mal had helped liberate his cousin from the Asters' laboratories in the Canadian tundra. Instead, the Pet had stayed behind. She had surrendered to Mal without protest. Every minute since had been a study in silence and frustration—silence from her, and frustration strong enough to consume his patience.

He didn't have time for this.

After removing his suit coat, he wadded it into a ball.

The expensive fabric served as protection as he vaulted one of the jagged half walls. Navigating one at a time, he hoisted himself up using the coat as padding for his hands. The ancient, crumbling rock was flaked and chipped like shale honed to razors.

He topped the last wall. A jerk behind his knees sent him sprawling onto the unforgiving ground. The Pet. She'd been pressed flat against the wall, waiting for him.

His head connected with a boulder the size of a large melon.

"*Bathatéi*," he shouted, using the worst curse in the shared language of the Dragon Kings.

The descending sun stole his vision. He jerked his head to the side by instinct alone. Metal scraped against rock. Sparks shot against his cheek. Those sparks might not have been visible to the naked eye, but he absorbed their minute flashes of power. He snatched them out of the air and armored his skin with the living equivalent of an electrical fence.

The Pet landed another blow, in the form of brass knuckles against his breastbone. Thudding pain shot out from the center of his chest, while she screamed. Electricity arced from the knuckles to his chest and back again. She landed on her ass, her elfin features enraged. Telltale quivers made her muscles jump and twitch. But she didn't give up. She landed two more hits, one against his temple, and as he rolled—again by instinct—one to the base of his spine.

Part of him conceded that the strike was perfect. Part of him was too enraged to care.

She landed atop his chest, squatting. Her boots were heavy. They fortified her slight weight. Beneath his dress shirt, Mal's skin was stretched by the industrial treads of their soles.

The Pet grabbed a fistful of hair and yanked his head off the ground. "You're bleeding."

"That would be your fault."

"The rock's fault. I take credit for making you fall." She shoved his head back down, then smeared her palm across his shirt. He caught the distinctly coppery smell of blood.

He was more surprised that her touch seemed designed to enflame and entice, as much as serve a practical purpose. Just how much had Dr. Aster, that psychotic fifty-something sadist, taught her in *all* means of combat?

Anger wasn't a strong enough word for the flames gathering in his hands. His palms felt as if beetles and maggots wiggled across his skin. The only way to banish it was to let the electricity build and burn—then unleash it.

He whirled away. She didn't lose her balance but had to jump to the side. She was petite and agile. The way she'd recovered from his initial blast was impressive. Both stood in loose fighting stances. Only now, she held a switchblade.

"You don't experience pain," he said, squaring off against her.

"I experience pain. You'd rather think that I don't."

He called on deep muscle memory to fight her hand-to-hand. Another concentrated, precise strike took time to build, but his was already prepped and ready to burst. He had always been more powerful than most of his clansmen—so quick to gather more and more energy into his personal arsenal. At that moment he could've blown up a mountain, but he didn't want to lobotomize her. Martial training was the only alternative.

He swept his leg to try and catch behind her calves, but she jumped straight up, then landed with the ease of a cat. She twirled to one side and stabbed him twice in the shoulder. The sharp spike of her assault made him grunt. Her control of the blade was faster than he would've thought possible. Was she of Clan Garnis? So scattered as to be nicknamed the Lost, the Garnis possessed amazing senses and reflexes, but her features were more delicate than those hearty nomads.

He had yet to determine the Pet's clan, or even her gift from the Dragon.

Still more mysteries he intended to solve.

Mal caught her trailing wrist. He yanked her against his body, spun, and used that momentum to slam her against one of the half walls. She caught her balance by gripping the razor-sharp shale. Her shriek was as wild as it was anguished. She dropped the switchblade. Mal tried to pin her, but the attempt wasn't fast enough. When was the last time he'd used his body to fight? His muscles were unfamiliar weapons, but they were weapons he relished rediscovering.

She launched off the wall, which added power to her punch. Brass knuckles connected with his jaw.

He reeled. His lip was split. More sparks crackled where her metal met his skin. She squealed as the electricity spiked up her arm. They circled one another like two starving wolves whose only option was cannibalism.

"I'm walking away now," she said simply.

"I can't let you do that."

"Then we keep fighting until one of us is a cripple. How long until you lose your temper and do too much damage? I'll be useless to you."

Mal breathed heavily through his nose. He would've rather dangled over a volcano than have his options so limited.

"Do you want to be caught?" he asked. "You could've bribed any bus driver and boat captain who helped you escape the mainland."

"I have nothing to use as a bribe."

"Women always do."

Her eyes became slits, her expression murderous. "Not an option."

"Why are you here?"

"I'm looking for something."

"For what?"

"I don't know."

"Nothing good will come from testing me," he said. "Because you're right. I might lose my temper. I might destroy the only link I have to the Aster cartel and the answer to Dragon King conception. Not that it'll matter to you by then."

"A tempest in a suit. Does the Council know who sits at the head of their table?"

"No." He stepped forward. "Do you think I need you in particular? You're convenient. You're valuable. Yet other Dragon Kings are connected with the cartels. I'll find them, one by one, just like I found you, until I get the answers our people need."

She tsked as if patronizing a child. "I'm sure altruism propels you."

"What do you mean?"

Standing to her full height for the first time, which wasn't very tall at all, she smirked. She packed so much disdain in the single lift of a midnight brow. *"Our people?* No. In your heart, Honorable Giva, you only want to win. At any price."

✢ CHAPTER ✢
TWO

Now I'm done with you," she said simply. "I have work to do."

The Pet once again turned from the Giva, although she would've been amused at finding a way to push him to lose control. Amusement was out of the question—and in this case, deadly. Her head throbbed and her fingers burned, as if the brass knuckles were fused to her skin. His electrical strikes still snaked under her skin, and the adrenaline of their fight was wearing off. What remained was a numb lack of coordination following his lightning strike. Her limbs felt leaden, her stomach a rage of nausea and pain. But she had to continue.

Forget the Giva.

Cadmin needed her.

"Why are you here?" he asked again.

She wouldn't have replied had his voice been wrathful, wheedling, or derisive. No, for the first time the Honorable Giva—such a cumbersome title to carry, like lead across one's back—sounded curious.

"To find something."

"Back to games?" He stood with the wide stance of a man used to commanding armies, not leading Council meetings. "You're all half answers and deception, keeping secrets someone would have to beat out of you."

"Someone?" She gestured to the empty vastness of that deserted plain. The labyrinth was its only feature. "Or *you*? Either stop me or help me."

"Help you?"

His indignation was nearly comical. The Pet wasn't used to smiling, but a fist made of fear in her chest loosened. Just a little. She wasn't sure she wanted it to; she held on to her fear because it kept her safe. No one could hurt her if she assumed that everything could cause suffering.

"Yes," she said, kicking aside a long, thin shaving of rock. "I'll know it when I see it."

She heard his strides over the rubble as if he were walking with his fancy dress shoes through the marble-tiled foyer of a magnificent palace, not the tumbledown remains of old ambitions. "Then how am I supposed to help you find it? Read your mind?"

"You're not Indranan."

Malnefoley grabbed her arm and spun her to a stop. "More fighting?" she asked. "I'm game."

"Look at me."

Her head snapped up as if she wore a collar that had been jerked by a leash. She'd known that feeling for too many years, publicly paraded as Dr. Aster's literal pet. She'd borne the humiliation by turning off a great many parts of her mind.

Only the children mattered.

And the riddle of the Chasm.

Although energy still pulsed from his skin like the hot waves of a mirage, he was merely frowning. Confused, maybe. Frustrated, definitely. But he was no longer angry. She was instantly on guard, waiting for the trick. There was always a trick.

"No more fighting." He glanced down to where blood still seeped from the knife strikes she'd landed. "And I'd rather have you talking than drooling."

"That pesky temper."

"Shut up."

"Touchy."

He pursed his lips around what might have been another raging curse. "You argue like a child and reduce me to your level."

"You behave like a bully and reduce me to yours."

Both of his hands clamped her upper arms. "Explain yourself, you servile *thing*. Why did you escape, only to stand here where anyone could see? Where *I* could see?"

A thing.

She'd never been anything else. No wonder some youthful, desperate part of her had interpreted his manipulation as flattery.

But she was free now. She would find Cadmin. *I knew your mother . . . I knew you . . .*

"What gift do you believe I possess, Giva?"

His frown was back. The jewel-like richness of his eyes wasn't a single shade but a thousand shades from aquamarine to midnight. His jaw was broad. The hollows beneath sharp cheekbones were like the plains that surrounded them—impressive and austere. Only where his mouth parted, with hardly more than a glimmer of white teeth showing between sensual lips, did he reveal any potential for softness. Yet those sensual lips spoke the words of the enemy.

"You've said you have the ability to see the future." He smirked. "So have others."

"You doubt it."

"I do." Despite the assurance of Mal's declaration, she never flinched, never looked away. Her eyes were almost too large for her face, giving her a childlike impression of false youth. Brows that could only be described as dynamic were her most expressive features. Subtle movements from those elegant slashes of black revealed more than she probably would've liked. With her small mouth and a heart-shaped face that was widest across distinctive cheekbones, she looked nothing like any Dragon King he'd ever seen. "No clan boasts such power, not even those that focus on the mind rather than the body—the Indranan with their telepathy, or the Sath, who steal other Dragon Kings' abilities."

"I was a foundling. Occupy yourself here by pondering my unknown genealogy. I have work to do."

"Something you saw about the future?" His words were drenched in snide disbelief.

"Yes."

No one had ever believed her abilities except for the occasional Sath, who temporarily acquired her gift to see would-be, could-be moments. The woman known as Silence had been one such individual. That singular warrior had come away from their few brief encounters—down in the Asters' Cages—with no doubts.

The Giva would need to be maneuvered differently. She didn't want to fight him again, because losing was a definite possibility. He might not liquefy her brain, but he could take her back to Greece. She'd lose the chance to help Cadmin, however the Dragon intended. Needing time to recover more fully from his lightning strike, she worked to appeal to his ego and occupy his mind. He was brilliant; she knew that much. No one had ever disputed his intelligence, which made throwing around the insult "Usurper" all the more believable. Had he been a simpleton, he wouldn't be accused of every plot devised in the last twenty years. Had he been any less arrogant, he wouldn't have fought to keep his title.

"Imagine this," she said. "An ancient endeavor, human or Dragon King, was built here. The sun is not blunted. Monsoon rains fall without impediment." She nodded to the east. "The slope of the plain invites the wind to gather along that rise, then hurls it with more force. So why here? Why build something so complex where it was destined to be sanded away?"

"All old buildings crumble. Half walls and curious humans aren't anything new."

"We're near no city. No village."

For the first time since his antagonistic arrival, the Giva seemed to focus his thoughts on something other than melting or recapturing her. He cut an elegant figure at a distance, but he was imposing at such close range. She stood no taller than his collarbones. His pristine white dress shirt had been ripped open so that two buttons were missing. Blood stained the shirtsleeve covering the arm she'd stabbed. The fine cloth was dyeing crimson. He was dusty and sweaty, as she was. A powdered grit had settled into the fine lines at the corners of his eyes and on either side of his slender nose. No matter the grime, he maintained the air of an angel who wouldn't deign to set foot on the ground. That would be too humble for a soul such as he.

She knew better. The Giva was the highest of their kind, but he was earthy and sordid as well. He didn't get his hands dirty while standing on high. But Malnefoley of Tigony could bleed and sweat with everyone else.

Now his mind was at work. While the Giva scanned the plain and seemed to process her questions, her observations, the Pet stared at the notch at the base of his throat where tan skin pulsed with life. His veins told tales of exertion and adrenaline levels as elevated as hers. A rivulet of sweat trickled down the side of his Adam's apple and settled in that notch, leaving a damp streak in its path. She wanted another to appear so she could watch its progress.

Enticing. That was the word. He was enticing.

"It was a prison."

The Pet nodded. "Good. The Minotaur. That sort."

"Minotaur? *The* Minotaur?"

"What other?"

"You're talking about a half-bull man who ate the human flesh of prisoners cast into his labyrinth."

"Yes."

"I don't know why I wasted so much time wondering if you have useful information about the cartels or the doctor's experiments." He straightened his cuffs and stared down at her. That shifting blue gaze must've intimidated hundreds, maybe thousands of people since he was chosen as Giva. The Pet only returned his stare, waiting for him to make his point, waiting for another chance to watch the trickles of sweat on his neck. "I might as well be talking to a chimpanzee who's spent the last few years being used for drug-test protocols."

"Am I a chimpanzee?"

He blinked and jerked his chin minutely to the side, as if he were the one waiting for a trick or a trap. "No."

"Then you only speak in insulting metaphor. I speak about the old ways."

He gave in to what must've been a painful injury by squeezing his hand over the meat of his shoulder where she'd stabbed deep. It would take at least a day before it healed. "The old ways? By telling tales about the Minotaur?"

"All the myths are true."

"You're joking."

"You'll know when I joke."

"How so?"

"I'll be as surprised as you." She sidestepped him and found her switchblade among the rocks. The steel was streaked with blood. She returned to the Giva. "Hold out your arm."

"You *are* mad."

"Hold out your arm."

"What do you promise in return?"

The Pet looked down at his patent leather shoes, which must've been shiny when he'd arrived in Crete. Now they were as chalk-dusted as the rest of him. He had caught his slacks on the rocks. The fabric was ripped along his thigh. Was he bleeding there, too? She didn't care about the injuries. He would heal. Quickly. But if they were together when night fell, the blood could attract whatever predators hunted these plains.

In return . . .

A promise in return . . .

"I'll tell you about Cadmin. Why I'm here."

"Will you apologize for stabbing me?"

"Only if you apologize for striking me with lightning."

Malnefoley twisted his lips, appearing rueful. "No."

Apparently an apology was more difficult than extending his arm toward a woman holding a knife, which he did with guarded strength. He was revealing more and more about himself—those things she doubted few ever examined too closely. The Pet looked at the expanse of white that hugged his strong forearms. A scant brush of blond hair edged out from his cuff and topped the back of his hand, which was curled into a fist crackling with electricity. He was ready to strike.

She lay the blade flat across his arm. He didn't flinch. With two swift strokes, she left streaks of brick red on the shirtsleeve. "All clean," she said, pocketing her switchblade.

She most certainly had his attention, which was more alluring than she was ready to admit. His expression was pure confusion. But she knew that with this man, confusion could quickly whirl into devastating anger. She saw it when she closed her eyes and caught glimpses of their shared future—the sensual future she'd seen since first meeting him amid the remnants of the Asters' ruined Canadian laboratory. She wanted to find that razor's edge and dance along it, daring him, daring herself.

Only, his anger dimmed. His skin no longer crackled in preparation for attack—or in retaliation for her mockery of his fine clothes and the injury she'd struck. He merely lowered his arm. "With your next words, you will explain yourself," he said with deadly calm. "Or by the Dragon, I will walk out of this maze with another murder to my name."

"Malnefoley, the Honorable Giva," she said smoothly, smiling. "I'd say how honored I am to meet the real you, but I believe you're in the mood to rip me inside out. So hear this. Cadmin was a fetus." She turned and spoke over her shoulder. "You'll come with me if you want to hear the rest."

Mal waited two heartbeats, so that he could discharge the flaring burn gathering in his fists. He shot it into the ground, which liquefied mica and shale. Liquefied minerals would cool into rough glass. Better to refashion the earth than to make good on his threat.

The Pet was a surprise. She had no rules. No order. She'd used his shirt to clean her knife—a knife streaked with his blood. She'd done it so simply, as if such a thing happened every day. She was dangerous, not because of what information she withheld or the allegiances she maintained, but because she spoke to him in the rough language of violence and spontaneity he'd long thought he had under control.

Polite political savages would just as soon scoop out his eye with a dessert spoon rather than speak plainly. He knew that every time he walked into the Council's meeting room in the Fortress of the Chasm, high up in the Himalayas. Sideways moves and plots within plans had been his language since childhood. The ultimate game of chess.

Sometimes he wanted to swipe an angered fist across the board and send the pieces flying. The Pet left him more tempted than ever. Few had ever heard him make threats. She now ranked among a rare assembly of people and Dragon Kings, most of whom were dead.

Mal followed her until he caught up, and they traversed the labyrinth side by side. She flinched, pulled away.

A flinch? What had happened to the woman who'd attacked him and crouched on his chest like a gargoyle in combat boots?

"There were many," she said, sounding as distant as the winds on the plains. "Fetuses. In the Asters' labs. And there were women. They'd earned the right to conceive—through their own actions, or because of a loved one who won Cage matches. I held the mothers' hands and looked into the years ahead. I told them the good and, if necessary, the bad." She stopped and crouched, tossing a few brambles aside from where they caught in a corner crevice. "For reasons I've never understood, those babies were born more robust and had a higher survival rate. My only explanation is that those glimpses of the future helped the mothers and fathers have more faith. They could do more than conceive. They would become parents. It gave them hope that was literally life sustaining."

"By looking into the years ahead?" Mal's head spun as he aligned the new information. "That's how Aster managed to achieve such a high percentage of healthy births?"

"Yes."

"No science? Just you? And . . . faith?"

She looked up at him with a sardonically arched brow. "Just?"

"This is more than you revealed in six months."

"Perhaps you weren't ready to listen." Standing, she shrugged. "We'll never know."

They continued through the labyrinth. Mal had thought the process of getting clear of the wreckage would be easier. He'd waded into the maze, having seen her petite form from across the plain. Now he was stuck with her in what should've been as simple as a child's toy. He loathed tasks where the details weren't his to orchestrate.

"Go on," he said. "Or you can tell me what we're looking for."

"You don't believe in the myths, so I won't."

"Back to the Minotaur? We seek his horns, maybe?"

She shot him a glare so sharp and cold that he forced himself to keep from looking away. She had green-gold eyes, as mercurial as a cat's, with a touch of frost that made her even harder to read. A wild, distant creature who moved like water, she held herself small and close, and spoke without pretense. Only subtle movements from those slashing brows gave him a clue as to her inner turmoil.

"Cadmin was not my first," she continued, apparently answering his barb with only her glare. "There had been dozens of others before her. I caught pieces of their lives. The Eiffel Tower. A bicycle accident. A first kiss. A rape. Tasting alligator meat for the first time. Anything that specifically hinted at a future meant they were viable."

"Even if you saw a rape?"

"It's life. Who was I to choose which lives should be lived? Only good ones? No. I only let it be known if it was possible. The parents, with all their love and devotion, did the rest."

The Pet veered to the left, then right again, as if she knew the way through the tangle. Her closed-off posture and quick yet graceful movements were unnerving. She walked with her head down as if someone might hit her if she looked to either side. Was that normal, or was it a result of Mal's presence?

"Here," she said. "This way. I know this wall."

"It looks like the rest."

"No. Here."

She ran her fingers along four grooves that traversed the length of the longest passage they'd found. She kicked aside a pyramid-shaped stack of rocks. "A funeral cairn. It's this way."

"If that was a cairn, why did you just destroy it?"

"Afraid of ghosts and lost souls, Giva? Are those acceptable myths?"

"Don't be ridiculous. Why did you do it?"

Those frosty green eyes roamed over his body, his face, but never reached up to find his gaze. "Do you feel like you're learning me yet?"

"No."

"That's why I did it."

"By randomly kicking the graves of the dead? That only adds evidence to the common wisdom that you're insane. Talk of soothsaying and reading the futures of unborn children doesn't help your case."

She touched the grooves again. "These were made by fingers," she said, apparently talking to herself. "Years and years. Centuries. It wasn't a prison but a means of execution. The archaeologists have it wrong. The walls were never high enough to support a ceiling. It was always like this. Just enough freedom to drive the prisoners mad. They were told of an exit that wasn't a door."

"Death?"

She nodded. "They walked and searched, marking places where they'd been, marking them again and again. They ate the dead and left cairns where bodies should have been laid to rest."

Mal leaned against a half wall and crossed his arms. Goose bumps rippled under his shirt. The picture she was painting was eerie. He could see the edges of their enclosure, but he couldn't escape it—not without dragging the Pet across the jagged spikes. He might consider it if they stayed any longer than another few minutes. He didn't like to be confined. To be trapped in this place when it was replete with a full array of defenses and entrapments . . . Yes, a man would go mad.

Tired of the riddles, he looked down at his shoulder. The pain was a numb throb. Drying blood stuck to his shirt.

The Pet stopped roughly ten feet away, her head bowed. She looked so vulnerable—tiny, slim, eminently feminine, and such a wonder of contrasts—but Mal knew better. Whatever she'd endured with Dr. Heath Aster had made her leather-tough and resistant to what would've crushed other people. He could try to overpower her again, but he'd come away with nine fingers and a woman without brains enough to speak.

More importantly, if she really was responsible for the Asters' high success rate, she was invaluable to understanding why Dragon Kings couldn't conceive. Generation after generation, the number of children brought into the world decreased to the point where desperate would-be parents sank into the realms controlled by the human cartels who promised the miracle of life—for a price. Otherwise obscure Dragon Kings trained to become Cage warriors and fought bouts for the entertainment of elite patrons and guests of the cartels, with the strongest granted the gift of attempting conception. Of the three largest cartels, the Asters had a tremendous advantage regarding success rates when compared to the Townsends and the Kawashimas. Most believed that high success rate was to Dr. Aster's credit.

Perhaps he had little to do with Dragon King science other than enacting hideous experiments on the weak, the infirm, and the losers of the Cage bouts—such a high price for wanting nothing more than a family.

That was if the Pet could be believed. There was no one else like her. Mal couldn't kill her. He could humor her a little longer, until retaking her into his custody didn't mean additional fighting.

Under normal circumstances, that wouldn't have been an issue. He lived in the straightjacket world and forced his baser nature to obey the rules. Having unleashed spikes of his energy on the Pet, however, left him edgy and ready for more violence.

"How do you know so much about the ruins?"

"Cadmin showed me," she said.

"A fetus showed you an ancient prison?"

"You asked."

"And you expect me to believe that?"

She shrugged. Her purple linen shirt seemed an out-of-place touch of softness. She was blade-sharp in her thinness, as if her heavy industrial boots were all that anchored her to the ground. "No, I don't. That's not your job, Giva. Your job is to recapture me and ask a couple hundred questions—the wrong questions. None of that will happen."

"You know that? As fact? As a . . ." He smiled, unable to hide his condescension. "As a soothsayer?"

"As a soothsayer, I admit you possess too many variables. The more volatile the person, the more difficult it is to see his path." She angled a glance that was nearly teasing. "And you, dear Giva, are the very definition of volatile."

"Then how can you be sure I won't take you into custody?"

"Once we find Cadmin's weapons, you won't want to."

"Did you ever even see her?" Mal pushed away from the wall on a surge of energy. "Do you even know if she was born?"

"I never met her, but I know she was born a few months after our minds touched. I didn't need to meet her in person. She was . . . different. She was magic."

"We're Dragon Kings. The majority of sentient beings on this planet would call us magical."

"No. We're just us. She was *magic*."

The Pet arched her neck and unexpectedly challenged him with her gaze. It was unwavering and fierce. But beneath the challenge was a sense of imploring. She wanted to be taken seriously, to be believed.

Mal couldn't do that. She was either insane or criminally clever.

Or she possessed other powers—perhaps along the lines of the Indranan's ability to read minds—and she was using his fears and hatreds against him.

All of her talk about the old ways, the ancient myths . . . He wouldn't tolerate much more. As a young man, Mal had inadvertently liberated his clan from its last, most hideous holdover from the times of gods and goddesses. He'd done so by losing control in the way he loved so much, sweeping the chess pieces to the ground. Only, he'd done that with living, breathing people. They hadn't been breathing when he'd walked away from Bakkhos.

"She showed me the past," the Pet said. "This place. She showed me the long-ago times. Don't you know? What was once will happen again."

"And that's predicting the future?"

"Of course not. But ask a Sath elder if I'm lying. They keep secrets not even you know, Giva. What was once will happen again."

"You're a charlatan. This ends now." He grabbed her arm and began to drag her. "We're going back to Greece."

The Pet snarled and fought, clawing his hands with her nails as she transformed from an imploring young woman to a fiend in the span of a blink. "You're a fool! A *fool*. It's here. Half of Cadmin's weapon is here."

"A weapon for an unborn baby who told you about a Minotaur and an ancient insane asylum. You need your own padded cell. I'll have one made up special for you."

She turned toward him as if he'd been leading a dance. Suddenly she was twirling beneath his arm. With her back to his chest, she reached up and dug her fingers into the stab wounds on his shoulder. Mal roared in pain and flung her away. The Pet sprawled on the rock. She sputtered on a mouthful of grit, then shoved black hair out of her eyes. Her shredded palms left a smear of blood on her temple.

"Do you know where the next Grievance will be held? Or when? Hm? Has anyone decided to share that with you, oh powerful Giva?"

Mal blinked. The annual Grievance was an all-out Cage match between the best warriors the human cartels had to offer—the days of gladiators made new again.

"No," he said, the word holding all of his suspicion. His pulse was crash upon crash of thunder. "My best spies haven't been able to learn that."

Neither had the underground rebellion of Dragon Kings who were slowly assembling across the world to battle the human cartels. To disrupt the next Grievance was their primary objective, but he wasn't about to share knowledge of their existence or purpose. Friends and even family were among their ranks.

"Then your spies aren't worth what you're paying them." She backed away from him. "*I* can find out. But only after we find Cadmin's weapon. *Some* weapon. She'll need it."

"Why?"

"She's eighteen now, and a Cage warrior. The upcoming Grievance will be her first . . . and it will be the last ever held."

❧ CHAPTER ❧
THREE

The last one," Mal said, unable to keep the incredulity from his reply. Incredulity—and maybe hope. If the rebels succeeded in their underground war against the cartels . . . But no, he couldn't start buying into the Pet's mad prophecies. She would say anything to keep from returning to Greece as his captive. "Grievances have been held for a thousand generations."

"By *our* people. The Five Clans. The Pendray stormed down from the Highlands to fight your Tigony followers for control of Europe. The Sath slinked off the African deserts to use secrets like weapons, while the Garnis appeared seemingly out of nowhere to prove they were not extinct. And the Northern and Southern Indranan proved to be as fractured as ever." Her voice was rich with passion. "The Grievances held purpose to leech bad blood and keep the Dragon Kings sound as a species, no matter our differences. They've only been co-opted by the cartels over the last fifty years. Old Man Aster is very good at using tradition against us."

"And this girl has to do with it how?"

"Fighting," she said. That's all I know."

"More variables?"

The Pet shook her head. "No. The fighting is a fixed point. How it happens is a mystery."

"But it involves you and me being here?"

"You? I couldn't say yet. Me, however—yes."

She shrugged free of his hold and continued her careful trudge through the maze. The sun continued its slow slope toward the western horizon. The deepening gold and pink cast color over her skin and clothing, but her black, black hair absorbed the light. It was a tangle of spikes and twists that could've been intentional, or a testament to some wild disregard for the outside world. Aside from her ability to fight, she seemed to live exclusively in a make-believe place in her mind.

Mal experienced a sudden flash of regret. He should've been at the Greek fortress to spend more time with her, to learn more about her. The Council had occupied his time, as had the bloody resurgence of the civil war between the northern and southern factions of Clan Indranan across the Indian subcontinent. Rumor had it that his late aunt's brother-in-law, Tallis, the Heretic, was involved in the explosion of new violence. Mal needed to get back to civilization in order to deal with problems that could wipe out the Dragon Kings even faster than watching each generation wither and flake away.

But now, the Pet had quickly rocketed to the top of his list of priorities.

"We're not going to make it to the nearest village before sundown," he said.

Her back was straight, but the furtive way she moved made her seem on the defensive. Although she stood at her full yet diminutive height, she gave off the appearance of crouching and readying for attack, that appearance of crouching and making herself seem smaller. Had life with Dr. Aster developed that means of self-defense?

Why did that idea twist in his chest? She was powerful. She was formidable. Yet, how many years had she spent watching and waiting for the next blow?

"I won't be heading into a village." She turned a corner, then another, and another in quick succession.

Mal could still see her head, but the path to follow was quickly lost to him. He had to double back when a dead end barred his way. He balled his fists, ready to punch solid rock. Had he wanted to, he could use his gift to disintegrate the walls into smoldering, charred heaps, but the Pet had reason to be there. Hauling her back to Tigony lands would be more difficult if he intentionally pissed her off—no matter her insane claims. Humoring her might be the better course until he was given no other option.

Some excited noise, or the closest to it the Pet was likely capable of, drew his attention. She must've ducked low, because he could no longer see her.

This damn maze.

"Over here," she called.

Eventually he was able to follow the sound of her voice and meet her at yet another dead end. "Tell me you've given up."

"No need. I found it."

From under a cover of rock and chalky dust, she pulled a slender quiver made of boiled leather. From the Dark Ages? Even older? A shiver worked up from the small of his back. The Pet pulled out an arrow. A flash of dying sunlight caught on what must've been gold. The dull, yellowed light glinted across her face in quick patterns. Her eyes were large and her mouth was tiny, but both features became more exaggerated as she examined the arrow. Eyes wider. Lips slack with apparent awe.

Mal crouched beside her. She edged away—from what seemed to be habit, not enough to put real distance between them. "May I?"

"Yes."

He shot her a sideways glance. "So willingly?"

"Because there are four more. I'd get this one back if you forced me to it."

"No more forcing for now." He extended his hand, catching sight of the dried blood on the forearm of his dress shirt. It was dark brown in the gathering shadows. What had made him trust that she wouldn't slice his wrist? What made him feel this affinity to be with her?

Fate.

The word was unwanted. It was heinous. Fate meant he had been intended to arrive at that moment, at that time, with this woman, despite every choice he'd ever made. That might've been a comfort when thinking of Bakkhos—that he hadn't been responsible for his actions there—but it also meant that he'd been fated to act as judge, jury, and executioner without any say. Why force that responsibility on him? Or burden him with the title of Giva? Surely there were more violent criminals to do the dirty work and more stable, sensible men suited for leadership.

He took the arrow. It was light . . . so very light. "Feathers hold more heft. How is this supposed to fire from a bow, let alone serve as a weapon?"

"I already said. Magic." For the first time, the Pet's voice sounded almost teasing. "But you don't believe in magic. Assume it's useless and give it back."

Yet Mal was entranced. Twenty-four-karat gold was too soft for crafting jewelry because it was relatively malleable. He would've been surprised had the arrow been made of anything less valuable. The gold was deep and lustrous, its orange-bronze gleam too dull to be considered attractive.

He held something unearthly. And this woman, this inexplicable woman, had known it would be among some forgotten ruins in Crete—the apparent ruins of a prison. Unbelievable, even when his senses couldn't deny the arrow in his hands. Its strangeness. Its great age and fascinating sense of purpose.

"Oh," she whispered. "Look."

Mal studied her profile first. The tip of her tiny nose turned up. Her upper lip was full at its apex. She had wide cheekbones and small ears. The upward sweep of haphazardly pinned hair revealed a graceful neck and a hint of delicate collarbones. She still wore the brass knuckles on her right hand. Softness and deadly skill. He was disturbed by his fascination, which was as unwanted as any thought of fate.

He hadn't noticed a woman the way he noticed her in . . . He couldn't recall a more visceral, compelling attraction.

"What?" His question was gruff. Had he spoken that way before the Council, the two representatives from each clan would've known a barb had struck home, or a protest had been met with his frustration. It was another rarity he shared with only the Pet.

"This mark." She tipped another arrow into the light. "What does it look like to you?"

Mal examined it more closely. Shining in the last of the light was an engraving. "The Pendray representation of the Great Dragon," he said, the hairs on his forearms prickling.

"Exactly. An Earth Mother. Fat and fertile. Yet winged with a tail. Breathing fire."

Examining the arrow in his hand, Mal found another engraving. "This one's Garnis. Thin and long, like the Chinese interpretation."

Sure enough, each of the arrows was marked with a clan's differing vision. Somewhere throughout the centuries, the idea of Great Dragon—their creator, their mother and father combined into one—had splintered until no clan could agree on its true likeness. They could find less vital topics to bicker about on any given day, but the image of the Dragon brought out fierce tempers. The most level-headed of their kind still mustered loyalties enough to argue the point.

"Which do you believe?" he asked. "Since you're so intent on believing in myths and superstitions."

"None of them are real, so it would be a waste of breath."

He handed the arrow back and watched as the Pet reverently returned it to the unassuming quiver. "None of them are real?"

"We split into five pieces. Do you think any one clan got it right?" She stood and shouldered the quiver. It looked good across her back, the weapon of a fey creature from another era. "I'm done here."

"Then you're ready to return to Greece?"

"I'd rather resume—"

Her answer was cut short by the sound of footsteps. She dropped low against the wall. Mal turned—just in time to avoid the downward arc of a huge, glittering sword.

The Pet hadn't known she could move so quickly. Just because she had been raised by a Garnis family, with their superhuman reflexes and animalistic senses, didn't mean she was blessed with their special skills. Her instincts said that didn't matter. Three Pendray wearing the collars of Cage warriors leapt over the wall in the throes of berserker rages.

She jumped almost straight up, landing in a crouched balance on the top of a wall. A sharp spike of glassy rock pierced the sole of her boot. Malnefoley had fallen backward, scrambling crablike away from his attackers. Had he not reacted so quickly, he would be dead—his head severed forever from his body. The glittering metal meant the Pendray wielded a Dragon-forged sword. Its metal had been honed in the fires of the Chasm. Decapitation by such a weapon was the only way to kill a Dragon King.

The Pet jumped off the wall and onto the back of one of the Pendray. With her knees on his shoulders, she clamped her thighs and squeezed. His rage was so intense that he resembled an angered wolf, spinning and snarling. He flailed back with his arms, trying to dislodge her. She wrapped her forearm around his eyes. His bellows were more powerful than an animal's howls, like a bear ready to swallow her whole. She used her brass knuckles to repeatedly punch his temple. He staggered, then caught her around the waist and flipped her onto the ground.

She landed on her side. The wind gusted out of her lungs. She reached behind her back and grabbed one of the seemingly fragile arrows.

The Pet exhaled and strove for calm. If the arrows were strong enough to serve as Cadmin's weapons in a Grievance, surely they would protect her.

Trust.

Belief.

The Pendray man leapt down to straddle her, with his fists raised to pummel her head against the rocks. With all her strength, she held the shaft straight up. His descending body did the rest. The tip of the arrow pierced his right lung. He screamed and landed a solid punch to her gut before rolling away in agony. Still winded, her stomach clenching in pain, the Pet jerked the arrow from her enemy. Blood flowed in its absence.

Goose bumps flared across her skin in the now-familiar feeling of an oncoming storm—not one made by nature, but forged by a very angry, very powerful Tigony man. She turned toward the force pulsing at her back, powerless to do anything else.

All around the Honorable Giva, sparks of frenetic electricity gathered and intensified. The color of his eyes deepened to a blue that was almost black, and blazed with an otherworldly glow. He made for a ghastly, primal sight, with blood from his torn shoulder soaking the sleeve of his shirt. He was a warrior in the midst of battle. He was wounded, but not on the defensive—not when he was master of one of the greatest of the Dragon's gifts.

Their eyes met. "Run," was all he said, aiming that eerie blue gaze directly at her.

A third Pendray, a woman, tried to catch the Pet as she darted past. She only managed to grab a purple linen sleeve, which tore away. The Pet clasped both hands into a knot of knuckles—one set protected by a row of metal—and swung her arms like an Olympian spinning to throw a hammer. Connect. Crack. The woman's jaw skewed to a garishly sick angle, like hinges coming loose from a door.

Heart pounding, with hair freakishly active across her skin, straining up from her pores, the Pet did exactly as the Dragon Kings' leader instructed. She ran. The quiver containing five arrows bounced against her back. Her direction didn't matter. The maze could consume her, but she knew what she needed to do to escape.

Those Pendray didn't stand a chance.

The air crackled and swirled. A slim tornado appeared from the clear dusk sky. She turned left, right, forward, dead end, back again, as the Cretan plain transformed into a battle between ozone and humidity.

Her gift served her well. Moments before the first lightning strike, she saw when it would happen, how it would happen, and who it would destroy. She pressed into a bleached stone corner, tucking between a small boulder and a wall. Vital organs protected. Head bowed. Only at the last second did she whip the quiver off her back and huddle over it, protecting it with her torso—as if her body could protect a weapon that had weathered countless years. Then again, it had likely never been struck by the full force of an enraged Tigony.

The sky lit like the explosion of a bomb. Heat ricocheted through the maze walls. The Pet huddled as energy washed over her hiding place. It wasn't enough to protect against the quick-burst fires that streaked her skin and singed the ends of her hair.

Sound came next—the loudest, nearest thunder eardrums could endure, whether human or Dragon King. She screamed, as if a bellow of equal fury could ward off the pain. She never heard the noise tearing out of her mouth, although her throat was abraded and raw by the time she took a breath.

Then . . . nothing.

She couldn't tell beyond the buzzing in her ears if the skirmish was over. She dared look back over her shoulder, peeking out from her meager shelter.

"Giva?" she shouted, although the word sounded warped.

Across the half dozen leveled walls between her and the Giva, the Pet could no longer see the Pendray. He held the first attacker's Dragon-forged sword, which was streaked with crimson. His eyes . . .

His eyes were lost to a fury she had never seen, not even from a Pendray at the height of a berserker rage. Yet his voice was utterly flat when he said, "They're dead."

"I know."

The Pet shouldered the quiver and ran back. The way was easier now. Flattened. A few pits and smoldering, lava-hot rocks meant she still had to be careful. Forgoing the risks, she nimbly hopped on a wall. Her balance faltered. She was standing on one foot, her arms pinwheeling. She breathed through her nose and calmed her pulse until she could lower her leg. Using the back of her boot heel, she kicked away some razor-sharp rock. Then it was a quick hop down to run toward the Giva.

Winded, her abdomen tight with continuing spasms, she landed and found herself in the midst of three fallen bodies. They were charred black, their skin peeled away and turned to ash. They'd been decapitated.

The Giva transferred the Dragon-forged sword to his left hand. His shoulder, which had been ripped open in the fighting, was now gashed to the bone. The injury only made him look more ferocious. He was pulsing with energy, even though he'd just aimed an electrical storm at three of their own kind. Maybe that was why he still pulsed with unspent aggression. The Giva was not meant to kill other Dragon Kings.

Then again, when was the last time anyone had attempted to kill an Honorable Giva?

"Hello?"

He lifted his chin. Blood smeared across his forehead and dampened the hair around one temple. The Pet jerked when his eyes met hers. She was looking at an entirely different man, one drained of civilization and hewn of primitive impulses. She'd suspected he was capable of such rage, but to see it in the flesh was overwhelming. Cadmin might stand a chance if she could turn this sophisticated, influential beast to her cause.

Moving with caution, she recalled the techniques Dr. Aster had used in his lab. He never wanted to lose his so-called patients. That meant each surgery was precise and careful. No mistakes. The men and women he'd captured were there for the long haul, and he needed them completely recovered after each experiment. The

Pet was as well versed in the use of sutures as she was scalpels, but the Tigony had other methods.

"May I . . . ?" She nodded to his wound.

He looked down at it as if taking notice for the first time. When he returned his eyes to hers, he had regained some hold on himself. The man was returning. The tempestuous beast few ever witnessed was retreating, gone back into hiding behind a cultured facade.

"Yes," he said simply.

"You trust me with your care?"

"I have no other choice. And others may try again. We can't stay here much longer."

"I've found what I came for."

"Guided by prophecy," he said with a sneer. "Do what you can for my shoulder and keep your mouth shut. Fate. Destiny. They doesn't exist. The only thing I care about is getting you back to Greece. I'll drag you there by your hair if I must."

She couldn't help a quirking smile. "Then maybe I shouldn't mend you after all."

"Are you surprised?"

"What?"

"You said you'd be surprised if you made a joke." He sat heavily. "That was close."

"I can promise more if you quit with this talk of returning to Greece. But that won't happen, and you told me to shut up."

Gingerly, he edged to the ground, still gripping the sword. She knelt before him. At that lower vantage, he was even bigger than she'd imagined, with long limbs and a sturdy, muscular torso, made even more apparent because of a long, singed rip along the midsection of his dress shirt. He was breathing through his nose, probably to process the pain. Each inhalation lifted his chest and tightened his exposed abdominals.

Gorgeous.

The thought was as quick as it was pointless, unless she chose to believe the most intimidating of her prophecies: that she and Malnefoley would become lovers. She'd known since first meeting him among the burning rubble of the Asters' laboratory. The fleeting image had grown stronger every day. Until that moment, she had never believed it to be more than curiosity born of her imagination. Now it blazed with the certainty of something that had already happened.

She looked into his eyes and shivered.

Fighting back to the present, she withdrew her switchblade. She cut his shirt into strips, and whipped off her own belt. "In your condition, how precise can you be with your gift?"

He lifted his left hand. It wobbled. Sparks shot in all directions. He made a frustrated grunting noise in his throat.

"If you don't help me," she said, "your fighting hand will be useless. I have the feeling you'll be needing it again shortly."

"I think you're right. Curious, what that quiver brought down on us."

"If you don't consider that an assassination attempt, you're crazier than you think I am." She caught his left hand and carefully aligned each fingertip along the deep tear in the flesh of his shoulder. "I'm going to hold you still. Understand? Dig deep, but only enough to cauterize the wound."

"It'll hurt you."

"You can feel bad about it later." She nodded to the torn shirt and her belt. "I can help you with those, but not enough."

He winced. His face was slicked with sweat.

She leaned close, closer than she'd been to another individual since escaping Dr. Aster. She pressed her forehead against his. "Malnefoley, you must. Did you hear me? I used your name. Do this, and you can help me pick *my* name. I'm no one's Pet. You know that by now."

He said nothing, but the upward press of his forehead was stronger. "I'm ready."

"Then do it, Malnefoley. Do it."

❧ CHAPTER ❧
FOUR

Beyond the blasted annoyance of his raw nerves,
Mal could feel two things: the Pet's forehead pressed
against his, and her fingers aligned with his. He could
see where he touched the gash in his shoulder, but his
nerves were malfunctioning. Pain and flesh had no barrier. They were one fluid entity.

But he could feel her.

The Pet smacked her forehead against his. "Concentrate. Do it!"

Mal surged.

He had never felt his own electrical shocks. He was
immune to the tornado of sparking lightning he flung at
his enemies. So nothing prepared him for the squirming
eels of static and sparks that burned his flesh. He cried
out a curse.

She didn't reply, likely because of the anguish reflected in her green-gold eyes. She was his conduit, the
equivalent of touching a downed power line when
standing in a puddle. On his own, he was grounded.
Gripped by her hands, with his blood as the lubricant
between their fingers, he was just as much a victim. His
body jerked. He kicked, fought, but kept up a river-wild

current strong enough to cauterize without paralyzing them both. Nerve damage. Crippling burns. So many risks.

She didn't let go.

He watched and watched as fireworks obscured where their palms twined. Surely his skin must be flaying away. So many said the Tigony power was exactly that: the feeling of having one's skin burned away one layer at a time.

"Enough!"

Yanking upright, she pulled their hands away. Sparks shot from his fingertips but they were soon exhausted.

The Pet was straddling his torso. She lowered her arms so that his hands lay inert on the rocky earth. She was wild, with her pinned-up hair in static spikes and her eyes full of daring. And triumph.

She leaned down and kissed him. An errant spark renewed between their skin, with slippery wetness to soothe the melding of flesh against flesh. The kiss itself was anything but soothing. The strong, sure push of their mouths turned everything unnatural . . . *natural*. They had done battle, and they would celebrate in the oldest, most pleasurable way. Mal used his good arm to clasp behind her neck. He pulled her closer and took control.

One of them tasted of blood. Perhaps they both did. There was dust and salt and hidden sweetness. She had an agile tongue, keeping pace with the bold strokes he swept through her mouth. Sharp, tiny teeth nipped his lower lip. He caught her lip in the return, this time with more force. He liked her wince. She shook against his hold at the back of her neck. Mal wasn't letting go; he

was enjoying this heat and sense of command. The Pet
changed tactics. She adjusted where her knees straddled
either side of his chest, finding a resilient balance. She
brought up both sets of knuckles—one skin, one brass—
and angled them against the sides of his neck. A pinch
of pressure against his carotid artery streaked washes of
black across his vision. He grabbed a tight fistful of short
hair at her crown and chuckled against her mouth.

Stalemate.

Neutral ground was the act of kissing. Keep kissing,
keep the peace.

Mal redoubled the assault he had so abruptly started,
where lip to lip had flared into a searing passion as hot
as the fire they had wielded together. He slid his hand
down her back and filled his palm with her taut ass. She
flexed her hips when he gripped hard—then harder still.
He would need her to surrender, eventually, but that
goal was far away as she moaned. The idea that she
might surrender more readily to their bodies' demands
than to his will was actually arousing, although it would
mean being defied.

No one said no to the Honorable Giva. The Pet did.

Would she say no to Malnefoley, the man?

"You'll live," she said, breathless. Her hazel eyes had
lost some of their triumphant defiance. They were
glassed over with a delicious fog that made Mal eager
for more. He had affected her. He could change the
direction of the wind, turn back the tide, and make the
Pet a picture of sensuality. "Better yet, you'll fight."

He pressed his thumb back across her cheekbone,
right where her heart-shaped face was at its widest and
most graceful. Dirt gave way to pale, luminous skin. "I'd

wager that wasn't on your list of advantages an hour ago."

Smiling tentatively, she quickly kissed the inside of his palm. "And I'll likely reconsider an hour from now." Off in a flash, she knelt beside him. The loss of her slight weight was as disturbing as knowing their kiss was finished—the first and last of its kind. He had liked the solidity of her body, as if this wildling could keep him centered. Deeper urges told him that being centered wasn't what he really craved. He wanted a return to their unique stalemate, when peace meant sharing space with her in the heart of a passionate storm.

It was then that he decided this kiss would not be their last. He would not give up searching out those hot, daring sensations again.

The Pet.

She needed a name. She must have one, or had one a long time ago.

"Your shoulder's a mess," she said. "But at least you caught the blade there rather than across your hand. I don't know if your wrist would've survived a cut this deep." She tipped his head and ran her fingers over the cauterized slash. "You are a handsome man. Your shoulder will not be. I recommend long sleeves from now on."

They watched each other. Together they'd come through a startling attack and a flash of unexpected passion. Their disagreements remained.

Mal rolled his eyes to the darkened sky. Three Dragon Kings dead . . . by the hand of the Giva, who was sworn to protect their kind.

Right then, he didn't care.

He was bare-chested and bloody in front of this

woman. Although she maintained an air of indifference, she kept flicking her gaze over his lips and torso, where he sat against one of the blackened half walls. He felt appreciated as a man, not an entity or a symbol, for the first time in years.

She leaned close, so close, as she wound strips of his shirt around his shoulder, then secured it with a loop of cloth around his back and chest. A neat field dressing. Then she used her belt to secure the scraps firmly in place. She smelled of copper and sweat, but he caught the scent of her womanly essence. A wild thought hit his mind with the strength of a boulder.

I could take her. More than kisses. I could have her, right here.

"It's still seeping," she said, businesslike. "You should wait to use it until morning at least."

Mal closed his eyes, although that forbidden thought followed him into the dark. His coat as their blanket. Her body his playground. Her kiss, furious and freeing. He'd never lost control of his gift when in the throes of passion, but something about this woman made him think control—of his desire, of his gift—would be the ultimate test when it came to taking her.

How long had he indulged in the idea of such a simple, straightforward challenge? No politics. Nothing but the feel of limbs sliding against one another, of lips warring for control, and sinking into her softness.

The images were as dangerous as they were compulsive. Whether it was because of their kiss, his long, self-imposed abstinence, her mysteries, or the violence of the moment, it didn't matter. The fact remained. Simple. Primal. He would have her.

Finding her gaze—a rather amused gaze, if his ego felt like admitting the truth—he cleared his throat. "We need to get out of here. A single attack won't be the only one."

Her amusement faded. "Because three random Pendray don't just decide to try and murder the Giva."

"I can't remember any history of its like." Eyeing her, with his veins icing over, he asked, "Can you?"

"No. But then again, I can't remember mention of any Giva being in your tenuous position of power."

"You're tactful. You didn't call me the Usurper."

"Because you're not."

She sat back on her haunches and wiped her hands on the dressing that crossed between his pectorals. Again, she seemed businesslike—but her dusky hazel eyes never wavered from his, and a new awareness shone in those depths. A dare. More than a dare when her fingers left the safety of the wrapped, stained cotton and trailed down his ribs. He nearly groaned, but held it back.

"Are you hurt?"

"No." Had the crooked tilt of her lips been a smile, now tucked away for another time? Nonetheless, a certain lightness in her demeanor remained. "I can see why you'd ask."

She stood and stared at the dead. Such a waste. Kneeling without fanfare, she retrieved one Pendray's head—the man who'd first attacked Mal. Was she the sort to kick the skull across the labyrinth like a kid with a ball? Or smash it with a rock?

Neither.

She smoothed the man's distorted features and

slicked what remained of his charred hair back from his warped, motionless face. She found his body, lined it up flat, and returned its head. Silently, without glancing at Mal, she repeated the process until all three Pendray lay like matchsticks across one of the pathways.

"Great Dragon. They're yours," she said.

Mal closed his eyes, overcome by confusion. She didn't crush skulls, but she didn't pray for them either—at least not using the traditional funeral rites of any particular clan. Just four words of benediction any Dragon King needed when he or she should go home to the Chasm, where dead souls went to rest. She did that for her enemies, no matter how plainly?

"If you suspect this isn't the last of the rogue hunting parties, then we need to leave," she said.

The belt, cinched tightly around his shoulder, was a dam. The pain was the water backed up behind it, building toward the point of overflowing. His gift built just as potently. He was going to burst, no matter how he struggled to rein in desire, screaming nerves, and the knowledge that other Dragon Kings wanted him dead.

She straddled him again—the most striking, stormy, beautiful gargoyle. She combined balance and fearlessness, with eyes deeply shadowed as the sun dipped lower. "You'll either leave here with me, or you'll tear yourself open, wondering if there's a grain of truth to all I'm saying."

"You've seen that, have you?"

"I've seen a lot of possibilities for you. Maybe one day I'll share." She actually poked his shoulder. "Our kind has survived worse. And for longer."

"In the labs."

"I know a dying patient when I see one, and I know a patient who will lose a limb. I don't see one here." She stroked the insides of his wrists with her thumbs. "Now get up."

They locked gazes. "As soon as you do."

She hopped away. Mal stood, dusted off what remained of his suit, and picked up the Dragon-forged sword.

They began the trek, picking their way to the north end of the labyrinth where Mal's powers had pried open an exit. Only when they were free of the strangely claustrophobic place did Mal take an easy breath, although breathing intensified the pain in his shoulder. He needed a day or two to rest up and let his Dragon King physiology work its wonders, but he needed to do so without losing his captive.

Captive. He chided himself internally. She was walking beside him because she wanted to.

But no matter her self-assurance, he refused to lose her again. She was an almost complete unknown. Now he had to contend with his reawakened sexual needs— and a possible assassination attempt. Could she be involved?

"Tell me about Cadmin."

"She's a redhead. Her parents were Tigony, but from the north. The Balkans. Only after I touched this quiver did I see her future more clearly. She was in the heart of the crumbled building. People everywhere."

"You hadn't seen that before?" He couldn't help keep the cynicism from his voice.

"No. We've taken one step closer. I know that when

she fights, she can do so with these weapons. *Can*. Many variables remain."

"Then there must be a bow, I suppose."

"Of course. The question now is whether you'll be with me when I find it." She shrugged. "I don't like surprises. You, Giva, are full of them."

"Maybe it's part of my gift," he said, half smiling.

"Then I *should* carry on without you." She shyly returned his grin.

"Not a chance."

He wasn't used to sounding so rough. His people were cultured—or he'd thought them so, long ago, when he'd first come into his own. His initiation into adulthood had disillusioned him of the idea that the Tigony were in any way elevated. He was a savage at heart. Maybe all Dragon Kings were—a people born of chaos and fire.

"You need a name," he said as they walked, with the last dregs of dusk at their backs. "I refuse to call you the Pet."

Her dark brows drew together. Her hands fidgeted with a belt loop. "I wouldn't know where to begin."

"Have you always been called . . . that?"

"No. I grew up with a nomadic family of Garnis."

"Garnis? Where?"

"We call them the Lost, but they exist everywhere. That way," she said, abruptly pointing toward a rocky outcrop barely visible in the distance. "We'll find shelter for the night, and a cache of supplies."

Her smile was sure and calm, not shy and quirking, as if she were a child seeking praise.

Dragon damn. *That kiss* . . .

He cleared his throat. "You were saying? About the Lost?"

"This family was native to the Yukon Territories. I stayed with them until I was twelve, but they didn't name me. It was thought that if a family named a foundling and that child died, it would haunt the souls of its name-bearers."

"What did they call you?"

"The Garnis word for *girl*."

"Then you became the Pet."

She stopped. Streaks of midnight and starlight made her skin seem to glow. "Yes."

"So . . . choose."

"I can't just choose out of thin air." She marched on, with an agitated gait and tight shoulders. "How does anyone do that? We're *given* names."

"Unless you've been given degrading names all your life. This is your chance to be your own person. Your terms."

She snorted a derisive laugh. "With you as my would-be captor, and visions of the future filling my mind, little about my life is on my terms."

"So take this opportunity."

She noticed how Malnefoley walked with the bearing of a king. And why not? He was the leader of the Five Clans. Because Dragon Kings had a natural life span of nearly two hundred years, he could be in charge of what remained of their dwindling people for another dozen decades, at least. She liked his long gait. He moved fluidly. Dr. Aster had always walked slowly, with so much deliberation, caught between the world of the living and his own demented thoughts. The Giva was a man of the present. A man of purpose.

He held the Dragon-forged sword as if it weighed nothing. That he strode beside her clad in nothing but dusty, blood-splattered slacks—his chest bare save her makeshift bandages—added an extra charge of awareness to her admiration. He was unspeakably handsome. Even the evening light conspired to make his features otherworldly in their masculine beauty. In profile, his brow elegant yet strong, with hollow cheeks and a nose as straight as the arrows in the quiver across her back. But his mouth was his most fascinating feature, by far. Glimpses of starlight and the moon on the far horizon outlined his mouth in luminescent white.

He was arrogant and handsome. He was royalty. He was devastatingly powerful.

And he was the only man she had ever kissed. Was he so special, or was it the novelty? Was their kiss proof of what she'd envisioned so many times since their first meeting?

Lovers.

Some futures were malleable. Some were set. That they would eventually make love was as certain to her as his presence at her side.

"I want a fresh start," she said quickly. "Something strong."

If she was going to be the Giva's lover, she needed to feel the power to keep up—or even lead the way. Having sex would be easy. Making him believe in her higher purpose was another matter. Although she couldn't pinpoint why, she would need him. Cadmin would need them both. Together. That was why she took no pains to hide herself from his pursuit. If only she could see a glimpse of why they were meant to travel this path together.

He walked in silence for a long time, until she gave up awaiting an answer. She fell into step. Every two of hers matched one of his.

"Avyi," he said at last. "What do you think of Avyi?"

She rolled it around in her mind, then gave whispered voice to its appealing syllables. "Avyi. What does it mean?"

"Maybe one day I'll share," he said, echoing her previous teasing.

He still hadn't looked at her. Just eyes forward, chin lifted proudly. But she got the sense that he was expectant. He wanted to know if his offering met with her approval.

If she would bear the name he gave her . . .

An exciting shiver crept over her skin. She'd been owned before. Literally. This didn't feel like ownership. It felt like he was doing his best to accommodate what she craved. Almost as though he was giving her a gift.

"I like it."

He nodded curtly. They walked on in silence, although her mind would not quiet.

I have a name.

Avyi.

The night was quiet except for the wind that whipped up the swell and buffeted their backs. She thought of that prison, and how the elements would be just as maddening as walls that promised only death as release. She could imagine men and women going mad, but she could also imagine them forging a certain sort of existence, as she had done in the labs. Dragon Kings, humans, animals of all kind—the strong adapted.

And now, she would need to adapt to her own new life. She was free of the Asters, but not free of the Honorable Giva. Of Malnefoley. He was her burden now, just as she had been his. Oddly enough, she didn't begrudge him the months of her imprisonment in Greece. She would've done the same, had she been in his position—with the vitality of their entire race at stake and the Giva as their leader. She wouldn't have trusted herself either.

She still didn't. Those Pendray . . .

And not even a flicker of warning. She'd known she would find half of Cadmin's weapon, but three cartel Pendray attacking them out of nowhere? Why hadn't her gift seen fit to share that important detail?

Although the night was sultry and scented with the salt of the distant sea, she was unnerved. They reached the rock shelter and settled into a craggy inlet. Being so near to him once again only renewed her awareness of the kiss they had unexpectedly shared in the maze. She was as curious for more as she was scared of the possibilities. They had a long way to go between her first kiss and her first time lying with a man.

They both slumped heavily against the rock. She was bone-tired, and knew Malnefoley would be equally tested. The quiver and the sword looked . . . *right* together, side by side on the gravelly ground. Avyi shivered, then began unpacking her cache of supplies. They ate and drank until the silence and her questions got the better of her.

"What if I'm wrong again?"

The words made more sense and didn't hurt as much when she gave them voice. When spoken, they sat in one straight line. A single sentence. In her brain, they circled like the electrical storm Malnefoley had conjured.

"Wrong?" His rough, low voice was voice eloquent, but it was deep and dripping with authority.

"They wanted to kill you. You're the Giva. That could mean it was political. Or it could mean a thousand other possibilities. Too many variables. That's why being around you is such a chore."

"Then you can continue not liking me back in Greece."

"You really don't understand. I won't be going back to Greece. Period. I have more important and frankly more dangerous tasks ahead of me." She grinned in the darkness. "Be it on your head if I die trying. You named me. If I die, I'll come back to haunt you."

"I'm not Garnis."

"You know how connected the Five Clans are, underneath it all. Just because you're not Garnis doesn't mean their curses and superstitions stop with their bloodlines."

Avyi exhaled heavily. If the Giva made a move, she would indeed wind up back in the Tigony stronghold. She wouldn't let that happen. She had to trust in her vision of their fate, that it simply wouldn't happen. They had only just come to know each other, barely, but they were inexorably linked as future lovers.

More than that, she hoped they would become allies. She shivered when she thought of facing so many important choices on her own.

"All the myths are true, Malnefoley."

She looked skyward and picked out stars. So many had been named by those who'd worshiped the Tigony. Hercules and Orion, Cassiopeia and Draco—their vision of the Great Dragon. She smiled to herself. The Tigony were known as the Tricksters, having deeply ingratiated themselves into the human population, until Greeks and Romans had become the envy of history—and of the other four sacred clans.

The Tigony had bested rival Dragon Kings by coming into a position of dynastic power when Pythagoras decoded the universe based on mathematics, when Gutenberg invented the printing press, when Fleming discovered penicillin. They had a reputation for preferring talk to action, which was ironic considering the bellicose nature of the Greco-Roman traditions: the velvet fist.

But they were just as wrong about the visage of the Great Dragon as every other clan.

What was once will happen again.

Her eyes grew heavy. She hadn't been so close to a man since her imprisonment with Dr. Aster. This was so different as to be one of those distant stars.

"They wanted you dead." She inhaled deeply. The blood he'd shed was the most prominent odor, but she would've needed to be born without a nose to miss his underlying masculine scent. *Malnefoley.* He wasn't clean and coated in fragrance—Dr. Aster's preference. No, this was the life-affirming musk of a man who had fought and conquered, the hallmark of warriors from the beginning of time. "Unfortunately, you killed them."

"Sorry." She could hear his smile—cruel and funny at the same time. The funny was new.

"But not all was lost. The head of the biggest man gave me a clue."

"The head? I thought you were performing funeral rites."

"I was searching what was left in their synapses. All I saw was the great dome atop the cathedral in Florence."

"Italy?"

"Don't be dense," she said. "That's not why you get to wear the fancy robes. Yes, Italy.

"It matches what I've seen before, a man beneath the dome of the Florence Cathedral. I didn't know it was you when I first glimpsed that image. That Pendray made it clear. Now I think the bow is there, and possibly more people associated with the plot against you." She inhaled and let the air out slowly. "That's how I see it."

"And that makes perfect sense to you." His mocking tone irritated her, as if she were a cat with its fur being petted backward.

"Yes. So you have two choices. Take me back to Greece, where I'm useless and you'll learn nothing about another assassination attempt until they come for you, or travel with me to Florence and find answers."

"What about variables?"

"They've narrowed. But I don't want to miss another surprise attack."

"Being wrong again frustrates the hell out of you, doesn't it?" The note of sympathy in his voice was new. From the Giva, she didn't know how to interpret it.

"Being wrong makes for a poor soothsayer."

"Another joke?"

"I'm trying."

"Why?"

Avyi hesitated. "Because you like them."

In the darkness, Malnefoley closed his hand over hers and gave it a squeeze. Maybe it was the struggle of the day and the weight of her responsibilities, but tears pricked behind her eyes. She hadn't been touched with such kind regard in . . . No, her memory wasn't that good. She couldn't remember a time. Their kiss had been combustion. This was comfort.

She accepted his strange attempt at comfort with a twitch of her fingers around his. It was lovely. But the last thing she needed was the impulse to please another man and seek his approval. Cadmin needed her, wherever she was and whatever she would do. That was what had pulled the woman named the Pet to Crete, digging among rocks and shale to find a quiver of arrows. Her mission remained clear, no matter that she was inexorably linked to the Honorable Giva who held her hand.

❧ CHAPTER ❧
FIVE

Mal awakened with a headache, a feeling of suffocation, and the Pet—no, Avyi—curled away from him. She was practically fetal, in a tight ball. She defended herself even in sleep.

He blinked against the rays of eastern sun beginning to creep over his face, Helios making his arc across the sky.

The old myths were called myths for a reason. Dragon damn, Mal *had* to believe in coincidences. Otherwise the last twenty-four hours would mean something greater than merely finding Avyi, finding those arrows, and finding his shoulder nearly hacked off.

They could've journeyed beyond the rock outcrop shielded by scrubby juniper bushes, but it had seemed like a welcoming inn. Avyi hadn't consulted him; she had simply made a pronouncement. He couldn't remember a time when decisions weren't made without contentious arguments where he eventually put his foot down, like a parent settling a score between squabbling children.

Avyi was definitely no child. She had such a strong mind of her own that he could barely reconcile her with the subservient Pet of the Asters' infamy. He'd only seen her once before the liberation that had freed his cousin and other Aster warriors from the Cages—and patients from the labs. The Pet had been dressed in skintight black latex, collared with leather and spikes, and led around by Aster by the will of his voice alone. Sometimes she'd squatted by the man's feet, holding his thigh, looking out from behind well-tailored slacks with those unreadable eyes, as if hiding . . . as if waiting . . .

Avyi, by contrast, was so changed as to be an entirely different woman.

Now, his body was tense. His mouth was parched. He tried to shift without waking her. A lance of fire shot from his shoulder to his forearm and back up again. But the effect was not so crippling as it had been. The Dragon's brilliant gift of quick physical recovery from injury was much appreciated. He could feel his left extremities, the subtle warmth of the sunrise, and how the rocks jabbed into his back in several places. He hadn't cared the night before, when the pain had burned to a crescendo.

As he sat up, dizziness smoked the vision at the corners of his eyes, replacing bright sun and bleached plains with a cloying gray mist.

After he took a deep drink of the water from Avyi's hidden supplies, he stilled and looked at the sun. He was unwilling but unable to deny that he was wavering. In no way did he believe her predictions, but there was a certain logic to being unpredictable. For the moment, at least, he had no doubt that she would stay with him willingly. If going to Florence turned out to be a wild-goose chase, he could always take her back to the Tigony stronghold.

And then there was his intention to pick up where their kiss left off. She excited him as few women ever had, which meant desire propelled his decision as strongly as any twist of logic. It wasn't responsible, and it wasn't something he needed to do, but he was actively pursuing a woman for the sole purpose of seeking pleasure.

He itched where she had used her belt to secure the makeshift bandages. The blood had dried. He was in desperate need of a bath—and a shirt. The sunshine on his chest and stomach made him potently aware of his bare vulnerability . . . and his awareness of Avyi lying so close. What would she do if he touched her? Jump out of her skin?

He wondered if there would ever come a time when she didn't flinch from touches she didn't initiate. Maybe she was too damaged for that to ever come to pass.

He reached up to peel back the maddening bandages but found his hands stilled in mid-motion.

"No."

She had turned and sat up without his notice. Was she made of smoke? Of liquid? No sound and no form. Except he'd felt her slight weight across his stomach when she'd straddled him. Her fingers had guided his into place. Her forehead had pressed against his, grounding him when pain and, yes, panic had threatened to warp his mastery over his gift. She'd helped him maintain control when that was something he took pride in keeping very much within his own grasp. He didn't know if he should be thankful for her assistance, or resentful that he'd needed it at all.

Both.

He remembered all of that like he remembered the rebellious tumble of her hair and her challenging defiance and the kiss that had changed the entire timbre of their time together. She spoke to him without words on such a deep, primal level.

"Not yet," she said. The pressure of her hand against his, where he held the belt buckle, brooked no argument. He frowned. She needed to use more force this time. The long, slender muscles of her forearms strained to keep him from his task. "I'll check, but we'll need to replace the same bandage and find new ones if the bleeding starts again."

"Out of bandages?" He eyed her with a mix of surprise and amusement. "I already sacrificed my shirt. Turnabout's fair play."

"I'm not stripping," she said bluntly.

"You had no problem stripping me."

"Next time, if you'd rather bleed like a butchered animal, I'll refrain from touching your precious clothing."

"So you foresee a next time?" Mal tried, but he couldn't help but smile. She was probably going to hit him—and part of him relished the chance to tussle with this frustrating woman. That didn't matter. He simply could not believe her talk about futures and prophecies.

"If you mock me again, I'll inflict the wound myself."

"I have a Dragon-forged sword."

She shook her head. "Don't make empty threats, Giva. It's unbefitting. You can't kill me and you know it. In fact, you're so curious, against your will, even, that you didn't bring reinforcements. You probably don't have any in waiting. Are you so arrogant, or are you so determined to find me compelling?"

"I only want what you know, including what you knew about those Pendray assassins."

"Which could be discussed right here, right now." She crossed her arms over breasts outlined by her thin, dusty purple shirt. One sleeve was torn off. One forefinger with a ragged nail tapped her annoyance. She was beginning to lose some of her icy, unreadable quality. "There's no need to take me back to some Tigony prison."

"It wasn't a prison."

"So I was free to go whenever I wanted?"

Mal grimaced in silent reply.

She leaned near, almost nose to nose, which meant she was once again closer to him than people ever dared. The title he wore was as much armor and barbed defenses as it was an honor.

He looked right down that filmy purple top and raised an eyebrow. "The last time you wanted to argue, you were straddling me. Let's pick up from there."

"Do you hear me, Giva? I need you because time is weaving us together. I won't bother telling you any more than that, because you won't listen. You know I've suffered worse than you could ever inflict. You won't get answers that way. As for your stronghold, I was free to go whenever I wanted. I proved that. The same held true with Aster. I am no one's prisoner and no one's pet."

Slowly, drawn to her softness, drawn to *her*, he lifted his good arm and brushed his thumb across a streak of chalky mica on her cheek. "That's right," he whispered. "You're Avyi."

She pulled back as if his touch were a brand rather than skin on skin. Within seconds, she had pushed away from him, shouldered the quiver and her pack of supplies, and stood facing the east. "It's a long walk to the village. We're vulnerable out in the open."

"That's the plan, foreseer of great and terrible things?"

She scowled. "You tell me, Giva. Do you remember the choices?"

"Florence . . . or dragging your skinny ass back to Greece."

For a moment, she appeared genuinely confused. "My . . . ?"

"Your skinny ass and your crazy hair and your unnerving cat's eyes. All of you. Back to Greece."

"We've already taken that option off the table."

He liked seeing her so ruffled. "Have we?"

"Yes."

"You know, the Aegean is beautiful this time of year."

"I remember thinking the same thing as I left it."

"You are my responsibility, whether you're a threat or an asset. That," he said, nodding to the quiver, "was a coincidence or a trick."

"You saw me find the arrows."

"I didn't see when you might have planted them."

She muttered something under her breath in a language he didn't understand. Garnis? If that was even her clan. All he had were stories. Why would she suddenly tell the truth, when months of captivity had yielded nothing?

"And predicting the future based on a dead man's final, what, thoughts? I can't believe that either. For all

I know . . ." His skin, baking under the rising sun as they began walking, suddenly went cold. Grabbing her entire delicate jaw in one palm, he forced her to look at him. She didn't meet his eyes. "For all I know, you knew about those Pendray."

"I saved your life."

"I have you and three dead Pendray. That's where this begins and ends."

She swept a boot heel behind his left knee and yanked, catching just the right spot. Mal sprawled onto the ground. He grabbed her around the waist and pulled her down with him. The quiver slipped from its place at her back.

He rolled. He was on top of her. They both stilled.

Mal's shoulder hurt, but he wasn't blind or dead or an idiot. He was stretched atop a confounding woman who looked up at him with eyes that were so perfectly gold and green, so wide, so chillingly distant. He got the impression that he could've taken her apart, limb by limb, and the same distance would've remained in her eyes.

Only a moment ago, she'd been teasing him. That was gone. Unfortunately, so was what should've been gratitude for what she had done to heal him. She could've left, letting him bleed, taking the quiver and sword without a backward glance. He should've been grateful, but more disturbingly, he wanted that brief moment when she'd opened up enough to try making a joke or two. He got the impression that was a rare effort.

With his elbow bracketing her face, he stared into those mesmerizing eyes. "You are a fraud. You come from some family of frauds."

She struggled and cursed, fighting until a sharp blow to his temple made him grunt.

"You're not getting away that easily," he growled.

"I only struck your temple. I could use my knuckles against your shoulder." She sneered. "That would take the fight out of you Dragon-damned quick."

"And you accused me of making threats I can't go through with." She didn't retaliate. She simply licked her lower lip. Mal couldn't have looked away had his life depended on it. Instead, he decided on a different tactic—one that needed to happen if he were to retain his sanity. "Kiss me, Avyi."

Mal ignored the lingering pain in his shoulder in order to grasp both of her hands. He pinned them above her head and took the kiss he wanted. It was heated and heady once again, but with a different flavor. They were celebrating; they were at war. She was driving him mad with frustration and indecision that felt like weakness. He wouldn't stand for it.

Avyi growled and fought his hold, but she didn't squirm away from his questing mouth. He needed her taste. With lips and tongue, he forced his way in. But that was all he needed to force. She met his tongue with every heavy pulse of blood in his veins as their duel was dictated by body and breath. Somewhere in the haze of that passion, Mal felt her hands relax. He dared release her. She gratified him by wrapping slender, deceptively strong arms around his neck, pulling him closer.

He was taken by surprise at how swiftly he was hard and aching. In less than a day, this maddening woman had proven that he could be stripped of the fundamentals of his character. He was a man who held on to control. Now his control was slipping. He thrust his hips, rocking their bodies together on the rough ground. They were even rougher. Take and take, with so little give.

He molded his palm over her breast. Such softness to be found there. Such temptation.

Avyi twisted at the waist and slipped from beneath him. He had been looking down at her pale, elfin face. Now he was staring at pearl-white shale. His hands were empty. His lips were slack, then tightened with anger.

"You don't touch me," she said bluntly, edging away from him. "You don't."

He stood to his full height, propelled by his flush of enraged frustration. "Then what the Dragon damn was that?"

"A mistake. I've made many since meeting you."

Without wasted motion, she hefted the Dragon-forged sword and held it in what looked to be a practiced two-handed grip. She turned her back. On him. The Honorable Giva. He had nearly given up trying to remember a time when anyone had treated him with such disregard. *Nearly*.

He ducked under her weak side—the left, where her elbow wasn't raised to the same ready angle. Two seconds and two swift moves later, he held the sword. They were face to face, body to body, breathing hard. He loomed a full head taller. He would only have to tip his chin toward his chest in order to kiss her crown. He realized that her view was very different. She would be staring at the hollow between his collarbones. She could lean forward a few scant inches and kiss his bare skin.

He tipped her chin up to meet his gaze. His eyes were filled with challenge.

"Have you made your choice, *Giva*?"

Hefting the sword, stifling every emotion but self-preservation—in all forms—he was the one to turn his back. "We should move."

The sudden coldness of the Giva's mood was no surprise to Avyi. How often had her wishes been met with disdain, anger, or even cruelty? Coldness was practically a relief, for its change of pace. She couldn't explain why she had acted as she had, either in kissing him or in ending the kiss. Too much. That's all she knew. *Too much.* Now he was walking, but his posture and expression were as hard as marble.

So often, she had been offered trust, friendship, or affection, only to have them jerked away for reasons beyond her comprehension. She was idiot enough to keep trying. Like a woman encased in ice, knowing the thaw would bring the paralyzing sting of pins and needles under her skin, she stepped without fail toward a source of potential warmth. Only, that warmth was always fire. Burning. Forcing her to shy away again.

While Malnefoley had slept, she'd resisted the impulse to curl up against his body rather than away from it. He was tempting. How much nicer would it have been to spend the night wrapped in his sure embrace than held by the chilly earth? How much more dangerous?

She wanted to like him.

She was an idiot.

In a mere matter of minutes, it became harder to think of him by his given name. He was back to being the Giva, standing tall, holding an intimidating sword that made him appear even more magnificent. Although bare-chested, he seemed to wear a cloak of arrogance only true leaders could shoulder—a leader who wasn't willing to consider anything but his own stubborn opinion.

He was no longer the man whose lifeblood had pulsed beneath her fingers as she'd guided him in the use of his gift. He wasn't the man who had kissed her with such intimidating passion. And he certainly wasn't the man who, without fanfare, had quietly given her a name she didn't want to relinquish. If he kept behaving this way, he would ruin the name for her, essentially taking it from her. She wouldn't want to be Avyi anymore, just as she wasn't the Pet or Girl anymore.

With deliberate footfalls, she once again walked alongside him. Cautious moves. The better to become invisible when those who saw her were more likely to beat her than talk to her.

"You are . . ." He broke off and shook his head. Strands of straight, bronze hair tumbled over his forehead.

"What?"

"Infuriating."

Avyi hefted the quiver. Some statements didn't merit notice. Some actions were better left to the past. But how could she forget what they had done when her gift insisted there was even more to come?

That was the future. For all the years she'd practically lived there, she needed to stay in the present with this man if she was going to have any chance of bending him to her needs—and fulfilling what her gift insisted would be their sensual fate.

"The job isn't done. More will come for you. The

dam has burst. Your enemies will jump from the shadows and they'll *all* come for you."

Malnefoley walked ahead of her with supreme confidence, as if he knew she always would follow.

The clear blue sky blazed off the perfect, taut skin of his back, which was naturally tan in the way of the Dragon Kings. *Most* Dragon Kings. She was as pale as sun-bleached sand and always had been. Malnefoley, though . . . And yes, she thought of his given name when admiring his body. Then, he was more man than symbol. Every muscle flexed as he strode across the wind-whipped plains. A sheen of sweat gathered to trickle down his spine. The belt she'd used to fasten his bandages reminded her of the straps Cage warriors wore to secure plates of leather and metal armor.

She didn't trust him. With strength like Malnefoley's came conceit and pride, and Avyi had never believed that the powerful could be just. The dominant influences in her life had been too cruel for that to be true. Unwillingly, she forced herself to put Malnefoley of Tigony in that category.

Let him think what he wanted about how the next few days would proceed. She only focused on the next few hours. She needed a means of getting to Italy. That would be much easier with a tall, overbearing man who carried a beast of a sword.

At least she knew that Florence was her next stop. Beyond finding anything in the maze, she'd been at a loss as to where to go next. Her gift was mercurial, playing hide-and-seek like the carefree child she'd never been.

"Deny what you will," she called after him. "Along

one path, you stood beneath the dome of the Florence Cathedral." Goose bumps climbed her nape when she stared the truth of her gift in the face. "Along the path back to Greece . . . you have no future. You will be murdered, whispering the name Pollakioh with your last breath."

❧ CHAPTER ❧
SIX

Mal had never been colder.

Pollakioh.

When his temper surfaced, he occasionally thought of Bakkhos, but he hadn't thought of *her* by name in years. There was no way Avyi could've known that name at all. She was pulling open his past in the form of a prediction.

For the first time, beyond logic or lust, he wondered if her claims had actual merit.

He needed to aim his suspicion away from the woman who had done so much, so quickly, to upend his self-assurance, to do her best to tend his injury . . . and to awaken a beastly sexuality that reminded him of the worst moments of his life. Being Giva meant the temptation to second-guess decisions, but he'd long ago established his means of dealing with politics. He was in charge. He didn't let up until he got his way.

On this rare instance, being in charge was a far and distant thing. He wanted to level entire plains, just to let off steam.

He stared across the rocky, leveled waste as Avyi

caught up and walked beside him. She had caused his old temper to resurface. He hadn't been so furious with another person in countless years. His revulsion toward men like Dr. Heath Aster—and the sadistic doctor's father, the Old Man of the Aster cartel—was an amorphous hatred with a rap sheet of offenses to back it up. What had this woman done except escape from the Tigony stronghold and help save him?

She'd kissed him.

Rejected him.

Shocked him to the core.

This woman he'd named Avyi was only the Pet. A tool of Dr. Aster's. A possible part of a greater assassination plot, especially if she claimed to know the circumstances of his death. She was no mythical prognosticator, able to see his future or anyone else's. She had no proof.

But . . . *Pollakioh*.

"You have become a living hell in my mind," he muttered.

Of course, that had to be the moment when she smiled. No teeth, no great change to the apples of her cheeks or the skin around her wide cat's eyes. Just the unmistakable and frankly alluring tilt of thin, expressive lips. She was breathtaking. She'd been Dr. Aster's personal plaything for so long that even if Mal had noticed her physical luminescence then, he wouldn't have seen her as anything but servile.

"Only for those who deserve it," she replied. "And I know you deserve a long stretch in hell, Giva."

He banked a shudder and closed off further thought of Bakkhos. Even if she could see the future . . . No. It was too unbelievable.

"Why let me find you?" He forced his frustrations down to his feet and out through the rubble. "Why wait out in the open?"

"I had no fear of your arrival."

Mal shot her an incredulous look. "You couldn't have known I'd come alone."

"To summon your personal guard would mean admitting a valuable prisoner had escaped your grasp, and that you needed help. You're a *lonayíp* fool, so full of yourself."

"No one but a member of the Council has cursed at me since I was a child."

"The privilege of the Giva. Never contradicted."

She was as graceful as a feline shadow as she transitioned from rock to the solid, smooth plains to rock again. After a half hour of silence, Mal was left with his thoughts, the ache in his shoulder, and the steady, calm respiration of his companion. This should've been so easy. Instead, he'd nearly been killed and he was no closer to untangling her riddles. Either she would tip her hand somewhere between Crete and Italy, revealing her tricks and her true allegiances, or . . .

Or what?

She'd find a bow? A young woman named Cadmin? See him in the shadow of a cathedral?

He would never believe what she claimed unless he was with Avyi when her predictions unfurled—or folded like a house of cards.

He would be better served to keep thinking of her as the Pet. She was too dangerous to make into some lost, wounded woman-child in his mind. But she was clever and blunt. She was exactly the sort of person he wished, almost daily, he could communicate with in lieu of the Council members.

"What would've happened to our people had I been killed?" he asked. "No so-called reliance on seeing the future. Just think it through."

"The Council would've collapsed in anarchy. None of the clans would've sent children to look into the Chasm and shout the name of another Giva. No successive Giva would've been chosen to take your place." She looked up at him with an expression of utmost sincerity, which layered a different sort of beauty over her features. "The end of order. The end of us."

"We came within inches."

"Do you finally realize this is bigger than your wounded pride?"

Mal flinched. Dragon damn it. She was right. He'd been so turned internally, toward his own aggravation, that he was only now parsing the fortune of his survival and the ramifications of his murder. He cleared his throat. It was necessary to find humility—not something he was used to needing. "Thank you. You saved more than my life."

"You're welcome." She wore none of the smug satisfaction he would've expected. A member of the Council would've reveled for weeks in his admission of gratitude.

She looked up to the clear sky, where sunshine glittered on her pale, luminous skin. Again he was amazed by the blackness of her hair, how it absorbed light, with no more brightness than the bottom of a well. She adjusted her grimy purple linen top where the straps across her shoulder had bunched the fabric.

"I'm not losing you again." He grimaced. That sounded far more . . . *intimate* than he'd intended. He hedged when he said, "With what you know about Dragon King conception, you could mean the difference between the survival of our people, and our extinction."

"So could you. Only, you don't trust me, and I won't trust you until you do. This will be a challenge, Giva."

"You know my name is Malnefoley. People of my acquaintance call me Mal."

"I'm sure the Council does not. They're 'of your acquaintance.'" She smiled again, to herself, face toward the ground. "We're not there yet."

She had a peculiar habit of simply ending her side of a conversation. Thoughts finished. Words ended. Mal walked on with his irritation at a low simmer. If he could get used to her odd, unnerving behavior, he'd be able to recognize when she spoke sense and when her fortune-teller's claims set off warning bells.

They arrived at a village Avyi called Septikos. It couldn't have housed more than fifty residences and a few rudimentary businesses: a leatherworks, a glassmaker, a pub. And a small hostel.

"Trouble." Without warning, Avyi took his hand and stealthily led him into a side alley between a small electronics repair shop and a grocery. "You don't know the shadows, Giva. I do. This way."

"That's because I've never had to hide in them. We have no fear of this place. We're Dragon Kings, and we walk in the open."

"Go ahead. Believe that our influence is what it once was."

Her words were so harsh, so certain, that Mal followed her. There was genuine pain in her voice and, more surprisingly, genuine fear.

Mal wanted to learn everything about her, with his reasons definitely blending into the personal. If he learned her fears, he could ease them—which was ridiculous. If anything, he should be using her fears against her in order to save his skin and accomplish his mission. Her secrets needed to become his hard data. Then he could make decisions for the good of all Five Clans, not for the sake of one woman.

Avyi crouched behind a rubbish bin, her back pressed flat against a wall Mal didn't want to examine too closely. He followed her lead by instinct. When was the last time he'd relied on instinct? Perhaps when he'd known, years before, that his cousin, Nynn, was a threat to the Five Clans' tenuous trust. If the other Leaderships had known of her potential, they would've disintegrated into factions so divided that not even the Dragon could repair the damage. Nynn was that powerful—even more powerful than he was.

He'd used his instinct to realize the danger she posed. And he'd sent her away. That she believed she'd gone by choice didn't matter. He had been the instigator—and thus the cause of her suffering.

Old bitterness would not see him free of danger. "Why are we hiding among refuse? Another attack?"

Avyi shook her head, her face a sickly shade of white beneath her shimmering skin. "Humans."

"Humans," Mal said flatly. "You're hiding from human beings?"

"Yes."

"Why in the name of the Chasm and the Dragon would humans send you running for cover? Humans are not our enemies."

"We aren't what we used to be—not to them. The myths are true, but they've stopped believing even when we still walk among them. Two Dragon Kings in broad daylight, even with that sword, aren't enough to cow a mob of enraged humans. Believe otherwise and find yourself strung up."

He grabbed her arm and gave it a shake, then pinned her against the wall with his forearm across her collarbones. "You're being absurd. We walk among them. They're awed by us and they leave us be. They're not a threat."

She fought back against his hold, but as in many things, his physical strength was overwhelming. "And if they attack? Are you ready to kill again so soon? Are you ready to learn what it feels like to take a bullet?"

"There will be no more killing, if it can be helped."

"Passive tense."

"What?"

"If it can be helped," she repeated. "You really mean, 'if I, the Honorable Giva, can help it.'"

"Why do humans scare you so badly? If you're blessed with the gift you claim, you should be able to see danger, not hide without cause."

She lifted her chin, trying to make him understand with her eyes alone. No use. He was beyond seeing anything but his own certainty, even when logic dictated that he was a potential—even likely—target for assassination. "How do you know the death I see for you isn't destruction by a mob of senseless animals? There are humans in Greece, after all. They can become animals."

Malnefoley leaned harder across her collarbones. "Your so-called gift comes with a lot of caveats."

"Let's try something you will understand." Not with her eyes. Not with her words. She would have to convince him with her past, although her past was not her favorite place to revisit. "When I was raised by that Garnis family, we traveled. Endlessly. After stopping at a village no larger than this, we traveled at a much slower pace."

She shuddered. Strangely, Malnefoley's hold eased. Rather than restraining her, he was almost holding her.

"Had the family accepted me as more than a burden, I might have been able to fit in. I might have even gained an adopted sister. Matako was her name. She was lovely, young, playful. She enjoyed traveling. I did not. I envied her ability to adapt." Avyi swallowed with some effort. Her tongue felt swollen, her lungs heated by fire. "We arrived in a small village in Kamchatka in far eastern Russia, populated by humans who believed in the old ways, including the existence of devils and witches."

"Your troupe of Dragon Kings must've fit those superstitions to a T."

"We did. Matako was stoned almost immediately. Her family fought. Half of the humans were killed. The rest fled. Matako . . . She was . . . *pulp*. Eventually she healed. As best she could. We had no sword."

He slowly shook his head, his understanding plain. No Dragon-forged sword meant no way to put Matako out of her misery.

"They'd smashed her feet. She couldn't walk. They'd collapsed her chest. She struggled for each breath. At night—" A shiver cut her sentence in two. "She gasped all night. I can't sleep sometimes, hearing her still."

"But your guardians didn't abandon her."

"They didn't." Avyi shrugged free of his loosened grip. "They never passed through a village again. They skirted around. Stole by the cover of darkness. I didn't sleep in a bed until the doctor bought me."

"Bought?"

It was her turn to shake her head, ending her reminiscence. She'd already revealed so much.

"Fine," he said tersely. "But don't think I won't ask again."

"Fine."

"Then why come here? It's daylight. Did you expect the village to be deserted?"

She was glad for the shadows because she didn't like to blush. She'd never been able to curtail that physiological reaction—as telling as a smile or a laugh. The doctor had liked to see her blush. She had been expressive until she learned to be expressive no more. But her blush had always remained.

Against all instinct, she stood. She looked down at the Honorable Giva, where he knelt in an alley. That had to be a first. "We need to get washed, find new clothes, and rest up. Comfort aside, we need to blend in as much as possible."

"Worth leaving this alley?"

She shivered. "It'll have to be."

Malnefoley rose with such slowness and grandeur that she thought he'd never reach his full height. He would hold her suspended in a state of anticipation for longer than time. He was so tall. Her forehead barely aligned with the top of his bare breastbone.

He touched the center of her chin with the pad of his thumb. "So, Avyi, now we explore the fine tourist destination of Septikos?"

"My name sounds better when you say it than it does in my head," she said quietly. He paused, scrutinizing her with unexpected intensity. A frown didn't detract from his heartbreakingly handsome face. He wore seriousness as well as he did expensive suits. Whether he realized it or not, he was meant for responsibility. Without need for her gift, she knew that much.

His hand slipped back to cup her neck. A shaft of sunshine caught the blue in his eyes and turned them into jewels, and spun his blond hair into thick, precious gold filaments. It took the entirety of her willpower to hold still. She was a rabbit in the grip of a wolf. She'd never wanted to feel that way again, yet with Malnefoley . . .

He held her possessively, but with something like respect. She'd never felt such a thing, so it was only a guess. An enticing guess.

"Do you like your name?" he asked, his voice so low and intimate.

"Very much."

He smiled at her, broadly, brightly, which was nearly as shattering as the powers he could rip from the sky. "I'm glad."

Enough of this . . . this . . . wiggling unease. She would wind up back in his arms, relishing his taste and his scent, wanting more than she was ready for. She ducked beneath his arm and walked out of the alley. Her knees were watery now, when they'd been steady and reliable facing off against three Pendray.

Full sunshine made her blink. She shielded her eyes, then set off to the north of the town. She angled a glance toward the hostel. "We'll stay there tonight."

"A prediction?"

"Sometimes it just *is*, like now. That's the only public place to sleep in town."

Avyi began to cross the barren street between the small whitewashed buildings. They must've looked like rats having crawled from a sewer, but perhaps the grime would cover the obvious—that, to humans, they may as well have been gods walking the earth.

❧ CHAPTER ❧
SEVEN

Malnefoley stood in front of the small, age-clouded mirror in his room in the hostel. He angled his upper body to get a better look at the damage done to his shoulder. The light was poor because of the oncoming dusk and the claustrophobically tight walls. The close heat of the hostel room, with its window that opened but a scant few inches, and his injury meant he left his new shirt off.

He liked being able to inhale fresh early-evening air, rather than the lingering damp-dusty stench of a room that needed a fierce cleaning. He would've preferred sleeping out in the open once again, except for the temptation of the mattress. It lay on a hardwood floor that pierced splinters into his soles. He'd donned his shoes and a new pair of jeans just after bathing.

Jeans, too, were a compromise. He couldn't remember the last time he'd dressed so simply. All of the supplies he'd acquired for him and Avyi were of the barest necessity. She had stayed in the hostel—and kept their weapons out of sight—while he traded with locals for additional supplies. He hadn't asked her to accompany him, not after the out-of-character fear he'd seen in her eyes and in her, like an animal readying to flee. What was he to make of her story? Just another clever ruse from a woman who spoke in riddles and insinuations?

But no matter how hard he tried, he could not escape one fact. She had predicted that with his dying breath, he would whisper the name of his long-dead mistress. The future was not to be trusted. That she knew Pollakioh's name at all was beyond belief . . . but very, very real.

He gingerly touched the skin forming over his injury, his mind re-creating a host of sensations. The initial slice. The throbbing gush of blood. Avyi's fingers holding his in place. And finally, the electrical strike he'd managed despite his slip toward unconsciousness.

It could have been far worse.

He had every reason to be more cautious than before, but that was a matter of physical and mental alertness, which he could supply in abundance. His foreboding now was different and inexplicable, with Avyi at its heart.

He'd been called the Usurper for his entire reign as Giva. They whispered the moniker in his trailing wake and thought he couldn't hear, or didn't know. He knew. But he'd never thought the resulting suspicion and resentment might boil over toward thoughts of rebellion— let alone an actual attempt on his life. Somehow, he had to make contact with Nynn and the underground rebel faction. Maybe they could shed light on the reasons behind violence that would mean far more than his death.

He kicked off his shoes and flopped wearily onto the mattress, which offered so little padding that his skull sank through to the hardwood. Grousing, he tried to find a comfortable position for sleep. He had food in his belly, and had swallowed bottle after bottle of water. A sponge bath and a fresh change of clothes should've been enough. Just *sleep*. He needed it, although he couldn't afford to let down his guard for long. Neither could he let fatigue cloud is judgment.

In the end, he had no choice in the matter. Sleep refused.

With a frustrated sigh, he turned onto his back once again. The ceiling was covered with dingy paint that might've once been white, where condensation had bubbled its texture. A large crack exposed wires that dangled across one corner. He refrained from lighting the room, even as darkness settled inside its walls. He didn't need another brush with the temptation of electricity in his veins. It was a drug unlike any other. Ecstasy was in its release.

The unapologetic knock at his door could only be one person. She was a demon stalking him as surely as a shadow.

The room was so small that he could kneel at the foot of the mattress and flip the lock. Why he had locked it . . . beyond him. Humans wouldn't last long if they intruded. Dragon Kings would bust through. He had his sword at the ready to deal with them.

Avyi opened the door and entered as if he'd invited her to an official Council meeting. Her posture was no-nonsense. She sat on a rickety wooden chair, the room's only furniture other than a small wooden sink cabinet with a faucet that leaked.

"Who tried to kill you?" she asked.

Her lack of preamble was as surprising as it was refreshing, but it was no longer so off-putting. Politicians and even human beings could spend minutes, even hours, building up to the point. Mal was ready to keep up, if only because he knew her bluntness was a limited engagement. He doubted he would ever meet her like again.

The thought left a hollow in his chest he couldn't explain. Didn't want to explore.

"Apparently you should've been able to glean that from their severed heads."

"You killed them too quickly."

"I was trying not to die."

She edged the chair toward a wall so she could lean back. She wore the same heavy boots. The sole of one was pierced. New pants made from tanned leather clung to her slim legs as if they'd been tailored to her petite frame. A simple black tank top did its part to accentuate her rough femininity by clinging to small breasts and revealing arms that were slender, gracefully shaped, and barely tinted by the Mediterranean sun.

She looked down at where he sat cross-legged on the mattress. He wanted to find his new shirt, but that would admit that her blatant appraisal of his body made him very aware of their contrasts. Man and woman. He was reacting to this strange, incredible woman in ways that made him edgy and . . . *more*. Needy. Eager. Perhaps it was simply intimacy. His sexual encounters were limited to brief affairs and the occasional lover, with whom he shared little but carnal exploration.

The Honorable Giva could share nothing more.

"So. Your enemies. Name them."

Mal laughed. The sound was warped and painful to let loose, but he laughed anyway. "Who *isn't* my enemy? Name a Dragon King, and he or she has a reason to want me dead."

"Avyi."

"What?"

"A Dragon King who doesn't want you dead."

Blinking against the gathering gloom, Mal lost track of the finer points of her features. Unacceptable. If he was going to have a conversation with Dr. Aster's Pet—a fact that didn't change because he'd given her a name— he would do so while being able to see each reaction and cue.

He snapped his fingers. Sparks of light appeared before the sound of the snap even registered. He tossed the sparks between his hands like a ball until the motion created a continuous arc of light. He threw the arc toward the ceiling, where it cast its glow throughout the room.

Avyi nodded toward a lamp on the floor in the far corner. "Why?"

"I wanted to show off."

He kept saying things to her that were dangerous. Not because of the words themselves, but because he hadn't checked his thoughts before uttering them. They shot from his mouth without reservation. Was that due to fatigue or just . . . her?

"I'm impressed." Her lips were curled into a smile as old as time. It was tempting and teasing, and frankly, he'd underestimated her ability to conjure such magic. "Now . . . think this through."

"Avyi, this is pointless. There's no sense in racking

our brains to identify which of hundreds of people, human and Dragon King, would benefit from my death, if only for their personal satisfaction. The trick is finding out how best to counter the next move." He stood and stretched, his back already stiff from the few hours he'd spent trying fruitlessly to sleep. "I'll call on my bodyguards and espionage experts to increase security at the stronghold before we arrive."

"The bodyguards who didn't notice my escape?" Mal flinched.

"And the espionage experts who told you where to find me? Did I present a challenge for them?"

Fatigue was a nasty rat in his brain. He didn't have the patience to deal with Avyi, even when he was fully rested—although the last time he'd been fully rested, he'd impaled her with a bolt of lightning. "No, you didn't. So if not my men, what do you suggest?"

"We don't hide, at least not from Dragon Kings. We wait for the next people who try to kill you. And we ask them. Unless you kill them first." She slanted her eyes in an expression of unmistakable humor. She *was* teasing him. He hadn't been teased so playfully, so innocently, in longer than he could remember. The Council didn't tease; they jabbed knives.

"I'll refrain if at all possible," he said, smirking.

"Plain sight will draw them out, and will have the advantage of showing the Council you're not afraid." She pulled her boots up to the seat of the chair and wrapped her arms around her shins. Mal hadn't thought her able to assume a tighter, more defensive position than her signature crouch, but she managed. This new pose struck him as so defensive as to border on vulnerable, as though she were a child crouched in the corner of a train station.

"And unpredictable."

"You're catching on."

"Miracles never cease."

"I wouldn't have thought you one to believe in miracles."

"It's just an expression."

She tipped her head. "Born of a kernel of truth."

He closed the scant distance between them and, on impulse, touched her black-on-black hair. The light he'd created still glowed overhead. He needed to feel the texture of such a wondrous feature. She was scrubbed clean, smelling of soap, water, and woman. Her hair remained in untamed spikes, pinned back from her face without care. Mal traced his fingers over a lock that brushed her cheek. It was far softer than he'd imagined, much like the woman herself.

She looked away.

"You deserve to be admired," he said, surprising himself. "I can't trust you, but you're one of the most resilient people I've ever met."

"Stop. Please."

"No. Uncurl for me."

"What?"

"I'm not asking you to take your clothes off." His temper shot to life for reasons that he couldn't deny or ignore any longer. He wanted this woman to feel comfortable enough around him to quit behaving as if he'd beat her at any moment.

Hypocrite.

He'd just about leveled her with the blast of his gift.

He had kissed her with so much force that she'd practically jumped clear of him. She had every reason to believe he could still do her harm. What she couldn't know was that his thoughts, his emotions, were beginning to change. Dragon Kings knew it would be simpler if they didn't, but he was *feeling*. A Giva didn't feel. He remained impartial and made impartial judgments. He recruited soldiers of good repute to infiltrate the cartels and work toward bringing them down from the inside. He fought the Council's recalcitrance and stubborn negativity, their petty infighting.

He certainly didn't feel . . . except when he was with Avyi.

"Here." He clasped her calves and slowly, with *aching* slowness, he pulled. At first she wove her fingers together and held her arms even tighter around her knees. But he was patient. He stroked her fingers, her knuckles, until they loosened. Her eyes held such a blend of yearning and fear. How often had she suffered that torturous combination?

Her entire life.

"Let go, Avyi. Let go."

She released her fingers, focusing that vise-tight grip on the armrests of the chair. The gold and green and wariness in her stare never wavered. She hardly blinked. Mal returned his slow touch to her calves. He pulled. The soles of her boots scraped the wooden edge of the chair with a sound that made her jump. But then her legs were free. Her knees eased. Her legs stretched. Finally, the soles of those wicked combat boots were flat on the floor.

She sat in the chair like a woman unafraid, although

fear still burned bright fires in her eyes. Her mouth was pinched to a tight white line that was even paler than her unusual skin. Could growing up in the labs have changed her complexion to such a degree? She should've been as robustly tan as the rest of the Dragon Kings, who practically glowed with the color of health and vitality.

"There," he said softly. "Now breathe. Deeply. Use the chair to support you, not that rigid spine."

"Only if you do the same." She nodded to the floor. "There, by the bed."

Mal sucked in air, then nodded in return. He was reluctant to let go of the firm muscle of her legs, but he had cultured far more discipline than the selfishness it would've taken to linger. He stood. For a moment, he simply stared down at her. He wasn't wearing his bandages. Although the gash on his shoulder remained deeply red, he was proud of his body. Some might call it conceited, but he didn't give a Dragon damn. Especially when Avyi looked up at him with an expression of pure appreciation. Her gaze traveled over every inch of his skin.

It should've been enough. But he wanted her touch to replace her perusal.

He returned to the plain mattress and pushed it halfway up the wall. The thing smelled of must and other scents he refused to catalog, but he did as she'd asked. No, she hadn't asked. She'd struck a bargain. He looked back at where she sat with her wrists still draped over the ends of the armrests. She had relaxed into the pose as if born to sit on a throne.

Mal sat, half on the mattress, half leaning against

what padding it provided. He stretched his legs. She took in the angles of his body with quick flicks of her magnetic eyes.

"Why did you touch my hair?"

"Because I wanted to."

"And you always do what you want?"

He laid his head back against the mattress. "Yes."

She shrugged, then examined the nails of one hand. The look she arched him from over her upturned knuckles was pure challenge. "One day, you'll put that stubbornness aside and you'll assume your place as the head of our people."

"I *am* the head of our people." His voice boomed through the small space. He forgot to keep his unconscious mind spinning that ball of energy. It flickered out, leaving them in darkness.

Avyi was on her feet in a flash, gripping the doorknob. She paused only long enough to toss a quick "Good night" over her shoulder.

Mal made a fist and stared at the closed door. He was left with the useless mattress, the tiny room, the memory of a grown foundling's silky hair . . . and her infuriating words.

He wouldn't feel this defensive if they didn't hold—what had she called it?—a kernel of truth.

All he'd wanted was rest. To heal up. Regain perspective. Yet sleep never came.

Avyi sat next to Malnefoley on the step behind the hostel, watching a trio of children running after a stray dog. The dog looked terrified. The children looked far too malicious for her liking. Perhaps that's why she'd been drawn to Dr. Aster. He was a cruel man, but she'd always found welcome in his expressions. She'd been at such an age and in such a desperate state as to take whatever apparent kindness was thrown her way.

The heat from the Giva's arm next to hers reminded her that she was in a similar situation now. The way he'd touched her hair . . . It had been even more intimate than kisses shaded by the fervor of aggression.

But that wasn't kindness, and neither was how he'd behaved upon their initial meeting. Trying to electrocute her after keeping her captive for six months wouldn't be considered gentle by any standard.

The sun had come up. They remained under a slight awning that kept them hidden from the morning glare. Malnefoley wore a simple white T-shirt that stretched across his wide chest and defined the undeniable masculinity of his body. A white linen overshirt was unbuttoned and hung open, sleeves rolled to the elbows. In profile, watching the same children, he was breathtaking. The slopes and ridges that comprised his brow, his nose, his upper lip, his strong chin—*perfection*. Hair a little too long had been combed back, still damp. Locks fell carelessly across his forehead, easing the stark beauty of his sharply masculine features.

"Florence," he said out of nowhere.

"Good."

"Just like that?"

"I saw it last night, after I went to bed. You must've made some decision. The image of you beneath the dome of the cathedral was as clear as glass. No variables now."

He grimaced, but she didn't know why. "Probably

based on the idea that Florence couldn't possibly have worse accommodations."

She smiled. "It wasn't the most restful night for me either."

"That's an assumption. Maybe I slept like a baby."

"Babies thrash and cry. So yes, maybe you slept like a baby. Was your bed as bad as mine?"

His smile was radiant, changing his face by shaping his mouth and cheeks with a new pattern of lines. She wanted to take a mental picture, so she could study this new version of the normally stoic Giva who harbored so much anger and frustration under his cultured surface.

"I can only hazard a guess," he said. "Yes."

She grinned. "Just *terrible*."

"Do you see a five-star hotel in our future?"

"*Our* future?"

"If word gets back that you were witness to the attempt on my life, you'll be at risk of retaliation, too. I'm not through with you yet. The question of procreation is still of vital importance to our people, and I know you're not telling me everything you know. I don't appreciate drips and dribbles of information. I expect that from the Council."

"Not from me?"

He looked at her dead-on. Eyes like the wind-tossed sea met hers, holding her as surely as he'd held her legs the night before. He'd stripped her of a defense she hadn't realized she resorted to so often. Curling into herself. Hiding by crouching and slinking. She envied the way Malnefoley strode into town, appearing for all the world like a dust- and blood-covered god, and carrying a Dragon-forged sword, no less. She had escaped

Dr. Aster, but she hadn't escaped decades of being treated as less than nothing or, a step up, as a plaything.

"No, not from you. I don't know why you should be any different from the polite liars and cheats who make up the Leaderships of the Five Clans." He looked away. "But you are."

"Does that mean you believe in my gift?"

"Don't push it."

"It weighs heavily on you—the problem of Dragon Kings' survival."

"Yes." He added that affirmation, although she hadn't intended her words as a question. "That everyone seems to be sticking their heads in the sand, all the while letting the cartels determine the future of our strongest warriors, is so Dragon-damned frustrating . . ."

He seemed to realize how much he'd divulged, because he stopped abruptly. His mouth was a pinched line, but nothing could erase the tempting slope of his upper lip.

Avyi permitted herself one indulgent thought. Just one. She wouldn't think about his firm, taut body or how much the wound on his shoulder fostered in her an urge to stand back to back with him, as his equal and his defender and his partner—everything a man and woman, a matched pair of warriors, could be. Those thoughts were too dangerous, too perfect, when she had no way to understand perfection.

No, she only indulged in the idea of kissing him again, this time with the gentle curiosity he'd demonstrated when touching her hair and unbinding her clenched body. He'd push her back until her body melted and let go of its ever-present tension. And he'd kiss her like a lover. It would be breathtaking with Mal . . .

Dragon be, she was thinking of him as Mal now?

She wanted a vision, a glimpse, but nothing came other than the same frustrating image of lying together with him, embracing, surrounded by gauzy white, their bodies pressed flesh to flesh. But when? How? Instead, she would have to rely on what she'd never given much thought to: the present.

He was arrogant, stubborn, inexplicably wrathful beneath his elegant exterior, and oddly powerless despite his personal strength and resolve. None of that mattered as much as one fact.

She *did* like him.

"Besides, Florence will hold more appeal than here."

She stood and adjusted her scant gear. They'd purchased another knapsack for Mal to carry their provisions, which included spare clothes and more food. It would last them until they reached Italy. "Appeal is as good a reason as any for making a choice."

He joined her in standing. "Really?"

"People do it all the time. Stay in. Go out. Fill their cupboards."

"You've been talking grand futures and old myths. It didn't occur to me that smaller choices would be variables, too."

She patted his cheek, as if humoring a child. "A small mind wrapped around a big brain."

She set off so that he couldn't see her smile. His expression had been too priceless—utterly stunned and affronted.

An hour later, they sat knee to shoulder on a bus to

the coast, and three hours after that, they reached the city of Heraklion.

"Considering what I've learned since," Mal said, "why didn't you choose Sitia as your point of arrival? This is a bigger city. More humans."

"More opportunities to be ignored. Even you, Giva—who knows who you are here?"

"Those Indranan."

He crossed his arms and nodded toward a pair of men by a dockside bar. Avyi felt their tap-tapping in her mind, as they revealed themselves less by appearance than by the invasive nature of their telepathic powers. She noticed Mal had felt that tickle, as the first sparking flare of his powers came into being. Already he'd gathered static electricity. She shut her eyes, frowned, and nodded. If Mal needed her help, she would be there.

She had his back. Stranger still, she would've laid money on the idea that he had hers, too. Instead, she wouldn't wage money. She was wagering her safety and untold futures.

"They'll recognize me," he said grimly.

"And me. I'm infamous, too."

"And proud of it?"

Her companion was grinning again. "When was the last time you smiled so much in a day?"

Mal frowned, as if the question were spoken in a language he couldn't interpret. "I don't recall."

"Good or bad thing?"

"Let's just call it a thing."

"Fair enough. But they don't seem out for a fight. I wish they'd mind their own business, though," she said, rubbing the base of her skull. "It's so rude."

"Agreed. Now try playing political chess with their kind."

"That's some poker face you must have if you can hide your thoughts, too."

He shrugged. "Long practice."

"Except from me. I read you like a book."

"I take exception to that."

The port was thick with masts, as if a misguided city planner had clustered all of its telephone poles in one place. A huge dock harbored long overnight tourist ferries. People unloaded crates and rolled goods up gangways. Passengers waited, sitting on their luggage or arguing with customs officials. Men from smaller ships called out their destinations and competed for business by literally out-shouting one another. Despite the necessity of blending in, Avyi was overwhelmed anew by the bustle of humanity. She'd been in isolation in the Tigony stronghold for months, in the labs for years, and among the wandering Garnis since before she could remember.

The present . . . It was a new, difficult thing to take in all at once.

"I arrived by helicopter," Mal said offhandedly. "Unless you happen to have a passport I don't know about, we won't be permitted into Italy by conventional means."

"You don't know a lot about me, but at least that's true. No passport. No records."

"I suppose that means the slow route after arriving in Athens. There's a cruise liner that sails from Patra to Venice."

"That sounds like Greece again, Giva."

"This is where I trust you won't run, and you trust I won't have you locked up."

Avyi adjusted the strap that held the precious quiver of arrows. "Sounds like you've made our plans already. I'm game."

They took a taxi to where Mal's personal helicopter waited to take him home. He called his pilot, who arrived within the half hour. His man was visibly shocked at the sight of Mal's attire. Apparently he knew his place because he stared, ducked his eyes, and said nothing other than, "I expected you back days ago, sir."

"I was detained. Back to Athens, Perdius. Then a refuel before we fly to Patra. Have Ginovosa meet us at the helipad. I want my suitcase ready for travel of all possible varieties, and another for the Pet."

Avyi hid her cringing reaction to being called that again—by Mal, no less. She had become so attached to the idea of her new name. But who among the Tigony— no, who in the entire world—would know her as anything else? Just Malnefoley. Suddenly the fact that she had no passport, no identification of any kind, struck her as more than a technicality. She didn't exist. She only existed as a commodity and a vendetta.

Taking the knowledge into her soul, she refused to be caught up in other people's definitions. She was simply Avyi. And she was on a mission.

She hadn't thought the mission would include climbing into a helicopter, yet there she was. She cursed her gift. Cursed and cursed and cursed, until Mal handed her a pair of headphones. An attached microphone allowed her to hear and speak during the noisy flight. Takeoff was dizzying. She gripped her armrest while keeping her expression as neutral as possible. She'd flown with the Asters, but their jets were practically windowless.

She shuddered, closed her eyes, and took a deep breath. That imprisonment was behind her now. She was flying. She was looking through a domed window, over the coast of Crete, where blue that matched Mal's eyes crashed in foamy white waves against rocky shoals and small fishing villages. It was daytime, with the fishing boats already at sea, their captains searching for the slippery creatures that would mean the difference between their families' survival or starvation.

There in the helicopter, she knew she would've been much more comfortable haggling with a boatswain to secure their passage aboard a simple vessel. She'd arrived by such plain means. It evoked images of long-ago days, when traveling by water was the only way to move from continent to continent. Had her age been closer to the end of a Dragon King's life span, she would've known those thoughts as centuries-old memories, not products of her imagination.

Then again, had she been born two hundred years earlier, she would've been able to bear children. There would be no cartels to serve, and no sick Grievances co-opted by human greed for Dragon King magic and violence. What sort of woman would she have become?

A family. A stable life. Eventually grandchildren.

And a husband.

She gripped the armrest tighter. Vertigo convinced her swirling mind that the helicopter was destined to fall into a sickly port's murky, gasoline-streaked waters. Her respiration ticked toward bursting her lungs.

A comforting hand settled over hers.

As he had in the small hostel, Mal loosened her death grip with patient fingers. He flipped a switch to exclude the pilot from their conversation. "What was that?" he asked, his voice humming directly against her eardrum.

"The hazard of bearing company with soothsayer."

"A prediction?"

"Something like that."

In truth, the word *husband* had evoked a mind-warping blend of images so overpowering that she couldn't sort fear from desire from resentment . . . from the unavoidable truth.

Did she want to avoid becoming Mal's lover, or take steps to ensure it took place?

Or would she finally accept, after so long, that conscious action made no difference? It was a prediction for a reason. There was no changing what would be. If even she had difficulty accepting that, how was she going to convince Mal to trust her?

She couldn't.

She and the Honorable Giva would part as soon as Avyi found her way to Cadmin and ensured her safety. The girl was important. That burned bright in Avyi's thoughts and guided her steps toward fulfilling twined destinies.

But the journey to meet the grown woman named Cadmin entailed more than a trip to Florence. She shivered and clasped his hand, but she refused to meet his questioning gaze or answer the questions he asked into her headphones.

Eventually the helicopter flew over the uncluttered waters of the Mediterranean. Without landmarks, Avyi's view was simply blue. That eased her dizziness. Although she wanted to be out on the sea, buffeted by the sun and the salt, she let that piercing blue do its best to strip the strange vision from her mind.

No. Impossible. Her future version of Malnefoley, wrapped naked around her in an unknown bedroom, was the same man who sprawled casually beside her in his seat. Watching the sea was like looking into his eyes.

"So tell me how this works," he said. "You see me clearly in Florence. Does that mean we're guaranteed to get there?"

"By one means or another."

"Meaning?"

"We will arrive in Florence. In the meantime we could be attacked or struck by a small aircraft or serenaded by clowns. There's no telling what awaits us in between."

"Serenaded by clowns?" He stretched his legs as best he could in the tight confines. "That almost sounded like an imagination."

"Do you doubt I have one?"

"I wouldn't have a clue. Not with you."

Oddly, she was offended. "Does my possession of an imagination detract from or confirm the possibility my gift is real?"

"Detracts from. You were more convincing when you were practically robotic."

"Robotic?"

Another shaft of hurt shoved between her lungs. Was she so . . . *different* than everyone else? Did she truly come across as a programmed machine rather than a flesh-and-blood woman? Had she been the Pet so long that no one assumed she had a personality of her own?

I was his pet. Who would expect anything but servile obedience to Dr. Aster?

Especially the Giva, whose job it was to investigate anything related to the cartels, particularly where they intersected with the issue of Dragon King procreation.

"I'm not a robot," she whispered.

She hadn't thought the microphone strong enough to pick up her quiet affirmation, but it had. Mal returned her whisper. "I know. I'm sorry."

Another shiver worked up her spine. Unwanted, unexpected tears pricked behind her eyes. *Fatigue. That's all.*

"How are you going to manage in Athens carrying that sword?"

"Better they see a man with a sword than catch notice of your skin."

Avyi looked down. Her arms were bare, but otherwise she was as practically dressed as ever. "What about my skin?"

He traced his forefinger up the inside of her wrist. "Pale. Luminous. Had I not seen otherwise last night, I'd have thought you could glow in the dark."

"I was being modest."

"Hiding your true potential?"

"If you like."

Leaning nearer, Mal tucked a spike of her exasperating hair behind her ear. "I don't want you hiding your true potential, Avyi."

"And you get what you want."

"I will when it's your turn to amaze me."

"In Florence. You'll see."

"No need to wait," he said, easing back. His gaze never left her face, until she was tempted to retrieve her brass knuckles and smack that perfect jaw. "I'm already impressed."

❧ CHAPTER ❧
EIGHT

To Mal's surprise, he meant his words. She was resilient and strange, but also wily, creative, and almost unwillingly funny. That didn't change their situation. He'd decided to go to Florence based on a number of sensible decisions, the most important of which was to see if Avyi's mission intersected with the plot against his life—or to see her discredited and put his mind at ease. He was not going because of his growing curiosity about more than her kisses and shy smiles. She was unique.

What if . . . ? Just *what if* . . . ?

Logic failed him when it came to Avyi, including why he'd bothered helping to name her. That name connected them. Bound them. Would she always be Avyi, because of him? The idea was almost primal. He had been granted the privilege of naming the woman who'd never had one of her own. It was a possessive act he couldn't help returning to, savoring as a small triumph.

Why am I drawn to you? Because on a very deep level, Mal knew their connection mattered. It was the strange feeling that another life vibrated just beneath the surface—all of it infinitely bigger than them.

He turned to her, where she had resumed her huddled position in the passenger seat. Had he not seen it for himself, Mal would've had a hard time picturing her standing to her full height, or lounging almost at ease in that hostel's wooden chair.

"What did you predict that was so overwhelming?" he asked. "When we took off?"

"That you and I would be lovers. But it wasn't new knowledge."

Had Mal been taking a sip of water, he'd have choked. "You hide so much, but not that?"

She hugged her knees closer. "I wanted to learn whether you'd be excited or revolted."

Not knowing how to respond, Mal only watched her. She was determined to avoid his curious gaze; she never looked up from the rubberized black flooring.

He could find her more than intriguing. He could find her *irresistible*.

"I'm . . . curious," he said simply.

She plopped her feet down. The boots hit the floor with a one-two thump strong enough for Mal to feel despite the helicopter's vibrations. "I could say the same about you. Curious."

The moment of odd intimacy was marked by its usual end: Avyi turned away. Had they not been confined, she would've turned on her heel and walked away from him. That he had to chase anything was novel. He'd been given everything since he was a child. Born to the privilege of royalty. Pushed to the point of such destruction that he'd become notorious.

Chosen as Giva.

He wanted her to stop hiding from him. But unlike

everyone else around him who bent to his will, this wouldn't come naturally. It was up to him.

Mal had so many questions to ask, although fewer and fewer pertained to Dragon King conception and the strategies of the cartels.

Why were you with Dr. Aster? What was the nature of your relationship? Why stay in his custody, flee, stay in my custody, and flee again?

He had the nagging feeling that she was comfortable opening up about blunt topics such as becoming lovers, but thornier questions about her past would remain forever barred.

He wouldn't give up on knowing her. Dragon damn, he wanted to know her completely. It was purely personal. It was purely selfish. He'd thought himself above all that.

He wasn't.

"Any idea what those two Indranan wanted? Did you picture them lunging after me with another Dragon-forged sword?" The tap-tap of a telepath probing his mind was never a pleasant experience. He still felt that tickle, as if he needed to scrub the inner folds of his brain. His mental poker face, as Avyi had suggested, only went so far. "Any ideas?"

"I don't like helicopters. That's one. Your hair is gorgeous in the sunlight. That's another."

"Your tricks are wearing off, Avyi," he said, although feeling a certain pleasant surprise at her intimate comment was unavoidable. "I meant about the Indranan."

"My tricks are just fine, because you still flinched." She smiled, a private smile seemingly meant for herself alone. "They were members of the Leadership from the

Southern Indranan faction. Their destination is Turkey, not Florence. The Sun goddess, Kavya of Indranan, has gone home to her place in the Himalayas, and they're returning to her in search of peace."

"Rumors, not predictions."

"Then call it hope. She'll heal their divide. She and Tallis, the Heretic. They are a volatile pair, but not when they're together. Two horses pulling the same cart."

"More rumors." His late aunt's Pendray brother-in-law had been on the run nearly as long as Mal had been Giva. To believe that the shady killer known as the Heretic had joined with a peaceful Indranan priestess was beyond his ability to give credence.

No way. Not Tallis.

Avyi adjusted the microphone and spoke directly into it. "Fact. They're going to meet us soon, but I don't know why."

"*Us* again? We're bound for so many adventures?"

She was smiling again, but this time for him. Few of her features changed configuration. She simply looked at him with a different brightness to her eyes. Keener, more gold than green. More fiery. More inviting. She was a woman who could smile without moving her lips. "Am I such difficult company to keep? Or are the adventures the issue?"

"I haven't done anything for the last ten years but mitigate disputes, split my time between Greece and Tibet, and target the cartels with every resource at my disposal. Adventure has not been a high priority."

"Perhaps that's why the Dragon has chosen us. Neither of us knows the world."

"Are you comparing my responsibilities to your years in Dr. Aster's labs?"

Her slight teasing fled from her expression. That speck of levity was replaced by revulsion so strong that had Mal been a telepath, he would've recoiled and done his best to turn his mind away from hers.

"Nothing compares to the doctor's labs."

They spent the rest of the flight in silence. No chance to open a window this time, as he had in the hostel. Perhaps he should apologize again, but her vacillation between accessible and impossibly cut off raised his hackles. And he thought *he* was the politician. Now he found himself on the receiving end of the most studied silent treatment he'd ever known.

He didn't want to acknowledge the haunted, stricken pain evident on her face when he'd spoken of Aster's laboratory. He'd seen it. He'd helped blow it to the ground. The horrors contained within those cinder-block walls in the Canadian Yukon were unspeakable. Dragon Kings had been held against their wills in cells akin to slab cabinets at a morgue. Pulled free of their narrow, coffinlike prisons, they'd blinked against the fluorescent light and hadn't known what to do with freedom.

Avyi had lived there as the Pet for . . . how long? He didn't even know. As with most Dragon King women, she was timeless. Her smooth features could've meant she was twenty or eighty. She was in the prime of their people's youth. Had she been in the keeping of the doctor for decades and decades, how was she even functioning? So long spent in the captivity of another person must be crippling.

His skin went cold. He sat up straighter in his seat and stared out to where the mainland of Greece was just coming into view. Although Mal hated giving credence to the idea, he needed to. She could still be in the Asters' service.

Avyi was not used to being waited on.

When she'd accepted a two-piece set of luggage from a woman on the helipad in Athens, she'd done so wearing what must've been a dumbfounded expression. That rankled compared to how easily Malnefoley slipped into his natural skin—that of the head of his clan, and the head of the Dragon Kings. She was reminded of his high-handed ways when he'd whisked her away from the ruined labs. So certain. Arrogantly certain. That same tone had followed her into the holding cells where the questions never ended regarding Aster's next moves, and the details of his crossbreeding program.

What she had offered—the truth about her role in conception—was disregarded as lies. She could lie. She'd been taught by a family adept at them, and she'd lived in the possession of a doctor who lied with every breath. That didn't mean she was lying about being Aster's secret link between the life and death of unborn Dragon Kings.

There was no point to lying now. She had too much to do before the Grievance. She couldn't pinpoint its exact dates until she took a few steps in an unknown direction. Then the future would flow through a vision of ideas into the facts of reality.

That left a smile on her face. Mal thought he knew so much. He'd see.

She always experienced a special moment when what she predicted came true. It was like a dream materializing before her eyes. But that didn't mean it was always happy. On countless occasions, she'd seen the imminent death of a baby or the certainty that a father wouldn't survive to see his child born. To know her gift was still active, true, and strong was reassuring—that she wasn't crazy, and that she wasn't deluding herself when she saw positive outcomes—but heartbreak always hit her twice: once when she saw it as a vision, and again when she saw it take real, immutable shape.

She glanced at Mal as they navigated the corridors below deck on a six-hundred-person ferry called the *Forza*, which would take them from Patra to Venice. From Greece to Italy. At least that hadn't been a trick. He hadn't told his men to shackle her and drag her up the mountains to the Tigony fortress. Her trust was paying off. She wouldn't have been detained long by the vaunted Giva's men, but she didn't have the luxury of time now. It was collapsing in on her.

Mal stopped at a door at the end of a cruise vessel's corridor. "This is it."

"It? Singular?"

"I said you'd have your own bed." After setting the cases on the floor, he retrieved one key. "That didn't mean they'd be in two rooms."

"You're trying very hard to make my prediction come true."

The key slipped across the face of the lock. He glared at her again. "This isn't about sex," he said. "This is about being able to get us on the same ship leaving today. As it is, we won't be in Florence until day after tomorrow.

I should've thought to have my people make you up a fake passport."

"You were too busy detaining me."

"Detaining. You meant something else by that."

"Interrogating? Getting nowhere with pointless questions?" She dropped her bags and snatched the key from his fingers. "Pick one."

Avyi opened the door and left her bags in the corridor. If she was going to be waited on hand and foot by a Tigony, she might as well start at the top. She hadn't let go of her anger. He didn't take her seriously, and she dearly wished her gift would align in a way that would prove she wasn't a fraud.

She glanced behind her as Mal rolled her suitcases into the narrow room. She couldn't help but smile.

"Not bad," he said to himself. "For last-minute tickets."

He wasn't wrong. The berth was wide enough for a center aisle with a single bed on either side. A miniature closet took up the space between the foot of one bed and the corridor wall, while the mirroring space was a very small bathroom. They wouldn't have to share with other people, but they would have to share with each other.

It's just overnight.

She sat heavily on the left of the two single beds. "At least I don't snore."

Mal chuckled. "How would you know?"

"I was rewarded when I stopped."

With the look of a man weighted by the whole of the ship, he locked the door and let the cases stay where they fell. He sat on the opposite bed and rested his elbows on his thighs. The glance he angled up from beneath his brows was poised between wanting to ask a question . . . and not wanting to hear the answer. That was the story of Avyi's gift.

"Rewarded?" he asked at last.

"By the doctor. He used hypnosis and drugs. Eventually surgery." She self-consciously rubbed the bridge of her nose. Her random comment had led to revealing just how subjugated she'd been. That wasn't a pattern she wished to continue with. "When I healed, I didn't snore anymore. He let me sleep on a mattress for the first time."

"He could hear you snoring in the first place?"

Avyi's hands had grown restless, touching the back of her neck. She'd worn a collar once, long ago, but not because she'd fought in the Cages. The doctor had liked how it looked. Mal's scrutiny added to her unease. She didn't like being unable to control physical reactions, but this topic was hitting well below conscious thought. She could smell the old-fashioned shaving soap Dr. Aster whipped to a lather in a cup. She remembered kneeling at his feet, holding on to his leg and smiling at his associates and enemies alike. She even recalled the soft crease he kept in his trousers.

The good pet.

"I slept in his room. After a time. The first few years I was kept in a lab cell. He had to figure out how to control me."

"Brainwashing."

"Initially, yes."

"But you slept without a mattress."

"On the floor," she said, grabbing the edges of the

mattress to reassure herself of the present. *Stay in the present.* The past was a tangle of evil, and the future was unreliable. "Until the surgery cured my snoring. But he never slept without me in my cage at the foot of his bed."

"*Cage?*" His voice was shockingly loud in that small space. Avyi flinched, then noticed the flicker of lights and how they matched the electricity in Mal's deep blue eyes and the sparks tingling from his fingertips. "He kept you in a cage?"

"Maybe you're more trusting than is wise. You volunteered to sleep in here with me." She narrowed her eyes and pinned him with as much ferocity as the memories of Dr. Aster always left her feeling. "Good luck closing your eyes tonight, Giva."

He stood and paced the three steps to the door, then back. Again. He shoved his hands through the long, straight strands of blond hair that fell across his brow. "Why did you remain with me after the labs were destroyed, when he fled?"

"I didn't want to stay anymore." She lay back on the mattress and pulled up a blanket. "And I haven't been brainwashed for a long time."

"How do you know?"

"I was in a lab room, where a Dragon King woman was being inseminated. I was ordered to talk to her and keep her calm. I didn't say much. Didn't have to. That's what pets are for. Be seen, be touched, be talked to. But it didn't matter. She was hopeful in a way I couldn't understand." She twisted the edge of the blanket around her fingers. "I hadn't known much about hope."

"Did you . . . ?" He stopped and braced his weight against the narrow width between doors. "Did you see your own future?"

"I know that I will kill Dr. Aster or he will kill me. Other than knowing about you and me, I've never seen another piece of my own future."

"I don't know what to do with that."

"Be glad you're the one I'll sleep with rather than kill?"

Mal smiled ruefully and let his head drop, face to the floor. She wanted to touch the place at his nape where the blond hair looked its softest, like corn silk beneath a heavier, thicker layer. "I'll take that, yes. So this woman . . . ?"

"She wasn't just going to conceive a baby. She was going to bear one. I held her hand and saw a moment in the unborn child's future when his father would hold him and hide his tears." Avyi shivered and curled into herself on the narrow bed. "Dr. Aster couldn't know what I'd seen. He couldn't know what I *knew*. No random hope. It had been a prediction of *joy*. The doctor only wanted the facts. Other predictions followed. The good and the bad. Children who would be successful. Children who would die by accident. Children who would grow up orphans."

She remained silent for a long time, as did Mal. He took off his suit coat and rolled up his sleeves. That seemed more intimate than if he'd stood before her nude. Rolling up his sleeves was like a prelude to undressing. There was potential and anticipation. He sank onto his mattress and leaned his elbows against his thighs once more.

"You should at least take off your boots," he said. "I'll be good."

"I know you will be."

He crooked a smile. "But these children. How did seeing their future break the spell of Dr. Aster's hold over you?"

"Can't you guess? If they had a future, good or bad, then I might, too. I decided I wasn't going to spend it with him."

CHAPTER NINE

Mal lay awake for several hours, listening to Avyi sleep. She didn't snore. Remembering their conversation, however, added a layer of anger and sympathy to what would've been a simple fact of physiology. That Dr. Aster had caged her, performed surgery on her, brainwashed her—likely through the use of torture—left Mal antsy and, more honestly, *furious*. The facts of Avyi's existence made the comfort of his life seem ridiculous, even wasteful.

He was the Giva, yet at heart, he didn't feel he was the self-sacrificing leader the Dragon Kings needed in this time of crisis. He talked the part, he oversaw what needed to be done to keep the human cartels in check, but had he truly put his back into the task? Had he done enough?

If the cartels were powerful—so powerful as to kidnap Dragon Kings such as his cousin, Nynn, from their home with impunity—what was the use of the gifts bestowed by the Dragon? Mal wasn't the only complacent one among their kind. He was simply the one who couldn't afford to be complacent. Ever.

He'd made the mistake of assuming that his assured

handling of the Council—only ten people—was the same as leading an entire race. It was time to stop delegating. It was time to take matters into his own hands. He could've used conventional means to follow Avyi, namely having his people take on the task and investigate her possible role in the assassination attempt. But he wanted to do it himself. He was finally, assuredly taking action, with reasons that had become thornier by the day.

Beyond even his growing desire for Avyi, he was all the more curious about her purported gift. If he were to believe it, he would need to see proof for himself. Without that proof, they were done. He would never be able to trust such a practiced charlatan. Which cartel held the woman? To what ends? That these basic questions couldn't be answered were a weight on his soul, if only because they layered suspicion over his growing regard for her.

He stared up into the near darkness. Glimmers from the large ferry's external lighting caught the panes of glass and refracted prisms of light into the double berth.

Turning on his side, he used the slight glare to watch her sleep. The almost-light cast deep shadows over her delicate features. She could be Pendray, with women sometimes as hearty as Vikings and sometimes as delicate as fairies. She could be Tigony, having brought forth legends of sirens and water nymphs. But none of that truly mattered. She was a foundling without a clan, claiming a gift that no Dragon King had ever dared boast.

She had only taken off her boots before groggily washing up and returning to her bed. In fact, washing up for bed included slipping on her brass knuckles and sliding a switchblade into her hip pocket. Had she learned that from life with Aster, or from her years as a migrant Garnis tagalong?

His guess was the latter. He couldn't imagine Dr. Aster forcing her to sleep in a cage while permitting her access to weapons. Despite Avyi's sleep-armor, Mal wasn't intimidated or fearful of her. His powers were vast, and he knew that Avyi believed their destinies intertwined. She wouldn't have cause to turn against him until her mission was fulfilled.

Was that before or after they became lovers?

Mal jerked awake from his half-sleeping state. He could barely imagine her naked, let alone beneath him or above him or kneeling before him, both of them seeking the heady release of pleasure. He could readily admit that she was beautiful. But her defensive posture and obvious distrust was a barrier to his imagination. She flinched whenever he was too near, when she wasn't the one to offer physical closeness.

That meant she was more likely expecting to initiate their sexual encounter. Encounters? No, the idea of one time was hard enough to grapple with. But letting her take the lead wasn't Mal's intention. If they were going to spend days, perhaps longer, in one another's company, and if she already expected a moment of supreme intimacy, he wasn't going to wait for her to come to him. Their affair would be brief and, at the center of his being, he knew it would be intense. The prospect stirred his blood.

Across the narrow aisle between their beds, she made a quiet mewling sound in her sleep. Mal took in a deep breath. He wanted breathy, sweaty, excited sounds.

He wanted her mindless.

And if she had lived a conjugal life with Dr. Aster, he wanted to wipe that life away. He wanted to replace those memories with newer, brighter ones.

Fool.

As if such damage could be erased with a couple good fucks.

That mewling sound became more intense. She thrashed under her blanket. She muttered in a language Mal didn't understand. He only understood when, in the darkness, she screamed. It was a scream to open the skies.

In a flash, Mal was out of bed and leaning across her mattress. Before touching her anywhere, he pinned the hand wearing the brass knuckles. She jumped to full awareness and fought him like a cat caught by its hind paws. Twisting at the waist, still screaming, she used the tight ball of her sleeping position as a coil to strike out. She reached for her switchblade, but Mal caught it from her hand and tossed it back toward his bed.

"Avyi! Wake up." He used the weight of his upper body to restrain her thrashing fury. Dragon damn, she was agile. "Stop! Wake up *now*."

He gave her a shake and caught the back of her head, where her hair was unbound and as slippery-clean as water.

Continuing to fight, Avyi's eyes flared opened. Even in those dimmed shadows, Mal recognized very little of the woman he'd come to know. She was feral. Blank. Absent of reason. Only intensity remained. She was the equivalent of a rabid animal fighting the captor who would put her down.

"Pet," he shouted with his most authoritative voice. "You will *stop*. You don't deserve this mattress. You don't deserve *me*."

She stilled. A sob hitched her chest. The fight dropped out of her body as if her bones were popped balloons. "Forgive me," she said, weeping openly now.

Mal had no choice but to offer what he could— invoking Dr. Aster—to bring her back into her true self. Did such a thing exist, he wondered, or would she always be so deeply, dangerously connected to the mad doctor of the Aster cartel?

"Avyi, it's me. Malnefoley. C'mon. Wake up. All the way, now."

He watched as the life came back into her eyes, first as suspicion. "Where am I?"

"The *Forza*. On our way to Florence, remember? To find Cadmin."

He didn't believe in Cadmin, and no way was he Dr. Aster. Both were benevolent lies to pull her free of the nightmare.

She blinked rapidly, then pushed the backs of her hands across her eyes. She hadn't been crying. It seemed more a gesture of frustration. "I remember. What are you doing holding me?"

"I was only trying to wake you."

She raised her brows.

Mal looked down as if he were watching another person. He'd taken up position on her mattress, lying beside her—almost on top of her. She'd pushed her upper body against his chest. His arms were around her back, cradling between her shoulders and down across her spine. *Cradling* was the right word, because the comfort he offered had little to do with the sudden realization that her lithe, compact form was nestled against his. It didn't matter that she wore her black tank top and a charcoal gray sweater that sloped over one shoulder. It didn't matter that he couldn't reach an inch of skin other than her face and neck. He'd only wanted her to stop screaming, to save her from whatever had made her so afraid—or so angry.

Realizing their closeness rekindled the cross between erotic and muddled thoughts. Her breasts were small but felt heavenly when pressed against his bare chest. He had chosen to sleep shirtless. They were only a few scant layers of fabric from being skin to skin.

Too many layers.

There were too many layers between them.

He would've laid her down right then, naked man to naked woman, had he comprehended her true intentions. He wasn't a noble man by refraining. No, he had been played a fool before, with his emotions amplified by physical ecstasy. The consequences continued to shred his soul—out of regret, and out of mortification.

That didn't mean he would let go of Avyi, especially when she rested her head back against the pillow with a sigh honed by pure relief. Her dark hair was midnight in their shared cabin, and it tickled his nose with its unexpected softness.

"You were screaming. Do you remember why?"

"I was hacking his head off."

"His? Dr. Aster?"

She nodded.

"But when I shook you and shouted for you to wake up, you didn't respond." He tipped her chin up and frowned. Had he been born Indranan, he would've used his gift of telepathy without shame. He wanted in her head that badly. Would knowing her thoughts be worth the pain he knew he'd find there? "But when I spoke to you as if I were the doctor, you responded."

"Words are powerful, and so is he."

"I'm glad the dream was to your advantage."

"Me, too. I prefer those to the ones where he wins our last contest." She patted his chest in a dismissive gesture. "I'll be fine now, Mal."

"You called me Mal."

"It was time. Go back to bed."

He touched the damp hair at her temples and trailed his fingers down to her parted lips. "And if I don't?"

Avyi knew she would never be able to get back to sleep, even if Mal had returned to his bunk. He was pressed fully against her, holding her when the worst of her terrors were ripping her apart. That she desired him beyond the point of curiosity made her still. Her breathing had just been returning to normal when his question amped her adrenaline again. She couldn't look away from his firm mouth, which had formed the words that would change everything between them, no matter her answer.

Yet her dream still haunted her. It wasn't a prediction, because victory shifted back and forth. She considered it a horror movie she wouldn't see finished until she met her former master again. Face to face. The last confrontation before they would be free of one another.

That was a prediction. He would kill her, or she would kill him. The field of battle, the weaponry, the method, the circumstances—they remained obscured, akin to knowing she and Mal would become lovers.

Would they do so now? He practically asked as much, while she was the one in control.

"Stay," she whispered.

Pushing away fear, she took Mal's fingers in her own and encouraged him to continue tracing her eyes, her cheeks, her throat. She felt safer by offering her overt permission, leading him to every inch of skin he touched.

Moonlight through the berth's single window high-lighted his profile and glimpses of the big body pushed flush against her. He wore his noble lineage well, with strongly defined muscles across his chest and down his abdomen. They bore the telltale striations of a man who knew how to care for himself. She had known so many Dragon Kings who relied on their gifts and let their physical assets deteriorate.

That wasn't the case with Malnefoley. He was chis-eled. Virile. Tempting bronze hair dusted his pectorals and formed a narrow path between the square ripples of his stomach, to where it disappeared beneath the waistband of his briefs. That hair would tickle her breasts if she lay on top of him . . . or if he lay on top of her.

Why shouldn't I?

His gift and his physical form were blessings from the Dragon. She would be well served by accepting those blessings into her deepest core. His negligent pos-ture and complete relaxation called to her in primal ways. She was taut and almost scared by what might happen between them. He was apparently willing to wait. Didn't he care? Or was he so assured that he knew it would happen eventually?

Well, that was easy enough to answer. She'd told him as much. "We're more enemies than allies," she said, her throat tight. "I can't believe in you, and you don't believe in me."

"Are we going to? Is that part of what you've seen of our future?"

"No . . ."

"People make love without needing anything but the release." His pectorals bunched as he adjusted his hold around her waist. "It's called pleasure, Avyi. How much pleasure have you had in your life?"

Frozen, she stared as Mal slipped his hand between their bodies and rubbed his right hand over his groin. Rather than embarrassment—she would've been mortified—he appeared as confident as always. His expression was intense. Desire shone from his eyes.

"I'm thinking about us," he said. "And I'm touching myself. Both give me . . ." He placed a delicate kiss just below her earlobe. "Pleasure."

"Then continue." She gave him a smile that made the constant pressures behind her sternum lessen, before changing sensation. Adrenaline was one thing. This was the slow pour of honey in her veins. Lassitude and a deep craving intertwined. "Unless I need to tease you. I have ten fingers, after all."

"*That* was a joke."

Her smile deepened. "Was it?"

"You show me." Mal tossed the covers aside. It was all Avyi could do to keep from gasping. His manhood was long, thick, bulging against the confines of his briefs. The head pushed up against the waistband, altering the intimate shape of the underwear and making it erotic.

"But lose the brass knuckles first," he said with a matching grin. With even less ceremony than she would have thought, she handed them over. She swiftly stripped out of her shirt and cargo pants. If she stopped to think about what she was doing, she would stop altogether.

She didn't want that.

She straddled him as she had in the maze, then dragged her fingertips along his muscled thighs and trim hips. The position gave her a measure of power she wasn't willing to relinquish. His gaze traveled over her breasts, her belly, and returned to her face. He bracketed her hips with his strong hands and elegant fingers.

"Damn," he whispered.

"Show me how." Her voice didn't sound like her. Husky. More deeply pitched. "I've never . . ."

"Never?" His stunned expression was replaced by something like resolution. She'd hoped for as much. The Giva would loathe to shirk his duties, but she only wanted the man named Malnefoley.

She lifted just enough for Mal to push down his briefs. They lost all hesitation. His hands became more insistent as he touched her. She feasted on the feel of his hard body. His arms, angling to form a V as he explored her body, were thick with tense muscles. His chest was taut. His stomach was a rigid playground for her tongue, lips, fingernails.

He lifted his head while pulling her nearer, then caught one nipple between his lips. Avyi gasped. Fear flickered, threatening its return, but she had known *real* fear. This was exactly as Mal had said. This was pleasure. She leaned into his wet caress as he circled sensitive skin with his tongue and teased her with gentle nips. With her hands threaded at his nape, she pulled him even closer. He switched to her other breast and deepened his kiss. Between his hands and his mouth, she was quickly succumbing to sensations that layered over each other until none could be named. It was just her and Mal—their surprising combustion.

"Here," he said, urging her hand between her spread legs. "Your turn."

She would've been embarrassed before, but no longer. Avyi was wet, aching. What began as a tentative touch quickly became more forceful as Mal worked magic on her breasts and she discovered her body's own secrets. Their respiration matched, not in cadence but in urgency. She briefly wondered what it would be like to see Mal's face hovering over hers, with his body in full mastery of hers, but that was too much. She needed to be above him. She needed to keep that fear of capture at bay, or she would lose these astonishing feelings.

They met each other in a forceful kiss that was unlike their previous encounters. This had an underlying shimmer of tenderness, as well as anticipation. Mal stroked his tongue across hers until she moaned. They shared rather than warred. It wasn't furtive, but a prelude to the dance yet to come.

Avyi wanted that dance, before that underlying tenderness became as chilly as fear. Pleasure. This was for pleasure.

"Now," she whispered against his damp lips. "It has to be now."

"Not yet."

Mal urged her to lift higher on her knees—then higher still. He positioned her pussy above his mouth. She had thought his touch was amazing. The hot flick of his tongue, however, blew away the last remnants of thought. He tasted, suckled, licked. Avyi thrashed her head, bracing herself with both hands flat on the inner hull of the ship at the head of her bed.

Her climax was so quick that she had no time to anticipate the onslaught of so much sensation. She grabbed the back of Mal's head and arched as waves pulsed up from where he still bestowed the most erotic kiss.

At his mercy now, she found herself straddling him again, but this time across his thighs. He covered her hands with his and showed her how to touch him, with strokes so strong that she thought they must be painful. Not so. He urged her to fondle his balls, massaging in a slower counterpoint to the heavy pulse they kept along his thick cock. It was fully engorged now, stunning in its rigidity and power. His eyes blazed. He grunted a curse and lifted his knees, digging his heels into the mattress.

"Now," he said on a groan. "Come to me, Avyi."

She braced a palm on his straining pecs. The muscles of her thighs trembled as she raised up enough to align his throbbing head with her sleek opening. Mal helped her, but only so much. Once Avyi had him fully in hand, he let his fall away. How could he know? *Did* he know? She needed to be the one to do this her way, as inexperienced as she was.

He was hot and pulsing as she sank down, so slowly at first. But need got the better of her. She enveloped him in one swift move. A surprised cry slipped from her lips. Mal was there. He had sat up, with his bent knees supporting her back, with his crossed arms holding her close. They kissed. They touched. They rocked together as that moment of pain dispersed.

"More," he rasped against her throat. "You can give us more."

She found that she could. There was nothing barring them anymore. Nothing barred *her*. She grasped the strong muscles that sloped from his neck to his sculpted shoulders. The pace she set was forceful and sure. Mal tossed his head back with a groan, like an invitation— one Avyi accepted by licking up from his collarbone until they were kissing again. Her world centered on him, on all the ways their bodies connected. The deepest connection was where man met woman with the most primal strength. She took him as much as he took her.

They locked gazes. Mal touched her hair, just as he had in the hostel. The surprise of that renewed tenderness was Avyi's undoing. She rolled her hips and rode the magnificence he offered. Fire burned behind her eyes and along her skin and down her belly, until it was a blaze of need. That need consumed her as sweat slicked her skin and stole her breath. She pinched her nails into his pecs when the first burst of release made her gasp his name. Another followed as he continued to pump up, gaining speed, holding back nothing.

He circled her body in a fierce grip. She sucked a patch of skin at his throat, then sank her teeth deep. Mal shuddered, then went rigid with a heavy grunt. After a few more lingering strokes, he flopped back on the mattress with a dazed, satisfied look on his handsome face. Avyi's inner thighs were sore as she slipped free and joined him on the bed, half lying across his body. They were both panting.

"That was . . ." She didn't have the words. How could she describe how right that had felt, in too many dangerous ways?

He hadn't taken her virginity; he had provided the freedom for her to give it to him. "Fantastic?" he offered.

She burrowed her face against his chest. It was as good a word as any, as she tried to completely shut down thought. The taste of his kiss remained on her tongue and the aftershocks of satisfaction still hummed in her blood. "Yes, Mal. It was fantastic."

❧ CHAPTER ❧
TEN

$\mathbf{M}$al didn't walk through the next twenty-four hours in a fog, but everything he did was hazed with new sensation and sidelong looks at his companion. She behaved as if nothing had happened in that ferry berth. Only the way she walked gave her away. She had a looseness to her joints that belied her previous tenseness. Although just as wary, with her eyes a constant study in the suspicion a wounded soul used to assess the world, she walked beside him with what might almost be described as ease.

As he and Avyi disembarked in Venice, Mal was dressed in Armani. He could've been a businessman headed to Switzerland for a G8 conference about the economic futures of the industrialized world. Instead, he was the leader of the Dragon Kings, hiding weapons in his luggage and trying to smuggle in a young woman without papers.

She looked both respectable and radiant in a pair of slacks, a gauzy blouse, and a tailored jacket. Her fawn-colored merino wool suit created a striking contrast with her midnight hair, which was swept back from her delicate features. Ginovosa had outdone herself in finding an outfit to fit Avyi's petite frame and help contain some of her prickly attitude.

Although it was a strange thing to feel, he wanted her back in *her* clothes, boots and all, but their possessions had been stowed in a train station locker in Florence. Although the Tigony he'd sent to complete the task was one of his most trusted men, Mal hadn't dared reveal that the chest contained his sword and the quiver. But now . . . this polished version of a beautiful woman wasn't Avyi. The off-kilter vivacity was still there for any who looked hard enough, but she was straightjacketed. He wondered where she had stowed her switchblade and brass knuckles. He had no doubt they were somewhere readily accessible.

No more, he thought. *Not for the rest of her life.*

The first Italian customs agents they met were typically Italian. They weren't ruled by clocks and hurry-scurry attitudes. They more resembled the humans of Mal's homeland, where family, good food and wine, and enjoying life's pleasures overruled pettier considerations. Greek, Italian . . . they were descended from the traditions taught by the Tigony. Mal's selfish heart spoke their language. He hadn't been raised to accept responsibility. There were always valets.

And priestesses. And victims.

He knew how deeply the craving for bacchanalia went, and how greatly the Tigony had been responsible for the worst of it.

"This is Avyi Tigony," he said in Italian, presenting his passport and a convincing business itinerary for his stay in Italy. "She's my wife and lost her passport on the ferry. We've looked everywhere. The ship's captain was still searching when we docked."

Avyi only raised her brows. She didn't seem averse to using any tactic. After all, she planned to search a world-famous cathedral for a mythical bow.

The customs agent was small in stature and wiry, as thin as the cigarette he let dangle from his lips. Not exactly the stuff of high-end airport security. He examined Mal's papers. He eyed Avyi, particularly lingering on her hair.

Under the agent's scrutiny, she assumed a placid expression that sent chills up Mal's back. It wasn't her.

It was the Pet.

She was everyone and no one.

The agent handed back the papers and passport. He took a drag on the cigarette and pointed it at Avyi. "The Greek Consulate will be your next stop. We can have you escorted."

Mal smiled benignly. "No need. We don't want to be a nuisance. Our ultimate destination is Berlin. Sorting out her passport is a first priority. Even more of a priority than the canals," he said, as if by way of apology to Avyi.

"Next trip?" Her plea had just the right timbre of petulant and genuine disappointment. "You promised."

"I did promise." He kissed the top of her head, then added steel to his voice. "Next time you'll remember not to misplace your things."

The agent smiled as if in agreement with Mal's harder tone. They were a people who would rather have wine insulted—as proof of good taste—than to bear obsequious courtesy. They understood and appreciated the attitude of a spoiled child. Mal could affect that without effort.

"Go then." The agent angled his head toward the area of the docks that extended to the marina, then the mainland. "If you're apprehended by *la polizia* and they find you haven't applied for a new passport, your stay in Italy will be indefinitely extended."

"*Grazie.*"

"And keep a close eye on this one."

He ushered Avyi away, with his hand at her lower back. They hired a porter to assist with the baggage. Soon they were seated in a rented town car, with a driver whisking them overland toward Florence.

She glanced at Mal, a cheeky bit of side-eye. "You didn't listen to the nice man. I see no consulate."

"And you won't. No papers, ever, at all, means you have no consulate. You're a woman without country."

"So I'm Greek by default, as your wife?" Her brows were so expressive that the rest of her features couldn't keep up.

"You understood that?"

"Some."

He watched her for clues, indications, but she only aimed that blankness at him. "How long until we arrive in Florence?"

"About three hours," he said. "Might as well get some sleep."

"It's two in the afternoon."

"Yes, but we were both up at all hours."

"Yes, we were."

Mal was left pressing his lips tight. So casually, Avyi tossed him that comment before leaning against the window. She didn't sleep, but she didn't move either. She simply watched, as she had during the helicopter flight. He picked near-invisible flecks off his trousers and adjusted the creases. This was his skin. The clothing that defined him. Yet he almost missed the freedom of jeans and a T-shirt.

"Was last night your prediction?"

"No," she said simply. "In what I've seen, we're surrounded by white."

Mal hovered between satisfaction and surprise, between greed and knowing the road they traveled together would not be tidy. It would never fit his former life of private jets and Armani suits packed for him by an on-call valet from his own clan.

Maybe that was for the best.

He'd left his life in the care of others for too long.

Staring at her profile, he was hit again by her unexpected beauty. She had cleaned up nicely for their entrance into Italy. But could no one else see the wildness bubbling beneath the surface of her forced calm? Of course not. She'd had years to become the Pet. Only Mal knew Avyi. And Dragon damn, he wanted to know even more about her.

"What we did was reckless," he said. "You were asking for trouble."

"You answered."

Mal turned in his seat and forced her to meet his gaze. Soon their faces were close enough that he could've kissed her again. He practically tasted her sweet breath. She tasted sweet everywhere. "You were a virgin."

"And now I'm not. Thank you." She smiled softly, with cheeks tinted pink. "Although I'd never known what I wanted, last night was it."

He accepted her compliment on a bone-deep level, but his confusion remained. He needed to say what was on his mind while she was still in the mood to speak. "You slept in Dr. Aster's room. He brainwashed you. You followed him everywhere—collared and leashed by his side. But he never touched you?"

"He touched me, but not that way. I was his trophy. Every man's deepest desire, but otherwise innocent. I think he liked the contrast."

Mal took hold of the back of her neck. She flinched. "You'll have to be stronger than flinching if you want to keep playing these games."

"Is this play? It feels like walking on the ledge at the top of a skyscraper."

"That, too."

She kissed his cheek with a teasing smile. At least he'd broken through the ice of her facade as the Pet. "So last night won't be a one-time encounter."

"A prediction?"

"An absolute fact." She smiled. "I'll make sure of it."

Mal decided to start right there. He clasped her chin and urged her to meet him midway. At first, their kiss was almost polite. Two strangers. But the swell of passion they'd shared was quick to follow. He swept her hair back from her face and held her head, taking command. With a few strokes of eager tongues and a playful war between teeth and lips, he was burning again. She breathed faster and clutched his lapels. Heedless of the driver, Mal swept his hand over her breast and fondled that small, soft swell.

He couldn't remember why they were in that limo, or why they were even in Italy. He only knew that he wanted to lay Avyi back against the lush leather seat and find his way inside her again.

She came back to herself far more quickly than he would've liked. Her petite hand pressed against his chest, and she pulled away as much as his encircling arms would allow. "We have a lot to discuss. Much to my disappointment, Giva, it has nothing to do with our sex life."

After a deep breath, he nodded. He planted a last kiss on her passion-swollen lips before releasing her. At least she didn't return to staring blankly out the car window.

"Blending is not your skill," she said. "No offense. It's not one of mine either."

"I'd argue otherwise. Is the look you gave the customs official what you gave Dr. Aster when he expected obedience?"

"I suppose. I've never thought of it. Most times he didn't want an opinion. He wanted a mirror that said he was right." She paused, staring at Mal with her unnerving capacity for directness. "Do you expect a mirror?"

"No."

"Are you certain?"

He began to protest, but stopped himself to consider. "No, I'm not sure," he said slowly. "I like being right."

"Do you expect failure when we reach Florence? That I won't find anything of value to either of us?"

She knew Pollakioh's name. How? Where is she leading me?

A chill bristled the hair under his shirtsleeves.

"I don't expect to find anything," he said stiffly. "So, yes, I expect failure."

She pulled her lips into her mouth, eyes averted.

That cold distance was back. She could raise it like an umbrella against the rain. "Perhaps I should continue on my own when we reach Florence, but you won't let that happen."

"I'm not in Italy for the sights."

"You have an assassination plot to unravel—which has nothing to do with me, you'll learn. But if the cartels are behind it, especially the Asters, and they know I'm with you . . ." She shook her head. "He'll find me."

Mal was more disturbed by his gut reaction to parting from this woman. "He can't simply find you. He's not a telepath."

"He had a thrice-cursed Indranan at his command, named Ulia. She was responsible for brainwashing your cousin for two months down in the Cages. If anyone can find me, she can." She kicked off her pumps and pulled her stocking-clad feet up to hug her knees. "You don't want me to be your weakness. I don't want you to be mine."

Mal didn't say anything, which gave Avyi the impression that he agreed with her assessment.

They would make love again. She knew that much. Sometimes her strongest predictions came about by means that would seem, by all logic, to be counterintuitive. They would go their separate ways after they reached Florence, but circumstances would play out as she predicted. She knew that, just as she knew she would see Dr. Aster again. Inevitably. Her future and his, twined, interlaced like the boughs of trees planted too closely. She much preferred sharing that connection with Malnefoley, yet fate was a strange ocean tipped with cold waves.

"I'll assume, for the moment," Mal said, "that you're innocent. Somewhat deluded, but innocent of any crime against me."

"How gracious."

"Do you believe there is any connection between your search for Cadmin and the attempt on my life?" Unconsciously, perhaps, he rubbed his shoulder where the impeccable suit hid the last stages of his healing. "Tell me that."

She turned so that her feet occupied the space between their seats. The town car was plush with leather and wood-grain decor. She'd traveled in such vehicles when Dr. Aster took her to Grievances in other countries—those hosted by the Kawashimas in Hong Kong, the Townsends in London. Only, despite years and years after having had her in his possession, he still handcuffed her to the door, with collar and leash around her neck.

Avyi rubbed her throat, feeling the ghostly shadow of that leather and all the years she'd borne its subtle weight against her skin.

"When you ask, 'Do you believe . . . ?' are you asking me to use logic or my gift? What if I revealed a prediction you couldn't understand or immediately quantify?"

"I maintain the right to reserve judgment."

The Italian clime was just as generous with its sunshine across his straw-blond hair as Crete had been. The light cast from overhead caught the fringe of his golden lashes and stripped the vigorous blue from his eyes. The color was icy now, but his intensity made the color somehow casual. He was practically basking in the beatific weather. The effect was powerful, radiating through Avyi's limbs until her heart filled painfully. She had to look away, or else she'd return to places of memory that were solidly in the past. Mal in blue jeans, sitting on the back step of a dingy hostel. Mal stretched beneath her in their berth. Mal looking her up and down on the docks of Florence, casually claiming her as his wife.

"You think you know so much," she said quietly.

"I know nothing, which is why I'm asking you—"

"A charlatan."

"—for answers." He cracked his thumb knuckles, then yanked at his tie. The silk and a few buttons fell away. "I'm tired of this *lonayíp* thing."

"You act like a human . . . what do they call them? Playboys? All money and privilege. You lead because it was expected of you, not like the Sun in India. That woman feels a call to service—an obligation to make life better for her Indranan brethren. You don't want the responsibility, but you're stuck."

"I'm Giva," he said, as if declaring he was a leper.

"There's no returning it when the children give you that title, even if they were quiet and few." She smoothed her hands down her luscious wool trousers. She'd never worn a garment so exquisite. "But have you ever considered the obvious?"

He glared at her, one hand pressed to his brow as if holding back a headache. "Which is?"

"The Dragon doesn't call on the weak. He doesn't call upon the feeble to take mantles of power. I don't like my gift any more than you do, but I try to understand it. I try to accept what it means for us as individuals."

"If your power is real, that means we live without free will."

"I would be a saner person if I could fully accept that."

"I am my own person," he said too loudly for the confined backseat of the town car. "I will not give up on that. Your insistence means decisions are a farce."

"No matter what you and I do when we reach Florence, we will wind up tangled in bed together, naked and satiated. And at some point, you will stand in shadow beneath the Duomo. How to come to peace with that is the hard part. To me . . . it's fact now."

"Let's make it fact then." His temper was burning brighter by the second. "We'll fuck again. We'll do it in the first hotel we find in Florence and be done with it. I'd rather track down Dr. Aster and fry him to dust one cell at a time than need to rely on you for answers."

"Do you believe in the Dragon?"

Avyi was so surprised by the heretical nature of her question that she shrank back from the Giva. He shimmered with electricity that emanated from the tips of his hair and the delicate whorls of each fingerprint.

"You forget yourself, Avyi. And you forget who I am."

"Oh, I could never forget that. You bask in it like a tragedian on center stage, relishing the best soliloquy ever written. You wear your title with such disdain. And your wealth. Yet what do you know of sacrifice and suffering? What do you know of getting your hands dirty?"

He snatched out from across the seats and grabbed her wrist. "*You forget yourself*. And you have no idea how dirty my hands have been. Tell that to the Dragon when you see him flying around the future somewhere."

With one shove, he pushed her back against her window and retreated to his half of the rear seat. She rubbed her wrist. "You don't," she said, voice rasping. "You don't believe."

He shot her a murderous look.

"No wonder you hate your responsibility so much. It would be like Catholics making an atheist the pope." Avyi slipped her pumps back on and crossed her legs. She wasn't hiding from this man anymore. He wasn't the doctor, who threatened her so regularly with his very presence that she felt like a woman half her height. "So will you believe me when I say that, yes, I see our paths connected? Of course you won't. But we'll part as soon as those obligations to the future are satisfied."

"We fought, survived an assassination attempt, pushed past a screaming nightmare, and had a few memorable hours. That's been plenty."

"You're not even curious to see how it unfolds?"

"Frankly, my only interest now is to see you discredited. Then I'll have no problem abandoning this little wild-goose chase of ours and—"

"—and handing over responsibility to someone else. Tell me, *Giva*, what will you do about the Grievance? Will you let it happen again? Will you let Dragon Kings kill each other for the cartels' sport? Of course not. You're in charge. You wouldn't stand for that violence again, not when the key to conception is supposedly such a priority."

Mal was silent for a long while. His jaw muscles were bunched to match the fists poised so tensely on his knees.

Avyi crossed her arms and looked down at them. It

wasn't cringing into a ball, but she still felt incredibly defensive. Mal was busily righting his appearance as the traffic slowed on their way into the city.

"How can you be so blind," she asked into the silence, "and discount all the possibilities that don't fit with your beliefs? Human beings would do the same to us. You of all people should be able to take the impossible and believe it possible."

Malnefoley of Tigony, the Honorable Giva, turned to her with the full weight and bearing of his title. "Go on, then. What does your mysterious, grown-up fetus of a Cage warrior have to do with the attempt on my life? Tell me, Avyi."

He'd given her that name. She would always hold him close in her heart for that simple fact. Suddenly their fight seemed like a pair of cats in a cinch-tied bag, squabbling over who knew the way out. They'd shared a very intimate act last night, more than she could process with rational thought. And now he used her name.

"I can't," she said. "I don't know."

"Now you hear me. I don't believe it. I certainly don't like the idea of it. But if this is your . . . gift . . . Dragon damn, does it really matter? After all, who'd believe what I can do with mine?"

"Yours is in the seeing. Mine is in the seeing, too, but sometimes it doesn't come true for years. Or on occasion, the future is cut short. I see that it's real. The dead don't."

"Are you saying I'm going to die?"

"One day you will. What was her name? Pollakioh?"

"Stop."

"For now, Cadmin's bow is the next cresting wave."

She found the strength to meet his gaze, although it had the potential to remain angered and irrational. Talking about the Dragon had been an unexpected sore spot that left as many questions as answers. "Random predictions and glimpses are one thing. This has significance, like when I found her arrows. Mal, I'm scared of what I'll learn."

"You started calling me that when you had your nightmare."

"It's fitting that we be on a first-name basis considering what happened last night." Her cheeks heated. "And how, according to the Italian port authority, I'm your wife."

A soft smile shaped his lips, slowly easing him back to the man she hoped he was—or could become. "I'll be with you, Avyi, when you find that bow."

"You believe that?"

"I was determined to take you back to Greece and wrench the answers out of you. Now I'm in Italy." He kissed her wrist, where he'd grabbed her with such force. "You have me so turned around, but I've never felt more in control of my own decisions. How is that possible?"

"I don't know. But if I ever meet the Dragon, I'll ask."

⚡ CHAPTER ⚡
ELEVEN

Mal had never been to Florence. He'd been to some of the highest reaches of the Himalayas, and to clan strongholds on the outskirts of Cairo and in the Highlands of Scotland. After his retreat from the outside world following the terror he'd inflicted at Bakkhos, he hadn't seen the point of travel beyond his explicit duties. He was the leader of Clan Tigony following his grandfather's death—his grandfather's execution, to be precise— which meant staying home in the Grecian mountains and the glittering Aegean Sea.

To travel for pleasure? He was a man of significant means, but the thought had rarely occurred to him. Too much responsibility. Too many reasons and resources to command from a distance. So, much to his embarrassment, he found himself gaping like a tourist at the scene laid before him.

They stowed the quality garments in the train station locker, where Mal was pleased to find its content in order. They changed into more casual clothes. Avyi was back in cargos and a gauzy blouse, while Mal took to jeans and a T-shirt again, as if reliving a comforting memory, and donned a black leather jacket. With brass knuckles and her switchblade stowed in a secret compartment in the sole of her boots, Avyi appeared at ease for the first time since leaving the town car behind.

Mal shouldered their pack as they walked to where travel by car was blocked to any vehicles other than those owned by locals. Every subsequent step in their journey to the Basilica di Santa Maria del Fiore, simply called the Duomo because of its unmistakable dome, was literally by foot. They followed the Via dei Calzaiuoli toward the cathedral, which was visible from miles off. Monochrome tiles of green and sienna decorated its facade. What had to be millions of bricks made up the eight-sided dome.

"It took more than one hundred and forty years to complete," Avyi said, her voice hushed despite the hum of countless voices and pressing bodies. Almost every face was pointed up toward the dome or down toward children who had the potential to bolt or simply be consumed by the crowd. "Can you imagine? Even Dragon Kings born on the day of its groundbreaking would've been into their twilight years before it was finished."

"With a significant break for the Black Plague."

"Strange that we survived that devastation unscathed, yet now . . ." Her gaze fell on a nearby family. A man and a woman shepherded tired children along the cobblestoned street. One was old enough to walk—a boy of perhaps eight. Another was carried in a sling across the father's chest, while the mother pushed a stroller. They walked with the stooped posture of pending exhaustion, yet they were smiling, absorbing the history and majesty. "That will never be us. None of us."

Mal stopped in the midst of traffic, then steered Avyi to a corner by a gelato vendor. He took her face in his hands, assessing, reading eyes made pale green in a flash of sunshine. "Do you *know* that?"

"You're asking me for a prediction?" Her tone somewhat exaggerated, which grated on his nerves.

"Do you *know*?"

She shook her head. Coal-black hair twisted down from her temples and hugged the curve of her nape. "I don't. Too many variables, remember? But every time I look toward the future, I see a human population expanding to the point of heedless destruction. And we're nowhere to be seen."

Mal spread his fingers, as if doing so might permit access to her mind, to the future he desperately needed to steer onto another path—a path where the Dragon Kings still thrived. "You mean it. You're not hedging because . . . because—"

"Because you've been an arrogant ass?"

He blinked. Pulled back. His palms burned.

"No, Mal." She sighed, her eyes returning to where that family had stood at the far edge of the Piazza del Duomo, but they were gone. A trio of what appeared to be college students had taken their place. "I'm not hedging. I would hide dangerous things from you if I wanted to act out of spite." Reaching up, she adjusted the twisted strap of his pack. "I can only hope that one day, events will change. Perhaps I'll see days when babies are born to surprised, thankful Dragon King parents. I'll breathe easier knowing such a future is coming, even if it's too far off for me to witness."

"Or to have children of your own."

She shook her head. "You mistake me. I don't want children."

"Self-defense," he said, grasping the hand she'd used to hold his. He tugged her toward the cathedral's massive bronze doors, which were adorned with carved reliefs depicting the life of the Virgin Mary. A line of tourists wrangled by ropes meant a long wait. He and Avyi took up their place at its end and shuffled along with the mass of humanity. "You don't want children because it'll never be an option. Why want something you can't have?"

She disentangled their hands and shoved hers into her pockets. "No, I don't. Not for any reason. I'll touch them and I'll know too much about their futures. I'll see accidents, weddings, disappointments, arguments, first sexual encounters, and maybe even the circumstances of their deaths. All the while I'll wonder what events lead to the terrible things and how I can prevent them. For the good things, I'd drive myself mad working to further them along."

"You say we have no free will," he said evenly.

With haunted eyes, she looked up at him. "But wouldn't you try?"

"Yes. I would try."

They reached the head of the queue and entered the dwarfing brass doors. He leaned closer to Avyi. "Most times, I don't take notice of human achievement."

"You're one of *those*. So superior."

"Maybe. But how is this any less magnificent than what we can do?"

"Perhaps that's our ultimate legacy, even if our race doesn't survive. We taught them the skills. They made . . . this," she said, hands sweeping up toward the doors' bronze reliefs. "Astonishing."

Upon entering the cathedral, Mal craned his neck to take in countless details, although he would've needed to be Garnis for his senses to keep up fully. Too many indescribable sights and ancient smells, all of which harkened back to the centuries when the Tigony dynasty had reached its zenith. The fresco that adorned the sloping interior of the dome was that of the biblical Last Judgment. Only, the painting wasn't distorted by the four-hundred-foot dome's sloping octagonal sides. The perspective was perfect, so that the scene appeared as flat as a canvas.

"How . . . ?" he whispered, his voice dipped to a reverent pitch.

"I don't know." Avyi shook her head. "More than six hundred years old. No computers. No Dragon-given gifts. Just human ambition and imagination." She gently elbowed him in the ribs. "Get your head out of the clouds and pay attention to the world. *You* have no excuse. You've not been trapped in a lab for twenty-five years."

He had his answer. She'd been Dr. Aster's captive for twenty-five years. A shudder climbed his spine.

"So where is this bow? Some exhibit?"

"It's not in an exhibit. It's in the crypt."

"There's a crypt?"

"It's a cathedral. Of course there's a crypt. And guess whose ruins were rolled over with rock?"

"Romans'."

"Your people must take personal offense when the Greeks and Romans get all the credit."

Mal was inclined by long habit to agree with her. But with a glance back up the dome, he reconsidered. "The Tigony don't deserve all the credit."

Following the signs to the crypt, which was accessible by rather civilized carved stairs and wrought-iron railings, they shuffled along with the rest of the curious.

"We should've come at night," Avyi said, her voice tight. "Fewer people."

Mal glanced down. Her face was ash white. Beads of sweat dotted her hairline. "I thought crowds would be good for blending in. Are there evening tours?"

"No."

"Then we made the right call. No sense adding to the dangers we've already faced by breaking into a national treasure."

The first memorial in the crypt was that of Brunelleschi, who had engineered the dome's theretofore unheard of structure. He'd also been the first human to introduce the concept of perspective. Mal couldn't imagine a world where perspective was a new concept that needed to be instructed by a singular individual. He nodded in appreciation toward the marble casing, before they moved to saints, bishops, and other artists who'd worked those one hundred and forty years to construct and decorate the Duomo.

"Down here?"

"So much doubt." Avyi took his hand again. He liked that. Too much. Every touch was a reminder of what they'd done and what they had yet to do—prediction or not. "The Giva must learn to trust," she said, slanting him a censorious look, "and to have faith."

"In you, the woman I shouldn't trust at all? And in

the mysteries of your gift? So far the power provided to you by the Dragon is to get under my skin."

"Don't invoke his name if you don't believe." Her voice held genuine castigation.

"Long-standing habit."

She stood on tiptoes and whispered in his ear, "Not habit. Deep belief. Now, a little distraction would be useful."

"Distraction?"

"Short-circuit something. Lights. Fire alarms." She nodded toward the ropes and barricades that marked the extent of the public's access to the crypt's excavation. "What we seek is not a tourist attraction."

"*You*, Avyi. What *you* seek."

"Rub your hands together," Mal said. "I need some heat."

"Flirt."

He raised his eyebrows, which tempted Avyi to smile. She nearly did. They were buried beneath the earth and surrounded by too many human beings for comfort. Surely someone would look at them both and spy the uncanny glow that visually defined their people. Enjoying Malnefoley's half smile was better than the unpleasant alternatives that walked bugs up her arms. She knew the pain that could come from being identified as a Dragon King.

That thought made her look down. They *were* in a crypt. They were standing among the dead . . .

"Avyi? Focus, wild child."

"Watch it. You already gave me one name."

She slid her palms together and rubbed with increasing speed until her hands were warm. Nothing could explain the touch of Mal's gift as that turbine under his skin sucked her scant static. His eyes glowed. Literally glowed. Twin blue beacons. She gave up on creating an energy source for him, because he was going to give them away. Instead, she grabbed his shoulders and turned him away from the bulk of the crowd. Glimmering golden skin could be rationalized into nothing: a really good tan, or that other human impression—that they were in the presence of a man or woman of exceptional, literally indescribable beauty.

There would be no hiding blue eyes that shone a light across his features and made delicate shadows of his pale lashes.

"Yes," he whispered.

The word was spoken with the satisfaction she'd heard in their ferry berth. Did he receive as much pleasure from his gift as he did from sexual release? Avyi would've been envious had she not been caught in the thrill. She grabbed his hands, holding on to a living electrical wire.

"On three." His voice was distant and rough.

"One, two, three." She said it quickly, intimidated by the strength of him, outside and in.

Mal grinned briefly. "Coward."

"Just not an idiot."

He released her hands and dropped his to his sides. With a quick turn, he released the gathered, amplified electricity and aimed it toward the nearest light fixtures. His precision was astounding. A bulb popped. Then another, and a third. The crypt went dark, before it was flooded with the bloodred of emergency lights. Warning sirens blared. People began to panic.

Avyi clung to the nearest waist-high railing—the one that marked the extent of the crypt's public accessibility—and held tight. Human beings astounded her, but this behavior was what had always made her fear them. *Panic*. Irrational fear that overrode calm common sense. If the tourists and docents kept their heads, they could walk slowly up the crypt's stairs and out to safety. That never happened. They were no better in such moments than a school of fish darting away from a shark.

"Which way?"

She opened her eyes and swallowed. Mal stood before her, his eyes no longer unnatural beacons of blue, but shaded black by the eerie red emergency lights. His hair beamed with orange highlights.

She couldn't move.

Understanding softened the urgency etched on his features. The lines of tension around his eyes smoothed to nothing.

He leaned down and kissed her.

Just a kiss. Barely a meeting of mouths.

But it jarred Avyi out of her haze. She licked her lower lip, catching the taste of him. "Was that some aspect of your Tigony ritual I missed?"

"In part wanting to kiss you." He grabbed her upper arm. "In part waking you the hell up. C'mon, before we miss our chance."

"I should be the one dragging you along."

"Who's in charge here?"

"Good question, Giva."

"We'll get along much better if you just listen for once."

"Back at you." She urged him from a recess between

a damp wall and a crevice that was barred by a metal gate, exasperated but reluctant to awaken his ire. He was tagging along for the wrong reasons, but at least he was with her.

Avyi nimbly scampered over the metal gate. Mal mimicked her actions, with more power and equal grace, joining her beyond the barrier. He stowed the backpack in a shadowed crevice, then set about rolling up his shirtsleeves. She remembered how he'd done the same in their ferry berth and felt a jolt of anticipation. Adrenaline was pumping, her imagination was in overdrive, and he was a Dragon-damned handsome man.

This wasn't the time. She was too near her goal.

Avyi stepped to within inches of his body. "Whatever happens . . . thank you for being here." She paused. "We make a good team. Except when you tried to obliterate me."

He grinned. "Something like that."

Heat traded between them. Her skin had pulled in on itself, dry, shrinking, needing wet kisses to ease an ache as old as time. Mal's stare had that effect on her. She needed to turn away, toward the opening of the deepest portion of the crypt, to remind herself why she was there. He was that distracting.

"No wonder these areas were barred to tourists," she said tightly.

"Not exactly on the guided tour." Mal pushed a thick curtain of moss away from where it dangled in its ancient home. The ceiling was sloped here, and the walls tighter, like a hand closing around them. The air was chilly and damp. "Could be anything down here."

"Just the dead."

"That's little comfort."

"At least they won't try to kill you."

"Good point." His smile was fast and delicious. "Now, off you go."

"How gallant."

"If you're going to be on your hands and knees, then I insist you go first. I'll enjoy the view much better."

She felt that Dragon-damned blush creeping up on her again. "If only the Council knew you as I've come to."

"I prefer being alone with you, although the location leaves much to be desired."

"But you forget." She slid a hand down his arm and clasped his hand, gave it a nervous squeeze. "We'll need to regroup here when it's time to leave. I'll enjoy the return view."

CHAPTER TWELVE

Mal had no time to appreciate the way Avyi's cargo pants clung to her ass as she crawled ahead of him. A wasted opportunity. He was too focused on the slick surface and its sloping dip into the earth, like a child's shallow slide. Securing his handholds and the grip of his hiking boots required all his concentration. Darkness overwhelmed them quickly. The red cast of the emergency lights at the opening of the tunnel was too faint to illuminate detail.

He stopped, straightened a little, and rubbed his palms on his jeans. Denim was useful for static electricity. The sparks he cast lasted a few moments until he needed to take a break and start again. The space smelled faintly of sulfur. He didn't risk using a stronger flash of energy, for fear of setting off an unknown underground element.

"Just think," he said, watching the shadowed waffle pattern on the soles of Avyi's boots. "Upstairs are hundreds of tourists being ushered into the sunshine. They're startled. They're upset because they paid for exhibit tickets and don't know if they'll get back in before dinner. I envy them."

Avyi threw a mildly disgusted look over her shoulder. "You're nearly whining. Unflattering, Giva."

"You're leading this expedition. My job is to make a little heat and remind you of how insane you are."

"I said one day I'll be right. You'll see. Today. Tomorrow. Your future will catch up with us." She paused. "And you'll hate me for it."

Mal fought to ignore the shiver that climbed his spine. Their connection was too tenuous to trust. "I don't know about that," he said, trying to maintain their uneasy peace. "You've only promised me one thing so far, and it's far from disagreeable."

"It will be if you don't shut up. I'm not doing this all by sight." She found a rock and tossed it out ahead of where she crawled on all fours. "A wall. Close. More light, please."

"Since you asked nicely."

He set off a charge of light and maintained it at a low glow just above their heads.

She reached the end of the crypt's descending slope and sat cross-legged with her back to the far wall. Mal joined her, hip to hip. Their clothes, streaked with earth, did nothing to detract from her radiance beneath his conjured light. She glowed with a luminance that nearly matched that fire. Memories of the night before might haunt him for the rest of his life. At the moment, however, they were as raw and fresh as if he'd just been so hard, so deep in her softness.

A sharp sound marked the first time Mal had heard Avyi laugh. She covered her mouth, but the sound kept coming. It reverberated off the walls, as the echo cackled along with her. She glanced at his jeans where his erection was coming to life. "You're looking at me like that *now*? Really?"

It was either grin or take offense. "I am."

"*Lonayíp* ass."

"You're stunning. And I'm arrogant."

She smiled, as if laughter still fizzed in her blood. Laughter at his expense. He didn't care. "Arrogance has its benefits. We're in a crypt because of mine."

Mal increased the burst of light above them in a lasting arc. "Where do we start?"

"Anywhere."

Together they searched on all fours within the antechamber, which was no taller than Avyi and not much bigger in diameter than a couch. Mal touched rock and dirt, feeling and digging until his fingers cramped. Avyi's breathing echoed in the small space, its pace exceeding that of their exertion. She sounded as if she were becoming ever more frantic.

"What if it's not here?" she rasped.

"Keep looking."

Mal frowned at himself, wondering why he was encouraging her to keep going. He didn't believe. But why were his hands dusted in dirt and his heart beating in anticipation?

Upstairs, the sirens went silent. They looked at each other. "I wish that had lasted longer," he said, dimming the glow over their heads. Then . . . "Here. Avyi, here."

In the near darkness, he pulled her fingers toward the curve of the wall to the left of where they'd entered the hollowed chamber.

Avyi knee-crawled forward. A hollow in the rock revealed a long strip of color that gleamed in the half-light. It was as if strands of gold had been inlaid between jewels, but the jewels were plain striations of earth. "It's beautiful."

"I'll be Dragon-damned." Mal pinched the back of his neck, struggling with his disbelief. "How did no one find it? It's *right here*."

She shivered. "What was once will happen again. Sitting here, I can see the past because it's a prediction of the future."

"A cycle?"

"Our clans have changed dynasties. There are patterns. Revolt. Reform. Corruption. Excess. Overthrow. It happens among the humans, too. Why think our cycles are any different?"

Mal tugged the rock away from the sliver of gold. Within moments, he'd uncovered the entire shaft, as if it had been waiting for his hands. "Surely . . . there won't be a bowstring."

Yet he was only muttering to himself. A part of him deeper than logic and older than his years—older, perhaps, than his clan—knew to shut the hell up. Because there most certainly was a bowstring.

He carefully set the ancient weapon on the ground, as if cautiously releasing a snake. He couldn't shake the eeriness. "You win," he said grimly.

"You think I like it?" She pushed away from the wall and knelt beside him. "*Do you?*" she whispered fiercely. "I have seen two glimpses of my future. *Two*. You'd think I could get a better perspective on my own life-yet-lived. Now that I'm here, I need to touch that bow.

I must learn what it will tell me. Because, Mal, we've made it this far. Step after step. I don't . . ."

She shook her head again.

Mal caught her face between surprisingly steady hands. This was absurd, but it hit a true, undeniable place in his gut. "You don't want to see what comes next?"

"I don't." Her vehemence was a surprise, as were the tears in her eyes. Mal caught her as she sagged against his chest and buried her face against his throat. "Stepping stones," she whispered. "Crests of waves. Think of whatever metaphor you want, but space exists between all of them." She turned a panicked gaze toward the glittering bow. "Traveling by helicopter. The ferry ride and making love. All of that was the space between finding the arrows and me touching . . . that."

"What will it tell you? The next cresting wave?"

"Otherwise, *you* win. I'm a charlatan, or insane, or worth treating with suspicion."

"I could think that no matter what you say."

"I wish you wouldn't," she said quietly.

Holding her upper arms, Mal took a deep breath. He could believe her, or he could crawl out and do this another way. He was tempted to turn away from the gift he still couldn't process. Only, what he'd witnessed so far was becoming impossible to ignore.

He picked up the golden weapon in all its gleaming perfection and held out his hands.

Avyi couldn't do it. She'd seen this moment more and more clearly since they'd arrived in Florence. Every mile, then every seemingly ordinary step forward . . .

she was nearing the last few seconds of innocence before she would know why Cadmin would need this bow.

Perhaps she would learn even more.

Perhaps she really was crazy, slowly driven mad after so long in Dr. Aster's captivity.

It would be a painful thing to come to that realization in front of Malnefoley. She very much wanted to be right, just so he'd look at her with surprise and admiration, not with so much suspicion.

His expression was etched with unexpected sympathy. His brows tucked together, laid over by streaks of straight blond hair that gleamed as golden as the bow he held. "Do you see the light above our heads?"

She matched his frown, then nodded.

"I spent four years on the top of what the humans describe as Mount Olympus. I stayed there until my gift had manifested. But more than that," he said, with such gravity that Avyi shivered, "I stayed until I could claim absolute control over every aspect of my powers, from a small glow to illuminate an underground crypt—"

"To being able to level a legendary rock maze."

He smiled softly. "Yes."

Again he extended the bow. Avyi raised her hands to take it, but jerked back. "Do you feel it? The humming? The ancient voices? It holds the screams of the dead."

"I don't hear anything, Avyi. I've shown you what I can do, in many of its incarnations. Show me what you can do."

Hands numb yet burning and bubbling, she closed her fingers around the shaft. A burst of sensation that transcended physical and mental, present and future, exploded through her with the force of a grenade. She could only cry out and clamp her eyes shut in the aftershock.

Cadmin stood on an arena floor made of crumbled concrete. Struts of pitted steel and decades-old iron strove toward the sky. She was surrounded by makeshift galleries where hundreds of people, both human and Dragon King, shouted and applauded. She held the bow in her left hand. Armor covered her shoulders and extended to form a thick lap skirt that reached her knees.

The doors opposite her lifted. A helmet obscured her peripheral view, but what approached her was unmistakable. Cage warriors from another cartel appeared, armed with a *nighnor* and a double-headed Mycenaean ax. Sath and Tigony, then. Their traditional weapons. Cadmin looked down at the bow she held, and reached back to touch the arrows in her quiver.

The warriors attacked. Dr. Aster smiled from the crowd in freakish delight.

And above them all . . . a shadow . . .

Avyi gasped and shook. "The Grievance," Avyi bellowed. "Dragon help us!"

Blood followed. So much blood. But none was Cadmin's.

Names filtered through. Rebels. Avyi knew them. She cried out as they were murdered, one by one.

"Avyi!"

As during her dream aboard the ferry, she found herself being shaken, rattled, shouted at. Mal stripped the bow from her bands, but he didn't fling it. He held a hand tightly over her mouth and cradled her close.

Believe me now, so that I can believe myself.

She clutched his forearm as if it were the only piece of flotsam remaining after a shipwreck. "You have a violent soul," she whispered. "I know. I know that it troubles you. But you're not like him. You can't be. I won't let you be."

"Avyi, you're not making any sense." His lips met her temple, and he smoothed a shock of hair back from her cheek.

"*Make* it make sense."

"I like to think I can do anything I want, but I don't think I can do that." He kissed her crown. "I would if I could."

He turned her in his arms so that she sat across his lap. Had she been sitting on her own, she would've clasped her hands around her shins and rested her chin on her knees—the pose of a woman trying to be small. Mal had shown her that in the hostel, how she hid within her own body.

She released Mal's forearm and found his middle. He was solid, immovable, breathing as quickly as she. The reassurance of his embrace was unlike any she'd ever known. He rubbed his hands on his trousers, getting rid of the loose gravel, and then petted her tears away.

"That didn't work," he said softly, so softly that she felt the words against her ear rather than heard them. "Let me try again."

He kissed one tear. Then another. Another. Until he was kissing her whole face, one sweet brush of heat after another. Avyi shuddered and pushed closer to the warm safety of his body. She kept her gaze riveted to the soft-enened light above their heads.

"Close your eyes." He kissed her mouth, then down her throat.

"I'll see it all over again."

"It's part of you now. Waking or sleeping, eyes open or closed. Tell me I'm wrong."

"You're not wrong."

She obeyed, closing her eyes—but she'd never obeyed like this. Voluntarily. She *wanted* to do as he said. She wanted Mal to be the one who directed the next few moments.

She moaned when Mal cupped her jaw, angling her face up toward his. More kisses followed. He started with each eyelid. These were no hasty jaunts from one place to another. He lingered, so that his breath became part of the caress. With every touch of his lips, she let go of a little bit of the tension crushing her chest. That rain of physical tenderness was a benediction. It was her reward for walking through fire. It was her reward for being Avyi.

The woman he'd named.

His mouth settled over hers and gave her more. The visions she'd witnessed were so violent, so vicious, that she welcomed Mal's turn toward more passion. The force of his lips increased when he returned to her mouth. His tongue pressed deeply, meeting hers, sharing his taste and taking hers in return. She hooked her arms around his neck while he crossed his behind her back. Their upper bodies were flush. She relished his warmth and the steady beat of his heart.

He's right here with me. Right here.

He tucked his mouth into the hollow between her

neck and shoulder. Lips tightened over that skin. His teeth followed—just a graze. He took the intimate kiss deeper, sucking, moaning against her skin. Avyi gasped, then gasped again when he unclasped her bra. Big, warm palms worshiped her breasts, roamed her back, and grasped her nape for another kiss.

Electrical currents followed wherever their skin touched, offering an unexpected charge. She trembled. Every stroke of skin on skin could be as dangerous as it was beautiful. How far could they take such passion?

"You're glowing," she whispered. "Malnefoley, look at you. Look at us both. You're making us glow."

He stopped only long enough to swipe a delicate fingertip down her forearm. A cool blue trail of energy followed in the wake of his touch. A look akin to confusion, suffused with awe, made him appear younger but no less daunting. He met her gaze, then cupped her cheeks. That glow swelled around the edges of her sight.

"Here," he said harshly. "Now."

Avyi pushed into his arms and kissed with all of her hunger for this man, but also as a means of erasing her fear. If she thought too much, she would be petrified by what was to come. Kissing Mal made everything go away—everything but the warm, wet thrill of his mouth on hers.

They fought for possession of the kiss. Avyi didn't stand a chance. She realized then how much control he'd permitted her on the ship. Now he took over. His hands were everywhere, just as he forced her hands under the hem of his T-shirt. She needed no encouragement there. He was a feast. A creature made to be adored. Each caress revealed a new delight, from hot skin to the pull and bunch of muscles that rippled down his back, his shoulders, his arms.

He stripped off the shirt. Avyi was faced with the perfection of his torso in all its golden glory. "Here," he said, low and harsh. "Kiss me here."

With a little tug on her hair, he pulled her closer. She kissed the skin just below his collarbone, before dipping down to relish his exquisite chest and taut abs. He breathed heavily, with a tight, occasional hiss when she found a particularly sensitive spot—or when she simply needed to bite. He was made of muscle and a vengeful will. He could take her teeth digging eagerly into his pecs.

Mal dragged her face to his and kissed her with equal fervor. He nipped her lower lip, then tugged her earlobe. She winced, then sighed as the sting became the sweetest agony.

"Turn over. On your knees. Like that, yes."

His voice was assured, as were his hands, as he turned Avyi to face away from him. He stroked her ass and thighs—roughly, so that the heat of his hands radiated through the cloth of her pants. Then he centered a rough grip between her legs. She stifled a moan as he massaged.

This was a test, although he probably didn't realize it. She had been on her hands and knees before. Now she focused all of her energy on remaining in the present, there, in Mal's keeping. She wanted to be with him. He would stop whenever she said to. But she didn't want him to stop, especially when he unfastened her cargos and pushed them down to her knees. She was bared to him.

The metal rasp of his zipper made her shiver with anticipation. She ached for him. She missed his hands on her body, grounding her. He didn't stay away long. One palm clasped her hip while the other roamed her skin, as if searching, as if he couldn't get enough of her. That thought charged her with heightened excitement.

Sure fingers discovered how wet she was. She let loose a little hiss before biting her lip. Mal was stroking her. He delved inside. He stroked outside. Swirls of pressure around her sensitive apex made her body shake. She pushed back to meet him—back arched, head lifted to the glow above her. Avyi whispered his name just before she felt what she wanted so badly. He positioned the hard, broad head of his cock at her slick opening. Without preamble, he glided deep inside. He shuddered and exhaled roughly. She shook her head when the sensation was nearly unbearable. How was she supposed to endure something so powerful without voice to let the intensity go free?

She reached back, needing to be part of how he guided their rhythm. It made her feel safer and more liberated to feel Mal's fierce, straining forearm where he grasped her hip. She dug her nails into his firm flesh as his pelvis met hers with increasing strength and speed. He was so big, inside and out, enveloping her, invading her in the most sensual, intimate way. Every sensation built and built until she gave herself over to the wildness of their desperate coupling.

Hair damp on her cheeks, she could say nothing. Everything was bottled inside as they stole this moment from the whole of time. Maybe that was for the best. As Mal began to kiss his way up her spine—kisses both spicy and sweet—she knew she would say too much to the most staggering man she had ever known.

❦ CHAPTER ❧ THIRTEEN

Mal tightened his hold around Avyi's hips. He adored the smooth perfection of her back where her shirt rode up. The pulse of their bodies was a revelation. She met him with equal force until he couldn't hold back. He steadied her, held her immobile with his arms wrapped around her torso. He arched until her hands came up off the ground. They knelt together when Mal showed her just how much he needed her.

Stroke after stroke, she took the full brunt of his power. He was aching, throbbing. She was so tight. Avyi was someone to be caressed and protected, not overpowered by the hard proof of his desire, but nothing about her spoke of fear, of the need to be coddled. She threw her head to the side to rest on her shoulder. Mal sucked the skin of her neck. Her pulse was almost heady in its intensity. She gripped his biceps where he clasped her flush against his chest.

More. So much more . . .

She barely made a sound as she came, but her body revealed every sensation. She shook and reached back to claw his nape as her inner muscles clenched around him. He fought the impulse to shout and to let the light above their heads bloom to its full radiance. That need for restraint did nothing to dim the explosive force of his climax. He swallowed a groan. His release was nothing short of madness as she stole every thought but the rightness of surging into her one last time.

They knelt together, panting. "Dizzy," she whispered, with a hint of laughter in her voice.

He hitched his jeans over his ass before rolling to the side, taking Avyi with him. She slumped with her back across his chest, still breathing hard. She found his hands and clasped them around her stomach.

Mal didn't want to think. He didn't want to ask questions about what Avyi had seen or why she'd seen it—or if he believed a Dragon-damned thing about it.

He was on fire. His body was steamy and fizzing in a way that had nothing to do with his gift. It was Avyi and her intoxicating nature—or, more like, it was their undeniable combustion.

He eased back from Avyi's tempting body and she fastened her pants. She shook out her hair, which was wild and damp. He followed suit. She was smiling, her eyes open wide and dazed. Nothing could describe her beauty. All the frescos and priceless works in Florence didn't compare. Would never compare. She was lace over titanium. She was pale fire with the softest skin and the most passionate nature he'd ever known. Who could ever have guessed?

Mal couldn't truly feel what she believed, and he might never be able to trust her, but that moment erased common sense. He petted her bare upper arms. She was shivering, and so was he. Kneeling before him like the foundling she was, seemingly fragile, she was also heartbreaking and enticingly wild. How was she capable of both, so completely blended into one sensual woman? He needed to be rid of her before his infatuation wrecked all sense of perspective, but he couldn't take that risk.

He didn't want to.

Destined.

"Fuck that," he muttered.

"What did I say?"

He glanced back over his shoulder. "Forget it. We should go."

Avyi eyed the bow as if it were a scorpion readying its lethal tail. "I can't."

"You don't have to. I'll carry it." He nodded back up the narrow tunnel where they'd crawled down into the belly of the crypt.

She let two fingertips hover within inches of the bow's upper nock, where time had impossibly left a string intact. What was it made of? It appeared no more extraordinary than hemp. But Avyi didn't touch it. She pulled her hand back and cradled it in the other. "One step closer. The power of the arrows was more diffused. This is becoming more concentrated with every new event. Each new discovery."

Unable to help himself, Mal touched his thumb to her chin. A spark flicked between their skin even before they touched. "Each discovery? Or just the ones you believe will take you to Cadmin?"

She took his hand in hers and watched the *pop, pop, pop* of energy as each finger aligned. "I don't know anymore. Is this . . . Mal, is this normal for you? This light and passion?"

"No. Not with anyone." He kissed her forehead, then slung the bow over his shoulder. "Let's go. I'm tired of feeling like we'll die buried alive."

They climbed out the way they came. Rocks pitted his palms, and the stench of old, decayed things was becoming a mold in his nose. As much as he'd been carried away by their desperate desires, he wanted to start clean with Avyi. He wanted a soft bed and her body in full light, not grasping for her in the belly of the earth.

He forced unspent desires to the back of his mind. There would be time.

Why did he believe that? Because he wanted to?

The bow slipped and hit the floor. "Wouldn't that cap off our little expedition? To find this thing after countless years and have the Giva bust it."

Laughter with an edge of mania colored Avyi's reply. "You could always convince the Council it was a sacrilegious item that needed to be destroyed."

"Do you think they'd believe me?"

"With that temper of yours, you could convince them or kill them."

Mal's fingertips turned to ice. She couldn't have known how close that comment cut him to the bone.

Voices brought him to full alert. "Shh."

Rather than find a group of tourists, they glimpsed workmen. They were busy setting up ladders to fix the lights Mal had destroyed. He whispered in Avyi's ear, "Grab the pack. And close your eyes."

Quietly, he rubbed his hands on his jeans while Avyi did the same against her cargos. It was a start. He gathered that static and added it to the swish and pull of the workmen's uniforms, the strikes of hammers, the swing of tool belts. Energy built and magnified in his body. When the men finally threw a switch to restore power, Mal struck. The light he emitted was bright enough to temporarily blind any human. He reached back for her hand. She already held the pack.

They needed no words as they hopped the barrier and ran past the men who scratched at their eyes and cursed in the Florentine dialect.

He ushered Avyi up the stairs leading out of the crypt. She darted away from him, pushing through a group of tourists who had reassembled after the alarms. Mal followed her up to the main floor of the cathedral, half convinced he'd never see her again. Had he been a means to an end, nothing more? Already she was lost in the crowd. The crypts remained barred off. Mal raced past two guards who stood at the top of the stairwell.

At least he'd thought they were guards.

They were from Clan . . . Garnis?

And they pursued.

Just what he needed. Two members of the near-mythical Lost, with their incredible speed and reflexes, chased him as he hunted a sexy, psychotic woman who believed she could see the future.

He didn't want to hurt anyone. He'd done enough of that in years past. Yet if these Garnis were another part of the plot against him . . . Sometimes a Giva was given no choice.

His own reflexes kicked up a dozen notches. He swerved past what had to be hundreds of people. Each of their expressions turned from annoyance to shock to fear as he pushed through the throng. Screams followed in his wake as the Garnis warriors did more than shove a few bodies aside. They were armed with maces, heavy six-foot chains tipped with spiked iron balls. When wielded with all their reputed force, the Garnis could use their clans' traditional weapon to sever a human in half.

Mal had to get clear, if not just for his sake, but for the countless innocents who might die because of his mere presence. He vaulted over a crying child and charged for the immense bronze doors at a full run. The Garnis were already there. They were so Dragon-damned fast. They both snaked out with the maces. Mal dove into a roll, lucky to escape being trapped by both. His heart thundered.

He burst into full sunlight and began working, working, working his gift as quickly as he could. A single blink later, one of the Garnis stood before him. The man was massive, hewn of muscle, and with hair so black as to rival Avyi's. They didn't have time to square off. The Garnis was too fast. He caught Mal around the ankles with the mace. Nothing stopped his fall to the ground. He smacked the back of his head on the asphalt. He barely kept hold of the bow.

The other warrior closed in at what seemed like quadruple speed, aiming to land on Mal's face. But he hadn't spent four years on a mountain for nothing. Throughout the fight, even having the wind knocked out of him, he'd been absorbing the strength of the sun—those blessed rays of pure energy.

A crack of lightning struck out of a clear blue sky. The man looming above his head bellowed as the bolt shot down from his scalp and through his feet. He collapsed onto the ground, unconscious and steaming.

"Mal!"

He looked up in time to see Avyi jump onto the second warrior's back in that squatting gargoyle pose. She battered him with her knuckles three times before the big man flung her off like a rag doll. Mal had just enough time to free his ankles from the mace. He snatched up the base of the chain, then used the remaining force pulsing through his body to turn the weapon into an electrical conduit. The Garnis who held it jolted and jerked as if he'd grabbed hold of a live wire. In truth, he had. Mal had created one just for his pursuer.

With both men temporarily dispatched, he knew he had mere moments to find Avyi and flee. One lucky escape did not promise a second. And there was no telling how many others might be in the area.

Avyi wasn't where he had seen her tossed into the crowd. He shouted her name, but there was too much panic and confusion to hear a possible reply, only human screams and the sounds of police alarms.

To Mal's trained eyes, she should've stood out among so many humans dressed for a casual day of sightseeing. What if she had passed out? Or was being trampled by so many scrambling feet?

Avyi would be terrified. She'd be ready to hide.

She *would* be hiding. If she wasn't too badly wounded. His heart lurched.

Mal dodged a group of tourists led by a female docent. He wove left and right, doubling back through an alley, until the shouts from the Duomo weren't so piercing.

Mind racing, he returned to the idea of Avyi hiding. She wouldn't run forever—*couldn't* have if her fall was too hard. As casually as he could manage, Mal returned to the scene of the attack. The Garnis were gone, which did his peace of mind absolutely no favors. He searched. He looked, started again, kept searching. The massive eight-sided dome loomed over him. The angle of the sun meant he stood in shadow.

There.

Across the piazza.

Avyi crouched against a low brick wall. Passersby obscured her face every other second. She held the pack's straps so tightly that her knuckles were bone white.

She flicked her gaze from him to the Duomo . . . to him again.

Mal shuddered as if an Arctic winter had settled over Tuscany. He looked up at the massive dome and found himself standing in the middle of a soothsayer's prophecy.

Avyi tipped her head to the east. Mal nodded.

In concert, they slipped between bodies and strollers and sun umbrellas, through what felt like the entire population of Europe shoved into a single piazza. Avyi gathered her breath, tried to stay calm. These weren't rustic villagers in search of witches. They were educated human beings with an eye for culture, history, and art. At least that's what she told herself as she zigzagged between families and a cluster of senior citizens wearing matching hunter-green jackets emblazoned with the words *The Globe Trotters*.

She found it in her heart to hope they were having

fun traveling the world. She would've traded places with any one of them.

But they'd also just witnessed a fight that could have been illustrated on ancient parchment. Dragon Kings fighting in the heart of Florence.

At the far end of a narrow alley, she found Malnefoley rubbing a hand over his hair. In unison they set a quick pace through narrow side streets and wide, crowded piazze. The shift from protected to exposed did crazy things to Avyi's self-control.

"Where did they go? The Garnis?"

"I didn't see. I was too busy scrambling to get free. Are you okay?"

"My ankles are probably hamburger. You?" His roughened voice was etched with concern.

"Bruised. I was more scared of the trampling feet than the Garnis."

"Different perspective," he said with a grin. "Those Garnis were Dragon-damned terrifying."

At least his self-deprecating smile leavened her fear a little. The rest of her concentration was shattered by Mal's long strides and the bow he wore across his back. The bow talked to her now. It sang and screamed and hummed. What she'd been forced to absorb all at once was beginning to align into images and more certain predictions.

And the Duomo . . .

No matter her injuries and fear, she had been hit with the full force of seeing her prediction come true. There was no denying the shock when the mind-blowing accuracy of her gift was reinforced. She swallowed hard, remembering how magnificent Mal had appeared, shadowed by the great dome, with his body fresh from battle, charged up like a thunderstorm, and that golden hair catching streams of sunlight. He was literally a dream come true.

Over the past few days, he'd nearly made her doubt the validity of her gift, but he'd become all the confirmation she would ever need.

They stopped in the doorway of an apartment, where a locked gate harbored a garden for its residents. Another locked door served as the building's main entrance. It was a place to breathe and to let Mal rest his injured ankles. Blood seeped through the denim of his pants.

"You win again." His voice was grim. "Satisfied? Me and the dome, just like you said."

His mouth was tight, his expression as powerful as his thundercloud gift.

She eyed him carefully. "Did you make choices?"

"Yes."

"Did they *feel* like your choices as you made them?"

"Yes," he said, more angrily.

"You only behaved the way you meant to at the time. It didn't feel contrary, like some marionette pulling strings. It was just you, until you and my vision became one."

"*No*. This is madness. Life doesn't work that way. You can't simply . . . You can't . . ."

"You're were holding me. We made love. Was that a bad thing?"

He grabbed her shoulders and pushed her into the corner between the brick building and the iron gate. He wedged her there. Kissed her there. His hands were aggressive, his intent obvious as he parted her lips with a forceful thrust of his tongue. Avyi only stayed his aggression to adjust the position of the pack across her shoulder, then dove into his embrace.

"We're caught in this together," she said, breathless, taking every kiss he pressed against her mouth, her throat. "I don't know where else to be but with you."

"I'm here by choice." His insistence was a growl that trembled down her chest and settled behind her sternum. The rhythm of her heart skipped.

"Even better."

She only knew the feel of his mouth as he took and took, offering no kindness as his lips folded over hers. He caught her hair at the crown, then angled her head to find better access to her neck. He sucked and licked. He nipped and kissed. His primal noises, all possession and need, sent shocks of greedy heat through her body and pooled low, lower in her belly. She ached. There was nothing to compare to being physically worshiped by Malnefoley of Tigony.

She spiked her hands into his hair, so that they wrestled for dominance in determining who kissed what, where, how hard. There was no question of softness. What they'd already done in the heat of passion had not drained the day of its adrenaline.

"I want you," he rasped.

"You're a fool if that's the only reason you're staying with me."

"I'm a damn fool no matter what I do."

She gave his hair a hard shake. "So you might as well sleep with me? Keep making mistakes with the girl you can forget once all this is over? I won't do this again if it's your means of revenge for having been shown a world you don't want to see."

"You're being ridiculous." He tried to kiss her again, but she flattened her palm between their mouths and shoved him away. His hold on her hip tightened almost painfully.

"Do you know what holding this bow reveals to me?"

"Magical fairies, crypt keepers, and a few Minotaur."

Avyi stood to her full height. Mal blinked, reminding her how rarely she permitted her body to unclench from its crouched, defensive position. "No, my dear, deluded Giva," she said, never looking away. "I saw through Cadmin's eyes the person responsible for the attempt on your life. She was aiming her arrow into the crowd, not at the Sath and Tigony Cage warriors charging at her in battle. *At* someone in the crowd. How she knew . . . I don't know. Dr. Aster was there, too, enjoying the bloodshed." Again she swallowed back an unexpected flood of emotion. The killer's features were obscured, as were Cadmin's. Avyi only knew what it was like to see the world through her eyes. "Your would-be assassin will be at the Grievance. So will a cache of captured rebels who will be slaughtered."

"The rebels? The ones who helped bring down Asters' labs?"

"Among them, yes."

"Hark and Silence? Leto and Nynn?"

"I don't know who exactly. But those who gather will die."

"Yet how and when and why—no clue. No picture of who will try to kill me. No reason why the rebels will be there." He glared. Frustration shimmered off him in powerful waves Avyi could physically feel. He grabbed the wrought-iron gate with both hands and sent shock waves of electricity up to the sky. Light radiated out from spearlike points at the tops of each bar. "You don't know a Dragon-damned thing."

"You speak of the Dragon, Giva. Be careful what you say." She lifted her chin. "Because there at the Grievance, I saw a dragon, too."

CHAPTER FOURTEEN

Mal gripped the iron gate and squeezed until pain radiated up his arm in a slow burn. "A dragon."

"Yes."

"At the Grievance."

"Four days from now."

Avyi glanced away, toward where water flowed beneath a grate at the side of the cobblestone street. No traffic here. Few people. A residential area where human beings left for work in the morning and returned home at night. Ordinary lives. They would never have any idea that he stood there trying not to demolish the whole neighborhood in a flash of frustration.

Giva. He was the fucking Honorable Giva.

And it didn't matter what he did. *Never had?* Choices that weren't choices at all.

"I saw its shadow. The shape of wings and limbs— maybe a tail, a head. But it was a dragon and it was furious. Flames everywhere."

"There aren't dragons, Avyi. Even if you buy into every myth and ancient tradition about the Great Dragon and the Chasm, you can't believe a random dragon will fly over the next Grievance. It's *insane.*

Time's up. Adventure over. You need to come with me, back to Tigony lands."

He grabbed her arms. She tried to fight, with her vicious weapons and her wildcat determination, but he was stronger and more resolved. A brief shock of electricity to her arms flared her eyelids wide, so wide that he could see the whites around bright green-gold irises.

So damn beautiful.

Why her?

Why some half-crazed woman who spoke about the future *and meant it*? A woman who might be so irreparably damaged by her years with Dr. Aster that every word she'd uttered to Mal was an unconscious falsehood—or an outright lie. She'd taken whatever scant certainty he possessed and pounded it beneath her killer boots.

"I'm not going back to your prison," she said viciously. "I will not be held captive and interrogated. I will not be doubted when so much is at stake." She stared at him with murderous accusations tinting her eyes nearly black. "I'm free now. Do you really believe you could get me back to Greece, let alone keep me there? You couldn't keep me there before, and you sure as hell won't keep me now."

He realized how tightly he held her arms, and how many shocks rocketed between them. When he held Avyi, he wasn't immune to his own twisted, nerve-jolting power. It hurt. It was unnerving. But it also fueled the dangerous impulses that charged his body—not his gift, but his body. He'd been kissing Avyi. Now he was brawling. They twined together in a heady cocktail.

"You'll do exactly what I want," he growled.

Avyi stilled. She touched his cheek, then lifted on her toes to kiss the corner of his lips. "Let me go. You know what I believe will happen. Do you really think your threats and bluster do a thing to dent my confidence?"

He exhaled heavily. "No."

"You've seen how this works, even if you turn away from what I've lived with my entire life. After all that, do you finally believe me? Please, Malnefoley . . . I need you to believe me."

Holding her waist, he rested his forehead against hers. It took more strength than he would've imagined to admit what had been building in him for days. But denying it now would be pure stubbornness in light of all that had happened. Turning away from the unknown wouldn't do anything to dissipate the gathering storm. If there was any chance that what Avyi predicted would come true, he needed to act.

"Yes," he said in a whisper. "I believe you."

She let out a cry and flung her arms around his neck. "Thank you. Oh, Mal, thank you."

He held her as she shuddered and shook. "What is this?"

"I've never . . ." She looked up into his eyes. "Do you know what that feels like? Maybe not. Maybe you can't know what *this* feels like. I never would've doubted myself for a moment had I known this day would come."

Mal was flooded with emotion he didn't know how to process. His only certainty was that Avyi clung to him with all of her considerable strength. She wasn't crying, but her body still trembled. His belief meant that much to her. In truth . . . it meant that much to him, too. A weight lifted from him as he held her petite body. When was the last time he had believed, truly believed, in another person?

"Come on," he said against her hair. "Let's get out of sight."

He used a quick zap of electricity to open the gate's lock, then ushered her inside. The private garden was even quieter and more secluded than their hiding place on the quiet residential street. Avyi angled her chin toward the vibrant sun of late afternoon. Summer in Italy. It wouldn't be dark for hours.

Once inside, he scrubbed his eyes with his palms, then ran his hands through his hair.

"Why did you stay in Greece for so long?"

"You. I needed you so I could be ready for all of this. You whisked me away from the tundra, taking me away from the labs. Even that small nod toward being rescued was enough to make me hope for a better future. And my prediction . . . about us . . . I didn't know when it would happen. It seemed more likely to come true if we were in the same vicinity, there in the stronghold. But then it was time for me to go. I felt compelled, or I'd miss my chance."

"And how did you escape?"

She patted his cheek, grinning. "Wouldn't you like to know."

He didn't want to ask, not after the moment of assurance and calm he'd felt, but one thing she said was too unimaginable to take on pure faith. "And the dragon? At the Grievance?"

"I don't know about that one either." She stood in a

shaft of sunlight. Her smile was bittersweet, almost cha-grined. "I'll believe it when I see it."

"It's a fixed point now? Like me and the doctor?"

"I hope so. For I'd dearly love to see a dragon in the flesh."

Mal nodded slowly. "That would be something to see."

Experiencing the relief of Mal's admission left Avyi both elated and exhausted. His belief wasn't something to be celebrated. She would never forget the heartbreak-ing pain in his eyes. He was a man whose world was blasting apart, and she was the cause. So instead of celebrating, she simply thanked the Dragon for giving her one ally—the first of her life.

Despite the contentious start to their journey, there in Crete, Avyi had put faith in the idea that, yes, one day their disagreements would be worth the reward of belonging—if not to him, then to the community she might return to at his behest.

She had wanted the sense of belonging she'd seen in the futures of the unborn. She had wanted what would never be given freely to a freakish foundling whose very gift was the source of her misery. Mal gave her that. No matter what happened now, she would al-ways be grateful for the events that had brought them to that moment.

No matter what happened now . . .

Too many visions had come true, especially when they were so near to the conclusion of each successive prediction. She could walk, run, scream, fight, set them both on fire. Cadmin, the rebels, a dragon . . . She and

Mal were deep into forces neither could control. All they had was each other, and that was a blessing she couldn't take for granted.

He was the leader of the Dragon Kings. He had been chosen by the Great Dragon to shepherd them through an undeniable crisis. She'd had faith, even when she was nothing but Dr. Aster's Pet. There was an Honorable Giva out there in the world, and he would save their people.

The backs of her legs tingled, as did the skin on her arm where Mal's anger had snapped and stung. He met her beneath the dappled shade of an olive tree and loosely held her hand between their bodies. His expression was quietly intense.

"I am not who you think I am. The good isn't as good, and the bad is worse. If you tell me no matter what I do, I'll still be your partner wrapped up in white sheets, what incentive does that give me to behave? I could slap you across the face. I could shave your head or steal that bow and arrow from you, never to be found again. We'd still wind up tangled in bed."

She shook her head, squeezed his fingers. "But you won't—not any of that."

"You can't be sure."

"This has nothing to do with gifts and predictions." She cupped his nape. "I deserve better. You've already given me that. You can give our *people* that. I've lived on hope most of my life. Let me have just this little bit more."

Mal swept her into his arms with such force and speed that Avyi gasped. "If I'm going to be forced up against choices that aren't choices at all, I might as well bend the inevitable to my will. I'm not going to make love to you by accident, just because we wound up trapped in the same berth . . . or hole in the earth, for fuck's sake. I'm going to do it now, because I want to."

"What are you talking about?"

He walked to the main door of the apartments. "Can you get through this gate?"

"The padlock is too big. And it's rusted. You could always conjure a light show."

"I'm not in the mood to risk more attention. Buzz each one instead."

"This is crazy."

A chuckle wove from his chest into hers, unfurling the last of the tension between them, as easily as one of Mal's tornado tempers receding to the point of clear blue sky. "Don't start with me. Buzz something."

Avyi pushed button after button, with Mal answering in perfect Italian. He lived in the building. The gate had been left open. There was a set of keys on the front step. "Are they yours?"

After the third such conversation, a young man grumbled and said he'd be right down.

"Your turn," Mal said. He set her down. "You're looking for keys when he holds the door open for you." He took the bow and was gone, secreting himself at the rear of the garden.

A minute later, Avyi was kneeling between the garden gate and the front door, rifling through the bushes and her hiker's backpack, muttering to herself in English.

"Hey," the man said in Italian. The rest of his words were a jumble.

Standing, shrugging, she countered his hostility in English. "I don't know what you're saying. I'm living here with my roommate. Quit yelling at me. I'm tired and I want to go to bed."

The young man, who looked worse than hungover, switched to his halting English. "The man. Said there were keys."

"I don't know anything about a man." She dangled a key ring—the one to Mal's town car. The flash of clinking metal wouldn't hold up under closer inspection, but the man remained confused and unwilling to keep arguing. "Now out of my way, please," she finished, pushing past him and into the building.

She walked up a narrow flight of stairs and waited at the second landing, listening. The young man grumbled with what sounded like Italian curses and slammed his door on the ground floor. She pulled a pin from her hair and searched the apartments. Picking locks had become somewhat of a specialty when she had checked on fragile patients Dr. Aster had insisted were beyond hope. Avyi had needed to know for certain, touching them, seeing the inevitable for herself. Never once had the doctor been wrong, but she'd tried every time.

Knock. Pick. Enter. Repeat.

Each was occupied except for a room on the third floor, which seemed to be set up as a bed-and-breakfast. There was a small kitchenette, furnishings, and a stack of city maps. A small makeshift souvenir area with miniatures of the Duomo and postcards featuring night views of the city took up one corner of the small living room. Three bedrooms were each outfitted with their own locks. A sign-in sheet was clipped by magnet to the

refrigerator, and a calendar of guests' comings and go-
ings hung beside it.

As did the keys.

Perfect.

She ran down to the foyer and opened the door for
Mal. He examined the bed-and-breakfast with an expression of frank approval. "The best no money can
buy."

"That must be a new concept for you."

He flashed his magnetic blue eyes without apology.
"We can't help how we were raised," he said. "Neither
of us. Good or ill. It affects every perspective."

"Did any of your perspectives imagine breaking in
to spend the night as . . ." She checked the itinerary.
"The Grovers from Chicago?"

"No. Your predictions?"

"Not a hint." They locked themselves in one of the
guest rooms. It was much larger than Avyi had imagined, considering the small, tidy nature of the kitchen
and dining area. A double bed. A wide-screen TV. A full
bathroom. She took the bow and arrow from him, winc-
ing at a surge of promise that drove into her marrow,
and hid them safely in a closet. Then she flopped on the
bed. "I'm impressed. We did well."

He crossed his arms, staring down at her. "Why did
you agree with me? To come here and do this?"

Avyi didn't like the grim curve of his mouth. She
wanted a smile at least. If he smiled, so would she. That
might take some doing, because although she was being
watched by the most potent man she'd ever known, she
was also being watched by the man who had the farthest
to go to reach his full potential—his best, most powerful

self. The leader that existed within the Honorable Giva had not yet matured. Believing her was the first step. Now she wanted to make love to the champion he would become—fearless, faultless, relentless.

"Just like you said. Because I want to."

❧ CHAPTER ❧
FIFTEEN

Mal watched as Avyi undressed without ceremony, but not without the awareness of his eyes as he stared, riveted. Her sidelong glances were equal parts tease and uncertainty. He liked both emotions. Although they had already made love twice, they would do so now with intention. Despite the electric kiss they'd shared while pressed against the wrought-iron gate, they were calmer now. More deliberate. The encounter promised to be slower and more intimate. Mal practically steeled himself for that, so strong was his connection to the woman coming to be.

At last, he could see the skin she bared to afternoon sunlight that entered through the twin windows on either side of the double bed. Nothing was concealed from him now. He wanted to see her. Ached to see her. They needed privacy away from terrible deeds and memories that wouldn't ever leave them be.

Maybe they could set them aside, if only for a few hours.

She stretched, languorously, and with a smile, rubbed her hair into a tangled mess, as if she'd already been thoroughly ravished. "As much as I'm looking forward to this, it will be good to get it out of the way."

"Get it out of the way?"

"So we're not trapped by it anymore."

Mal frowned as he turned the blinds and shut the curtains. "Trapped?"

"We can dispense with one of our fixed points and move on, so . . ." Her bra dropped to the floor, and she stepped out of her panties. "We get it over with. Prediction fulfilled. No guideposts to tell you and me where to go next. We choose, with no more obligation."

He knew he heard her speaking, and on some level he registered the words as being sensible, if not mercenary, but he was beyond true conscious thought when looking at Avyi. She was naked. Pert, small breasts were tipped with nipples a shade darker than her golden-pale skin. She had no markings. Not even Dr. Aster had left behind physical proof of his abuse.

"Don't you think?"

As if lured, Mal moved to within arm's reach. "Thinking has stopped."

"I'll consider that a compliment."

"Meant as one."

He pulled her closer, with his hands at her waist. "You're beautiful."

With a slight frown, she tensed.

Mal was going to lose his mind within minutes, and he was going to do so with a bone-dry mouth and a throbbing hard-on. "Why the frown?" he managed to choke out.

"Beautiful. It's beneath you. I know you can do better."

Mal grinned, then let it disappear just as quickly. "You make me want to try. To sacrifice. To believe the impossible."

"All because I took my clothes off?" She stood plainly before him, no crouching posture, no sensuous pose. Just the thin lines of her limbs, the breasts that hinted at a deeper femininity than her slim hips, and a small black thatch of private hair she didn't bother to hide. She didn't hide anything. Her expression said, *I dare you to look away*.

"Because you brought us here," he said. "*We* brought us here."

"It's just life. Good or bad. And you know this will be good."

"Good? I know you can do better."

He unbuttoned his shirt and pulled off his belt. Every piece of clothing that was flung onto the floor added to a sense of shedding his skin. He was the Giva, and he was a man who was finding his way. Even his body seemed to be cooperating with his newfound sense of inner determination, because his ankles were healing at record speed. Was it because he was using his power more frequently? Because he simply couldn't be hindered by weakness, now or ever?

There was no knowing what to do when so much was already in motion, especially the moment when he and Avyi lay facing one another, completely bared.

Avyi stretched her arms toward him, her expression softer than he could have imagined of the woman everyone else still thought of as the Pet. "Come show me."

She snapped her fingers, where sparks of static flickered like miniature fireworks. He'd already given her those bursts of power from what he struggled to contain. "Enjoy my body, Malnefoley. Let me enjoy yours."

He nodded, resting his forehead against her stomach, reveling in the soft way she stroked the back of his neck. She had sure hands, finding places of tension and working them to nothingness. He was aroused to a staggering degree. A great deal of it had to do with curiosity. She *was* beautiful. But her mysteries flipped his brain. Their previous encounters were preludes to these moments. When she'd predicted them together, had she known how they would kiss? What position they'd assume? How they would reach the conclusion of their passion?

No. Those weren't fixed points. He liked that. When it came to these intimate moments, they still had free will.

She wrapped her hands around Mal's shaft with such swift assurance that he hissed his shocked pleasure. "Damn, Avyi. You go so fast."

"We make the rules now."

He stared down at her, to where her eyes shone with unearthly beauty. Her skin was aglow with pale gold, as if her veins pulsed with the energy he consumed, amplified, released. "If you were making the rules, how would you want this?"

With two fast strokes, she threw her head back and laughed. Mal couldn't decide which had unmanned him more thoroughly—the rough, sensual treatment of his cock or the unexpected melody of her laughter. "I want you any way I can get you," she said. Then, with more tenderness, she lifted her head off the pillow just enough to kiss his forehead. "That's how it's been since we met."

She clenched him hard, setting a rhythm he enjoyed too much. He groaned and dropped his face between her breasts, kissing and gasping against her skin. "I want it like this," she said against the top of his head. "With your big hands on my ass. With your mouth on my breasts. Until neither of us will stand for anything less than magnificent."

"With the pace you're setting, magnificent won't last long."

"Your tornado tempers don't last long either. They tear the heavens in two and leave everyone utterly amazed, even terrified." Without gentleness, she pulled his prick until he bowed his hips toward hers. She notched his engorged, aching head where she was wet, hot, and just as eager. There, she waited. "I'm not terrified, Mal. Not about this. But I do want to be amazed."

Avyi looked into his storm-cloud-blue eyes and wondered just what she'd invited. Mal's moods were unpredictable in ways she was just beginning to comprehend. This was the pinnacle of sorts, but she'd only ever envisioned the aftermath. They would be tangled together, sweaty, satisfied. Nothing else was guaranteed. At the moment when the future would change between them, she wanted promises. Promises that neither of them could make.

So she concentrated on Mal, on his tension and the energy that literally thrummed in his blood, humming, making him even more extraordinary.

He tipped to the side and cupped her face in his hands, kissing, kissing oh so deeply, with so much passion. They were strikes of flint, flinging sparks, shooting off fireworks and sending lightning across the sky. He made her feel those images rather than see them. Her skin tingled where he touched. He was ahead of her every time. She'd want his hand on her breast, and he would already have his palm opened wide across her sensitive flesh. She'd crave the wet suck of his mouth against her throat, and he would already be tasting, nipping, inhaling her scent and whispering her name. Avyi. Her name—his claim on her, in a way that no one ever had exerted, and never would again.

She lay belly to belly with him, pushed into the mattress by his firm body. He grabbed her thigh and brought it up and over his flank. The sound he growled just beneath her jaw was untamed and possessive. Whoever he was outside of this room, or high above the Chasm when arguing with stubborn politicians—that was gone. He was ramping up faster, with more intensity, his hands everywhere and his mouth following.

"You stopped gripping me," he rasped.

"You seemed convinced this would end too quickly."

"I changed my mind."

He took hold of her wrist and pushed it between their bodies. Their fingertips knotted in a fist around his shaft, which was fuller and heavier than before. Avyi moaned and closed her eyes. He was going to fill her. More than that, he was going to fill her over and over, until the pressure of his thrusts was all she knew, all she wanted.

"Yes," she said on a long, hissing exhalation. "More."

"Greedy."

"So are you."

"Yes." He moved her hand with his, up and down,

until their flesh created rhythmic, erotic sounds in that still bedroom. "You make me crazy. You . . . *strip* me."

"I want you stripped. Nothing else comes between us now."

Mal grinned against her cheek. "Not much room for that."

He slid down her body, reversing the slow, sensuous climb of when he'd first crawled onto the bed. He stopped midway down her body. With the slightest lift of his eyebrows, he asked silent permission. Avyi couldn't answer with words, only nodded with a dip of her chin. Mal parted her knees, leaned in, tasted.

"Oh!"

Avyi couldn't control her hips when his mouth fixed on her pussy and used every weapon in a full-out assault. "Amazing," he whispered against her heated flesh. "That's what you wanted."

"You think a lot of yourself—" The words were a gasp, cut short when he flicked his tongue inside her channel, then swirled up to encircle with fissures of pain-sharp pleasure.

"I do. Too much. But I can't get enough of how you taste." He nibbled the tendon up the inside of one thigh. "I could stay here all day."

A groan edged primitive need into the room—her groan. She'd never heard anything half so erotic, let alone feel it backed up with action. Mal inserted two fingers into her slick channel and established a rhythm nearly as quick as what they'd shared when stroking his erection. Then lips, then tongue, then the barest scrape of teeth. He alternated fast to slow, rough to soft, until Avyi grabbed two handfuls of his straight blond hair.

"Pick one," she gasped. "And stay with it."

"I like teasing you."

"Why?"

"Because you'll do the same to me when you get the chance."

Avyi uttered a quick shriek when he followed his words with a long, deep suck on her clit. The pressure, matched with his swirling tongue, forced her to the breaking point. His relentless fingers never stopped— even when she shattered. She surged her hips up and toward him, and he took everything. Her thrusts never altered the position of his head, which was rigid and selflessly giving her a place to grind out the last of her stunned sensation.

Again using his hair, Avyi pulled him up so they could share a kiss. She wanted the proof of her release—proof that he'd given and taken at the same time. He tasted sweet, salty, both mixed on his tongue. The combination was beyond sensual, as was the slow, promising way he withdrew his fingers.

"You know what happens next."

She smiled, feeling like melted wax. "For once, I really don't."

"What happens is . . . everything else."

He positioned himself at her opening. Avyi already had her legs lifted and hooked around his low back. She was open to him, vulnerable and yet in the care of a man intent on making these hazy, gorgeous sensations last as long as possible.

With a mighty, breathtaking move, Mal surged into her body. She gasped. He cussed. And there was no stopping either of them. Avyi kept her legs around his hips and her hands planted flat against the padded head-board. She took his driving pulses, both accepting and fighting at the same time. Her beaded nipples rubbed against his chest as he shoved deep. He, too, used the headboard, but not as support. He curled his fingers around the top and found extra leverage—hips and body and the unrelenting force of his arms bracing for even deeper thrusts.

Avyi had never thought there could be such a thing as being too full, too magnificently stretched, so ready to give everything to another individual. Mal made her reconsider. *Made her*. Because he didn't relent.

"I've done it," she breathed, her respiration far too fast. "I've made you forget. Your body is mine. You want me too much to hold back."

"I *am* holding back."

He slowed only briefly, to catch her gaze. Avyi found fire in his eyes. Power. Unimaginable power. Yes, he was holding back. It was like comparing a firefly to a strike of lightning.

"I'll hurt you," he said. "I don't want to."

"Hurt me how?" She glanced at where he held the headboard. "You've given me your strength. I can take anything."

Still keeping up a steady rhythm, he let go with one hand and used it to pull her chin in place. She couldn't look away if she wanted to.

"My strength, Avyi, is only part of me. My control is another." With a dozen quick, fierce strokes, he brought her right back to the cusp of orgasm. But he only gave her those dozen. "I can stop when I need to."

"Pull out right now? Be done?"

An expression of supreme arrogance transformed his aristocratic features into beautifully depraved variations. "If necessary. Just like I'm holding back the use of my gift."

"Right now?"

"We're having sex. Lots of friction. So much energy. You have no idea what this feels like to me."

She reached up and threaded her fingers through his hair, which crackled with static. "Better than orgasm?"

"I don't know. I've never tried."

"Why not?"

"You felt what happened when you held my hands to my shoulder, the electricity that flooded us both."

"All I know is that you look sensual after you use your gift. You look satisfied."

"It's another way of letting the body have what it wants." He swallowed, pushed back the insistent pulse of his hammering need to come, and braced his weight on either side of Avyi's neck. Arms straight. Arms tingling. "I just can't have both."

"I don't believe that." With a wry smile, she leaned up and licked the left side of his jaw. "Give me a taste."

CHAPTER SIXTEEN

Mal shuddered. "Why?" was all he could manage.

"I want new. I want experiences I've never had." She slid her hand down to grasp his buttocks again, reinitiating their quick, thumping rhythm. "And I want to see the look on your face when it happens."

He groaned. "Avyi, no."

Without waiting for any further resolve-crumbling inducements, he leaned low over her. He shoved one hand between their hips and found her clit. With the other he dropped to his elbow, still holding his torso up from hers—but not so far up that the sweet scrape of her nipples didn't greet him with every forward thrust. He put the deep pull of his mind aside. No gift. No powers. No losing control of anything but his body, which needed appeasing until Mal thought he'd go mad from the screaming in his mind.

Take. Have. Own.

The last of his gentleness seeped away as he used Avyi for his satisfaction. She grasped him, chanting his name, scraping fierce nails up his back and down his ribs. He found the rhythm he needed, the depth and pressure, and climbed steadily toward the moment when his mind winked out and only feeling remained. Avyi thrashed her head, then snapped taut. Her inner muscles clamped around his cock in a surprising flood of new sensation. It was what he'd needed. Mal buried himself to the hilt, glorying in how well she accepted his invasion—how she welcomed it with so much passion.

Sweating, he slumped down so that his head rested on the pillow next to hers. Their cheeks met, while their chests, now pressed together, heaved in time.

"*Bathatéi*," she whispered. "That was . . ."

"Yes, it was."

After endless moments of glorying in their bodies drained of tension, and their respiration leveling to a softness near normal, he rolled to the side and pulled her with him. She lay partially over him, with one knee hooked up toward his navel.

"You held back after all."

"You sound disappointed," he said.

"In theory. But . . . I was being selfish, even reckless. You protected me. Thank you for that." She stopped and pushed damp hair away from her temples. "It was wonderful."

"Amazing?"

Avyi smiled against his chest and nipped a bite of his flesh.

Her silent distraction didn't work. She was pliant and soft against his body, while he disliked knowing—even if she wasn't going to discuss it—that she'd wanted more from him than he'd provided.

"I can't, Avyi," he said quietly. "It's dangerous."

"Have you with . . . with other women?"

"Not exactly." He shifted to pull a coverlet over their cooling bodies. Briefly he wondered if this was the scene she'd predicted, but he didn't want to ask. If it was, it could mean the end to their acquaintance. Worse, it could mean any number of futures had just opened up.

"Will you explain it to me?" She pushed up, then crossed her forearms over his chest and settled her chin there. "So I can call that *undoubtedly* amazing, rather than feel like I missed out on something."

"You missed out on me making the wrong call," he said. "On me truly forgetting myself for one second. You know how fast light travels. Imagine if I did so much as blink, with my concentration gone for only that duration. I could kill us both."

"Show me. Now. When you're in complete control."

Mal exhaled and looked into the most tempting eyes he'd ever known. The urge had been so strong, to give her the burst of his body and the jolt of his gift. He'd never had both. Never together. He'd always feared losing too much of himself to a woman who could accept both—and feared what would happen to a woman who couldn't.

But she was right. He was calm now, if he didn't glance down to the beautiful tangle of limbs covered by a thin white coverlet. Or acknowledge that how Avyi stroked his skin and ran her fingers through his chest hair were the most comforting sensations he'd ever experienced. It was calm and promise and a dare, all at once.

"Very well."

Her lips curled into a sweet half smile.

Momentarily distracted, Mal took that smile into

himself until the memory of it would become as intrinsic as the composition of his cells and the beat of his heart. Tentative as it was, that smile was a gift. He'd learned that much. Revealing her emotions was something she reserved for him. The full crest of her upper lip flattened as her mouth widened even further. She was more than beautiful. Full of mystery and intrigue, all in the guise of a half-grown woman, she was the ultimate puzzle for a man who'd given up on solving much of anything. The problems he faced were so insurmountable as to make trying as difficult as doing. He'd come to the stomach-dropping conclusion that she was just as burdened. Yet her delicate appearance and moments of vulnerability, even accessibility, hinted that maybe, just maybe, with enough time and dedication, he could unravel her secrets.

If he could do that, he could be the man to lead their people. Why did it take a single woman to make him realize something so basic?

He was delusional, but it verged on possible. In a moment of clarity—one he imagined was akin to her predictions—he knew Avyi's contradictions would draw him back, again and again. It would be the equivalent of chopping off a limb when it came time for them to part. And there were some wounds from which a Dragon King couldn't recover. A missing limb was one. And like human beings, heartbreak was another.

"Very well," he said again, with authority in his voice. If she wanted to see the man she'd taken into her body, she needed to know who he really was. "Sit up."

Together they arranged themselves so that they sat facing one another. His legs crossed behind her back, while hers angled over his so that her heels pressed against the tops of his buttocks. Modesty was not an issue. Becoming aroused again was.

He stayed focused on her face. "Brace yourself on my shoulders. Don't look down. Straight into my eyes."

Avyi did as she was told. He'd enjoy her obedience more if there weren't the lingering questions as to whether she actually wanted to go along with him, or if her conditioning by Dr. Aster had stripped her ability to resist. Perhaps she didn't say no to Mal because she *couldn't*.

No.

Even at the end, moments before they shared that astonishing orgasm, she'd fought him—fought for what she wanted from him. She was obeying now because she wanted to. That made him breathe more easily and hold on to the slippery certainty that she was her own woman.

She remained still, her stare trained on him.

"Ready?" he asked.

"Yes."

Mal slipped the fingers of his right hand down between their torsos, where the sweat hadn't yet dried from their blazing encounter. He didn't stop until he rested the pad of his thumb against her clitoris. "Don't move," he said, using the moment to gather his will, his strength, the entirety of his being as a Dragon King.

He leaned forward and rested his forehead on hers. Eyes bright. Clit so slick. And Mal holding his breath before a surge.

Avyi jolted on a breathless shriek. Her fingernails tightened along his ribs, deepened, until she broke skin. Her eyes lolled back.

Mal's fingers were flooded with the moisture of her climax.

He caught Avyi against his chest and held her close. He buried his face in her hair and crossed his arms around her back.

"What"—she gasped—"was that?"

"I don't know." He held her closer, genuinely confused and upset at himself for being so. Yes, he'd mastered his control, but perhaps not all of his gift's possibilities. That was unsettling. And knowing she could take his power—take it and *enjoy it*—was earthshaking. "I'd intended it as a warning."

She laughed against the stretch of muscle between his throat and his still-healing shoulder. " 'Here, Avyi,' " she said, mimicking him with a breathless voice. " 'This is what would happen if we mixed business and pleasure.' "

"Something like that."

"Backfired on you. Because *that* was amazing." She smiled again. He felt it on his skin without needing to see it. "Are all Tigony this dangerous?"

"Dragon damn, Avyi. I hope no one is as dangerous as I am."

"Good, because womankind would never be the same." She clasped his fingers in hers, where sizzles of power still sparked tiny lights, like a sparkler held between their near faces. She kissed his thumb and gasped. She did it again, finger after finger. Mal was speechless, even as his power increased with his arousal. His cock jutted up between them. She licked the sweat from the tense column of his throat, stopping just behind his earlobe. "I want another."

"Avyi . . ."

She glanced down and grinned. "Don't even try lying to me."

Without pretense, she lifted on her knees just enough to align their bodies and sink down. They both moaned, and Mal knew he was both lost . . . and found.

Avyi struggled to catch her breath as Mal grasped her ass in hands that fizzled and tingled. He was still holding back, and she knew that was for the best. She knew what he could do, how dangerous he could be. But every gift from the Dragon had degrees and varied uses. She felt like she'd discovered a new toy. There was no way she would let him take it away from her.

Using his upper arms for leverage, she lifted and lowered, relishing the feel of his return each time she sank toward his lap. Her body was made for this—for him—and she'd never known.

He could take her mind and throw it to the stars. That's where she wanted to be.

"You're so anxious," he groaned, as she picked up the pace. His hands were strong, commanding. He slowed her to the point of sensual agony. "Dawn will come soon enough. This is worth savoring."

"Says you. One touch and you could make me come again. Don't blame me for being hungry for you. And don't tell me that ability is anything less than heady. You were surprised—" She gasped when he hit a particularly sensitive place deep inside. "And you enjoyed the result."

"More than I can say."

He thrust up, harder now, his skin electric and

tempting. Avyi petted to feel his masculine textures, his flexing muscles and his glistening skin. How much of him could she take? She already knew she could take the full measure of his passion, no matter how thick and hard and demanding. She wanted to know how much she could take of his other skills. He was so reluctant that she knew she was the first woman to experience him this way. *That* was heady.

They were breathless and slick with sweat. They sounded beautiful—erotic animals who craved and craved, so primal now. She was close. His eyes were glazed with passion, but also with the concentration she'd seen when he summoned the majesty of the heavens. Avyi grabbed his thick wrists and brought his hands around so that he gripped her thighs. His thumbs arrowed toward her sex, where friction edged her so near to another shattering climax.

"No," he groaned. "You can't."

"You want to. I see it in your eyes. And I want you to."

She pushed his hands closer together along her skin, until his thumbs closed over her clit from both sides.

"*Avyi.*"

She wrapped her arms around his neck and buried her face there, using his strength as her anchor. "It'll be just as powerful for me, too," she whispered. "Are you scared, Giva?"

"Fuck you." His voice was that of another man—or maybe not a man at all. He was a Dragon King in the most pure, potent sense.

Biting his earlobe, she rocked her body, faster, more urgently, as her breasts scraped the barest static along his chest hair. They were charged, on the edge of exploding. "I'm so close, Mal. You want something even more potent? Something more powerful to soak into that arrogant ego of yours? I've never begged. Not ever, no matter what's happened in my life. *Never*. I'm asking you, please. I'm begging you. Do this. I want to be free."

For the briefest moment, he stilled. He looked into her eyes. "So do I."

He flipped her onto her back and angled her legs to open wide. She dug her heels into the mattress while he bowed low over her body, his forehead heavy between her breasts. He looped an arm behind the small of her back, bracing them both as he took over.

She cried out. She'd thought what he gave her before—that force—was all he was physically capable of. Not even close. One wave crashed over her until she was a shuddering, heaving mess beneath his relentlessness. She almost wanted to tell him to stop. Instead, she grabbed his ass and dared fate. Rend them apart. Die in his arms. She didn't care anymore.

He began to moan, low in his chest. With his free hand, he slid lower and lower down her body, until he gently held her clit between his thumb and forefinger. The control he must be exerting—the thought was enough to send tremors of pleasure to chase her orgasm.

"Please, Mal, *please* . . ."

He drove deep with an animalistic groan. She barely felt the explosion of his release before the electric effect of his climax shot down his arm, down his fingers, and directly against her most sensitive nerve endings. She arched on a scream. She thrashed when he didn't let up, didn't let her escape, as one, two, three—endless pleasure—made her an animal, too. She scraped him, bit him, cursed him in the ancient language of their people. The world shook to pieces as his gift tingled and shocked her to complete mindlessness.

He gently eased back until he was petting her with nothing but skin to softest skin. "Avyi." He stroked her nipples and the tops of her thighs. "Come back to me. I need you to come back to me."

"Here," she mumbled, smiling. "I'm here."

She flung her arms around his neck and pulled him close. It was the last thing she could manage with limbs so heavy and limp. But she needed him all around her. There was a moment . . . a moment before he had spoken . . . when she'd been certain he would pull away completely. Why? They'd just shared something uniquely beautiful.

The tension left his upper body as he encircled her, arms and legs and his big, strong frame. The sheets were tangled around them. She smiled secretly against his chest. *This* was the moment. Telling Mal would probably freak him out again, but she thanked the Dragon. There she was, living in the present. Maybe seeing something this earth-shattering in advance would've scared her off. She grinned more deeply. Or it would've spoiled the fun, taken the surprise out of such an unexpected present.

She thanked the Dragon for that, too. Her present. Mal was her present.

She'd never been given one before.

"I don't know what to say," he said, voice rough, lips against her crown.

"I do."

"Enlighten me."

Ah, there it was. The return of his humor. She needed it. She needed to know he was still with her, not pulling away as she'd feared.

"That wasn't just something to get over with."

"No?"

"Amazing," she breathed on a long sigh.

He laughed and kissed her lips, softly, but with the leftover intensity of what they'd experienced. "Finally."

"You said you spent four years on a mountaintop mastering your powers. That you held on for me, and made it good for me even before . . . And then to concentrate and keep me safe even as you came . . ."

Grinning, he slid his hand down her back to cup her ass. It wasn't sexual. It was merely comforting. And nearly possessive. He was so strong. Avyi couldn't have gotten away from him had she wanted to. She didn't. They were entwined physically just as they were entwined in destiny.

Good. She couldn't think of a better partner for facing the challenges that lay ahead.

"See? Even you can't find the words," he said.

"I could go back to being silent and mysterious. Slinky and devious." She angled up on one elbow. "Or I can be the woman Malnefoley of Tigony rendered speechless."

He eyed her with that curious distance again. She shuddered, and even shuddered again when he pulled her back into his embrace. "Thank you, Avyi."

❧ CHAPTER ❧
SEVENTEEN

Avyi lay awake, listening to Mal breathing. She had nestled her head in the hollow between his good shoulder and his chest, and had yet to move. The afternoon was long gone. So was early evening. They should've been hungry or restless or . . . anything. At least, that's how she imagined she would feel. Yet she didn't move, as if the smallest inhalation or reflexive sigh would break what had become an overwhelmingly seductive spell.

Stay.

Like this.

She shouldn't want it. Shouldn't even be thinking it. But Mal's hand on her hip and his mouth tucked against her temple were achingly beautiful. The more time that passed between their shattering lovemaking, the more time she had to realize the truth. She'd thought this the peak of a mountain, but she had no vision to replace it. She'd been thrilled and bold when they'd dared each other so roughly. The real dare was how long she could lie in his arms and still be able to walk away when the future inevitably caught up with the present—a future she couldn't see.

Did she need to walk away?

She couldn't, she realized with a sudden shock. She couldn't when the emotions were all wrong.

Dragon damn. That was it. The emotions. She'd seen the image, but something was still missing.

No, no, no . . .

It couldn't be. Her gift said they wouldn't just be lovers tangled in sheets, but that they would be *in love* when that moment arrived.

Her heart quickened. She was halfway in love already—and had been for a long time, thanks to the long buildup provided by her vision—but he would never love her in return. In all honesty, she didn't think him capable of love.

It couldn't be true. *This* was the moment.

Wasn't it?

Yet no matter how she tried to look through the mists, the same predictions remained, including her and Mal lying tangled together—but not there. How to get from here to there? She didn't know how to operate with so few clues.

Maybe that was why Mal had come into her life. She needed to trust him. Fate—no wonder he hated the idea so much—said she needed to adore this man. No matter how much she doubted herself at that moment, she knew one more thing with utter certainty.

The Honorable Giva needed to believe—in her, and in the Dragon—or their people were doomed.

No one needed her powers to understand that. They only needed to understand *him*. He smelled of such a strange, almost endearing combination of scents. Male sweat. Sexual release. Sunshine from the piazza. Shadows from the crypt. She inhaled slowly, taking in as much as she could. The present tended to be an afterthought. The future was her curse and her gift. If she saw a clear, undeniable glimpse of what was to come, she knew how to prepare. Steel one's heart. Be ready to smile. Brace for a punch. They were mere confirmations that, yes, the Dragon still wanted her to see three steps ahead of every other being on the planet.

The spaces in between . . . they were the joys. Living for the sake of living, not in fear or anticipation of some moment yet to come.

So she enjoyed Mal, as night claimed them in the room they'd broken into.

"Now what?" he asked, the timbre of his voice startling her with its low rumble. Abrupt. A little too loud. As if he'd been contemplating what to say for quite some time. That was the awkward, endearing result of what they had done.

"I don't know."

Mal shifted until he sat halfway up against the headboard.

Lights in the garden terrace down below shone shades of orange and blue across his torso. Every muscle was deeply defined by the sideways illumination, as if he needed to appear any more alluring and powerful. Avyi was left with the feeling the mortal women of old must've experienced when the Dragon Kings were finished with them. The distance. The sudden feeling of loss. The knowledge that she'd reached heights that would never be repeated, and that she should be thankful for having had the opportunity.

But Avyi would not turn away from Mal's mouthwatering body. She had suffered too much to deny herself anything so perfect.

"What do you mean, you don't know?"

Avyi lay on her stomach, propped on her elbows with her forearms crossed. She tried for lightness. "I say we go for a repeat performance."

Mal's pale brows drew together. He always appeared so somber when he frowned. She'd since learned to take the expression as one of frustration, not stately prowess. Anyone who was intimidated by his scowl was a fool. She was no fool, except when it came to him and desires she couldn't control. Maybe she didn't even want to control them anymore. When had she ever wanted anything so completely, so selfishly, just for her own safety and pleasure? When she'd been held by Aster and owned by that long-ago Garnis family, she hadn't known what it was to want. The concept had been completely foreign . . . until she'd met Cadmin, and all the children to follow.

Now she knew. Wanting to belong simply wasn't enough anymore.

She wanted love.

"Repeat performance? Is that what you predic— You know what? Right now, I don't think I care."

"Good," she said, smiling. "Then we try it again and again until we get it right."

"Get it right?"

"You and me. Tangled together. White sheets. Even the sunlight from earlier. It was all as I'd envisioned. Only . . . This wasn't it."

"What?"

She shook her head, then turned on her side so as to

push her frustratingly unmanageable hair out of her eyes. "I get these feelings. That's the best I can explain. *Feelings*. The moment when a prediction of the future meets the present. The children I've seen, for example. One twisted the chains of a swing, twisted and twisted, then let it go. He spun in circles, laughing as the chains unwound. Then he threw up. Too dizzy. I was in one of the doctor's operating theaters when that moment happened. Somewhere out in the world, that boy would've been seven years old, and he'd just finished vomiting after spinning too quickly on a swing." She exhaled and took another breath, unused to putting her nebulous sensations and impulses into words. "A chill came over me. I closed my eyes. And I knew."

"But not now." He said it flatly. His expression was made of stone.

"Whatever stands between us in the future, this wasn't what we thought it would be."

"We?"

She ducked her head, blushing. "It wasn't what *I* thought it would be."

He grinned, looking smug, cheeky, and tired—beyond the fatigue of their lovemaking. "So much for getting it over with."

She sat up to join him against the headboard. "You have decisions to make now. I can't be any more of a guide than you are."

"You've already seen the Grievance, the rebels being killed, Cadmin shooting toward the faceless person behind my assassination attempt, Dr. Aster, and . . ." Mal scrubbed his palms down his face. "And a *lonayíp* dragon?"

"Yes."

"A bunch of futures and no idea how to get there."

She took what felt like a tremendous risk by touching his arm. She stroked the fine, hot skin down to where hair like gold dust textured his forearms. "Maybe now you can see how it never feels like I've been robbed of much along the way. There are too many—"

"Variables. Yeah, I got that one now."

"I had no idea how to get here. Had I run from the first day, the Dragon still would've brought us together."

"Why didn't you?"

She looked away, until he caught her chin. "I wanted you to chase me."

"Did the trick."

"So here we are. And we haven't even reached the moment I foresaw when we first met at the doctor's labs. You were on a snowmobile."

"And you were wearing black latex."

She shivered. "I prefer my own clothes. One of the perks of being free."

Mal pulled her back into his arms. She sighed deeply. "So, no guideposts," he said. "Just when I was getting used to having *some* sort of map."

"Only choices, Giva."

"Giva." He practically spit the word.

"That's what you are. The Dragon wouldn't have chosen you if you weren't the man to bring us out of the darkness. Where we go is up to you. Who we tell is up to you. Which problem we tackle first, be it Cadmin or the rebels or confirming the location of the Grievance—"

"Up to me." He shook his head as if weighted with

terrible purpose. "I almost preferred it when you were smug."

"You were ready to give up your duties so quickly."

"Yes. A thousand times yes. But that isn't my fate."

"No. But we keep getting good news every time we make love. This won't be the last time. I just didn't feel it."

"Didn't feel it? Woman, you felt quite a bit."

She hooked her leg across his and sat up, straddling him. "Then we should definitely try again."

Mal awoke in the middle of the night with a feeling up his spine as if someone watched them from the dark recesses of the room. He moved only his eyes, trying to peer through the shadows. Perhaps a dream. Perhaps his imagination. But the ache in his shoulder was still a nuisance. The attempt on his life could've been the end of him, and as he was beginning to truly accept, it could've been the end of their people. He couldn't afford to take chances when that buzzing feeling grew stronger.

Avyi mumbled something in her sleep. Mal was tempted to place his hand over her mouth—not enough to wake her, but enough to keep her quiet. That would require movement he couldn't afford.

He decided the only way to get back to sleep was to take the offensive. Either he'd breathe a slightly embarrassed sigh of relief at being so jumpy, or he'd take an attacker by surprise.

Lying there, he concentrated his senses on the room itself. He looked for any place he could find static. Any hint of energy. He reached out to the shift of water in the pipes threading through the ceiling, and from the opened window he gathered the movement of the curtains and the hiss of streetlights.

The open window? His heart leapt to triple speed. Someone was definitely in the room.

Focusing, he found the air current that indicated respiration. The steady lift and fall of a chest rubbing against clothing. It was another touch of static, as well as an indication as to where the invader crouched in wait.

The corner by the bathroom. A trick of the light cast that small area completely in black. The perfect hiding place.

Mal closed his eyes and used his gift to gather the bits and pieces of electricity he'd grabbed from the air, even the friction from his opponent's own body. He pictured that corner, while trying to contain the glow of power that filled his veins and supercharged his muscles. With a last breath, he jerked to a sitting position and leveled a blast of blue-white light.

The light reflected off a surface with such intensity that Mal was momentarily blinded. Avyi was awake instantly. She jumped off the bed, out of sight. A scraping sound meant she'd grabbed her knife and her brass knuckles. She'd donned her T-shirt and panties after having taken a shower, as he had, but he couldn't see a hint of her body. The flash of white blindness completely obscured his vision.

The scrape of metal against metal was no surprise. Feminine grunts and hisses were. Mal fumbled for the nightstand lamp and flipped the switch. He blinked.

The Cage warrior named Silence had pinned Avyi's

torso against the far wall, using a shield ringed with serrated edges—the mirrorlike surface that had turned Mal's power against him. But Avyi wasn't completely helpless. She grabbed Silence's free hand. The razor-sharp switchblade was poised to slice Silence's wrist.

"In the name of the Dragon, drop your weapons," Mal shouted. "Both of you!"

Neither moved. They didn't look away from one another, their expressions fierce in the midst of combat. They were motionless but still fighting. A standoff.

Mal flung the blanket aside and whipped it over Silence's face. She whirled. The blanket was shredded with one slice.

The distraction was enough for Avyi to change the balance of power. She tripped Silence's feet out from under her, sending the warrior to her knees. Avyi stood over her with the switchblade against Silence's carotid artery.

"You'll bleed out. You know it. And you won't die unless we decide to kill you."

"You have no sword."

"We do. In luggage at the train station. You'd be in agony, because we'd take our time in retrieving it."

Mal saw the flex of Silence's shoulder. She was adjusting her grip on the shield's handle. "Don't, Silence. Stand down. Last time I ask."

"You didn't ask, Giva," she replied.

"I'd heard rumor you can talk."

"When I need to."

Avyi's eyes blazed with the heat of battle. "Enough," he said quietly, deadly serious.

Avyi lifted the switchblade and stepped back in one

fluid motion, her hands lifted as if in surrender—but with so much more attitude. Her body language said she'd stab Silence in the eye if the woman so much as sniffed.

Mal nodded to Silence's shield. "And that. On the ground. We know what powers you can muster if you feel threatened."

"I'd use your Dragon-damned electricity against you. Don't think because you're the Giva that I'd hold back."

"I don't think that at all."

Silence was a Cage warrior from Clan Sath who'd fought for the Asters. The Sath were known as Thieves because their gift from the Dragon was the ability to temporarily steal the powers of another Dragon King. That made them helpless on their own—thus most were well trained in physical combat—but unpredictably powerful when in the company of another of the Five Clans. The best were able to acclimate to the sudden influx of another's gift, assess its vitality, control it, and use it as a weapon. All in a matter of seconds.

"Introductions," he said simply. "Silence, you remember the Pet."

"I helped her find a very special relic." Avyi smiled sweetly, but with steel behind it. "And her husband."

"Not the time to trip down memory lane," he said. "And we're beyond those monikers now. Neither of you are in the Asters' custody anymore. And I'm a man as much as I am the Giva. So . . . . I'm Mal. This is Avyi. And you are?"

Silence scowled. She had peach-pale skin like Avyi, but with hair so bright blond as to be silvery white. She was tall and slender, fit for the rigors of combat after having spent five years as a Cage warrior. "Only Hark knows that," she said simply.

Her husband.

Mal sat on the corner of the bed. His heart still thudded in his throat. If Silence had wanted them dead, they would be. That meant she was there for reasons other than violence. She wasn't another potential assassin.

He had to believe that, or else he'd be jumping at shadows for the rest of his life.

"Fine," Mal said with a wave of his hand. "Where is he, anyway? I got the impression you two were a matched pair."

He nodded to where Silence's bare forearm was marked with a small but permanent needle that curved just under the skin. The Sath called it the Ritual of the Thorns, their mating commitment. She and Hark were bonded for life.

"He's been kidnapped."

"Kidnapped . . . By whom?"

"I don't know."

She finally set the shield on the ground, as Mal knew she would. She was a vicious fighter, but she was a good woman. From what Mal had gathered, she'd voluntarily stayed with the Asters as a Cage warrior long after she'd needed to. Following the raid where Mal had helped free his cousin from the Cages, Silence and Hark had thrown in with the group of rebels Avyi predicted would die.

"We were on assignment," Silence said. "The Grievance is only days away, in London."

"London?" Avyi edged away from the wall, her eyes still wary. "Where in London?"

"The old Battersea Power Station."

Understanding spread over Avyi's expression. "So that's what I saw. Crumbled and abandoned. On the Thames in an industrial area. It's perfect. You found this out with Hark and the others?"

Silence nodded. "He and I were separated. That Indranan witch, Ulia, who works for the Asters—she played games with the minds of every rebel until our cohesion broke down. Everyone was captured but me and a man, Grandio of Indranan. He remains in hiding in London. I . . ." Her voice choked off. "I ran. I needed help."

Mal nodded. "You did the right thing, although I would've preferred a different way to reunite."

Silence glared up to where Avyi had moved within striking distance, yet closer to Mal. "The company you keep made me wary."

"You trusted my predictions well enough to stay in the Cages two extra years," Avyi said harshly. "I had nothing to do with Hark's kidnapping. Had I known how to prevent it, I would've got word to you."

"I wasn't talking about you." Her words were plain but as sharp as the razor edges of her shield. Mal flinched. "I was overruled when it came to seeking your predictions, because you'd been a Tigony prisoner for so long. Even Hark thought better of it. I'm sorry, Giva," she said, pointedly using his title rather than his name. "But you hold little authority over anyone, especially the rebels. The attempts on your life made the situation worse. Someone wants you dead. None of us wants near that sort of trouble, not when freeing as many as we can from the cartels remains our focus."

Avyi smiled softly. "In all these years, that's the most I've heard you speak."

Silence ducked her head, looking up through pale, pale lashes. "Blame Hark. The Dragon-damned chatterbox."

But her voice cracked. She closed her eyes.

Avyi set her weapons aside and knelt, holding Silence's shoulders, the malice of moments ago drained from her face and replaced with sympathy. "I've seen a future where the rebels are killed."

A soft hitch in Silence's breathing was her only response to the harsh news. "And Hark?"

"I didn't see him." She petted Silence's shortly trimmed hair. "His death is not a certainty. Did you bring the Dragon idol?"

"Yes."

From a leather satchel draping from her waist, Silence brought forth an obsidian idol. It was carved in the Sath's interpretation of the Dragon. The idol was a dead ringer for the engraving on one of the arrows: wiry like a snake, with three heads, three forked tails, and six paper-thin wings in pairs along its back, sticking up like a butterfly.

"Where did you find that?" he asked.

"Half in Hong Kong," Silence said softly. "Hark had it. The Pet—Avyi?—said he would have it. The other half was buried in the Asters' underground complex. By joining both pieces, I was able to use it to unlock the collars that keep Cage warriors' powers in check. When the collars are activated, they're no better than trained animals. I should know. There's nothing like feeling that part of you stolen away."

Mal was stunned that the idol, so delicate, could survive the journey its pieces had taken through time and across the world, but then he remembered the bow. Although ancient and buried in a crypt for countless centuries, its string remained intact.

"You were going to return this to the Sath Leadership and clear your name of having stolen it," Avyi said.

"We thought better of it." Silence offered a rueful smile. "*Hark* thought better of it, after the Leadership tried to have us killed. A story for another time. Likely, he'll be glad to tell it." Almost cradling the idol, she looked up through her lashes. "Please, help me find him." She paused and cleared her throat. "Avyi."

❧ CHAPTER ❧ EIGHTEEN

As with Cadmin's bow, Avyi didn't want to touch the idol. She'd predicted the locations of its pieces, but she'd never seen it united, and she'd certainly never held it. The Sath considered it sacred. It *felt* sacred, emanating a strange vibe that resonated at the base of her brain. To touch this would change her life.

She reached out to accept it, but thought better. After donning her cargos and sitting cross-legged on the floor, she looked up to where Mal still sat on the edge of the bed. The sheets were a jumbled mess.

"Hold on to me?"

Mal inhaled deeply. "After what happened last time . . ."

"At least we may have another direction."

"You insisted it was time I make those decisions for our people."

"Then choose. With Hark's life at stake. Those rebels. Everything. Do I touch this idol or not?"

"No matter what it does to you?"

His voice was like a last caress before parting. Then his face hardened. He was immutable and commanding, with no weapon but his expression. He arranged his legs so that he bracketed either side of her shoulders with his knees. The whole of his calves braced her body. His hands were solid and strong on her shoulders. Silence joined Avyi on the floor, also cross-legged, but without touching her. That was Mal's responsibility. She offered the idol again. "You helped me find it," she said. "It's so much to ask that you help me again."

"The Chasm isn't fixed." Avyi blinked, as did Silence. Mal's grip stiffened on her shoulders. That same old phrase. That same *Dragon-damned phrase*.

"Do it," Mal said—an undeniable command.

Avyi blew a breath out of her nose and took the idol in hand.

She stiffened. She saw so many images as to make Cadmin's bow just another piece of junk. This was history and power distilled into obsidian. She gasped as more poured out of it and into her mind, threatening her consciousness. "Orla, don't leave me."

She closed her eyes, but felt reinforced when Silence, the woman born Orla of Sath, twined her fingers with Avyi's around the snakelike dragon. So many pieces. Far more than the two that had been united to form this portal to the past and future.

With a gasp, she wrenched free of that mental hold. She found herself in Mal's arms, stretched on the floor. Her face was damp, her whole body sticky with sweat. A chill wouldn't let go. Her teeth rattled, and he held her even closer. Hot and cold. Near and far. The earth tilted as she tried to make sense of what had happened.

"How long . . . ?"

"About four minutes," Mal said quietly by her ear. He kissed her temple. "Scared me."

"Scared myself."

She tried to sit up but needed help from Mal as dizziness washed over her vision in a haze of red and black.

He rubbed her arms. "Easy now. No fast moves."

"Oh!" The idol was broken in two. "I— Silence, I didn't mean to." She looked around. "Silence?"

The young woman was sitting on the floor in the far corner, arms hugging her shins as Avyi was prone to doing. She was pale and covered in a similar sheen of sweat. "You called me Orla."

The name sent fissures of fear and something akin to joy down Avyi's spine. With caution, she met Silence's eyes. Dark eyes. Black on black. But in her features, in her posture, Avyi saw what she couldn't deny.

"Orla of Sath," Avyi said. "I'm here for you."

She pushed away from Mal with gathering strength and purpose.

Although her legs were still too unsteady for walking, she crawled in a way that reminded her of how Dr. Aster had liked to see her move. Slinky and lithe like a cat. She pushed that memory aside in favor of one much more complicated and potentially beautiful.

Because Orla met her halfway. They joined hands. Each inhaled sharply.

"Frakohn," Avyi said. "Our mother's name was Frakohn."

"Pale like us. Thin but strong. So beautiful."

"I touched her stomach. I was maybe three years old. 'Mama, you'll have a girl. She'll be Sath like you. Hair like sun on the sand.'"

Orla dipped her head on hitched breath. "How can you know this? You see the future."

"What was once will happen again." She squeezed Orla's hands. "Look at me. Why did I help you? I had no reason to. In fact, it was dangerous. Dr. Aster could've . . ." The tightness in her throat wouldn't let her speak. She swallowed past the pain. "He would've punished me. I couldn't find the idol, but I needed someone who could. Someone I could trust without reservation, although I didn't know why. And why in the name of the Dragon did you trust *me*?"

"That affinity. From the first. I never doubted what you told me. I would lie awake at night wondering why I still fought in the Cages, when I had the means of escaping. I couldn't understand why I trusted the one woman I should've killed rather than believe. I only had your word, that I needed to be there. Why would I give that much of my life into your care? You were Aster's Pet!"

A wash of calm swept over Avyi. Her sweat cooled, and her shivering stopped—like a fever breaking. "But I was your sister first."

Mal stood and began to pace. "What is going on?"

"We're half sisters," Orla said, her voice filled with awe and acceptance. "You were sent away."

"And I was crying as Father took me out of the city, knowing we'd never be back. That I'd never see your face."

Orla's smile was crooked but welcome after the overwhelming confusion and deep emotion. "You ever get a prediction so wrong?"

"Not that I know of," she said harshly. "But in light of what I've been seeing lately, I dearly hope for more mistakes."

Crouching beside them, Mal was wearing his customary frown—the one for when he was deep in thought. "What was her name? Frakohn? She was the youngest daughter of the Sath ruling family. This would've been about forty years ago? I heard the gossip after . . ." He dipped his eyes, then cracked a thumb knuckle. "After I came down from the mountain. She married a Garnis and was already known for her eccentricities. Then she caused even more scandal. Another man? Something like that. Everyone disappeared. Secreted away as the Sath do." He glanced at Orla. "No offense."

"None taken, Giva."

"So my Garnis father took me away," Avyi said. "What about Mother and your father . . . ?"

"My father was Sath. I was always told they went down in the Cages. The assumption was debts. Maybe it was to hide her family's disgrace. Then I was placed with my Sath guardians. Everything hushed up." She nodded to Mal. "As you said."

"And I was placed with mine, to be raised by my father's clan."

Mal rested his broad palm on Avyi's knee. "What do you remember of him?"

A shudder overwhelmed Avyi's body until both Mal and Orla needed to hold her steady. "All I hear are raised voices," she whispered. "What if— Oh, Dragon be. No. What if the family that raised me was my real family? Those Garnis were my father's people? What if they punished him and scorned me? *Then they sold me to Dr. Aster.*"

Mal wrapped her in his arms, his body enveloping

her as she curled against his chest. "Does it matter now, Avyi? We have so much to do. That idol held pieces of your past. The past for both of you. But it won't help us with Hark or Cadmin—"

"Or you," she said vehemently. "Someone tried to kill you. We've known from the start that they won't stop with a failed attempt."

Orla was so quiet, so still, that Avyi pulled away from her lover to look at her sister. They had been drawn together their entire lives, until they sat together on the floor of a bed-and-breakfast in Florence.

Avyi reached out for Orla's hand, and then they were embracing with a strength born of decades of separation and pain. "Every unborn child whose future I predicted," Avyi said, "gave me the feeling that I'd done so before. Not in the labs but somewhere long ago, so distant. I think I was remembering how I'd first foreseen your birth."

Orla took her face in hand. "Is your gift so strong? To have known at such a young age?"

"I don't know. I hate that I don't know. But Mal's right. We need a plan for the future. This," she said, hugging her sister around the waist, "will be waiting for us after we've protected those we love, when we fulfill what the Dragon has been planning for us both since our earliest moments."

"You'll help me rescue Hark?"

"That shouldn't sound like a question, because there is no question about it."

"What if Hark . . . ?"

"Orla, you have to trust me again. I would tell you if

I knew. I would do you that mercy, even if it felt like a cruelty."

And I would fight fate no matter what.

She had accused Mal of being resigned to his role as Giva, never giving of himself as much as he could. Had she been doing the same? Was it possible . . . just *possible* . . . that she could change her visions? She had been trapped for so long with Dr. Aster that seeing the outcome of a pregnancy had been her only guidepost— the signs of *any* future. What if life with him had taught her not to hope for anything better? Had she ever truly rebelled against the future?

More resolved than ever, she embraced Orla again. Avyi drew strength from the rightness of fitting two pieces back together. "But how did you know your name, before this? Avyi. Did you remember it from so long ago?"

"No," Avyi said with a shake of her head. She glanced toward where Mal had stood, gathering their weapons and possessions. "I was still the Pet. He named me."

Orla tilted her head in that way Avyi remembered from the days when Silence was her only name—a woman who never spoke. "What does it mean?"

"In the Tigony language, it means dawn. East." Despite his slight smile, he appeared haunted and struggling, as unnerved by all of this as she and Orla. But he was stronger now than she'd ever seen. Certainty looked so very right on the man intended to lead them all. Her heart swelled until she couldn't breathe for pride. "It also means new beginnings."

Tears filled Avyi's eyes. He said he might tell her one

day. He didn't say that it would hit straight to the heart of her, fulfilling every wish she could have for the name she would bear with pride and love for the rest of her life.

"I thought it was meant for Avyi alone," he said. "Now it's for all of us."

❧ CHAPTER ❧
NINETEEN

Mal was tired of being on the back foot. Really tired of it. He had a lover, his lover had a sister, and that sister's bonded mate was going to be killed. Or was he? Avyi didn't know for sure, which meant Mal erred on the side of being able to do something for Hark. It was time to stop reading runes. It was time for action.

He called the only person on the Council he could trust, his adoptive grandmother, Hobik. Within twenty-four hours, she'd procured fake papers for Avyi and plane tickets to London. She'd also arranged for a collection of weapons to be packaged as antiques, including the Dragon-forged sword, to be held in the belly of the passenger jet. Mal didn't ask for particulars. He didn't want to know how the cagey old woman had managed.

She was the only person yet living who knew the truth about Mal's behavior at Bakkhos. That she accepted his failings while lauding the changes he'd made to Tigony culture—for the better—was the reassurance he needed. She didn't think he was a saint. But she'd always believed what he was only now taking into his own skin, and breathing with his own lungs. His temper had fueled the destruction of Bakkhos, but countless others would've been destroyed had he refrained. The Tigony would still be hiding and perpetuating the last terrible secret of their clan.

He and Avyi disembarked from the plane, with Orla following close behind. Security at Heathrow was its usual mess. Three large planes had landed in close succession, from Mexico, India, and the United States. Avyi was bouncing on her heels while they waited to pass through customs, while Orla had pulled deeply within herself. Silence. He'd only ever met her in passing, there at the liberation of the labs, but the name suited her uncommonly well.

Hark could be anywhere, but the Townsend cartel was the obvious place to start. They controlled the Cage warriors of Europe and North Africa, with the Kawashimas claiming domain over East Asia. The Asters practically owned the western hemisphere and any place where a slight toehold meant an avenue toward more power. They needed to be destroyed.

Mal had stood by for too long, working through the politics of the Council, relying on the idea that a solution would produce itself without effort beyond arguing with the other clans' representatives. In truth, he'd been the same spoiled brat as always, and the same fool who'd fallen into an ancient trap. He blamed the world—but mostly himself—for the tragedy that followed.

He glanced down at Avyi. She was the change he'd needed.

Perspective. Vision.

He didn't just mean the ability to predict the future. Her strange optimism and childlike faith were the flip side of his jaded apathy. Together they made for an interesting team.

Interesting.

The word was so insipid as to be insulting. He wanted her. More and more. That their stolen night in the bed-and-breakfast hadn't been the vision she'd pictured for their future actually lifted his spirits. It meant they would be together again. No telling when. How far into the future? How long would they know one another before the future spread out before them, undefined?

What would they do then?

Mal cleared his throat. The security officials checked their passports, including Avyi's doctored papers. Everything in order. Even their weapons, crated and safely delivered, were stacked among the oversize luggage. He glanced around the baggage claim, where several hundred human beings hurried on their way.

None of them had any idea of the cataclysmic events happening all around them. There was nothing they could do, nothing they would know to do. The cultures established by the Five Clans would continue as if their originators had never existed. What would the world look like without the influence of the Dragon Kings? What would the world become without them?

Mal hoped it wasn't a world for the better. He needed to know his people were a force for good. He would make it so.

He snorted under his breath. Avyi pulled her luggage alongside him and shot him an assessing look. "What was that for?"

"I'm thinking more like you than I want to."

"Do you believe in the Dragon yet?"

"Avyi, don't."

She shrugged. Some of that feline grace had returned to her poised movements—part teasing, part defensive mechanism. "I'm not worried. You will, Mal. Or we'll all be dead. Either way."

"Now you're a fatalist?"

"No," she said simply. "I've never been a fatalist or an optimist. Otherwise all those unborn children would've driven me crazy. Seeing the ones who would live. Seeing the ones who would never survive. They just were. That was the only way I could manage. That's the only way we'll get through the next few days. It just is." She glanced to the side. "Except for Hark and Cadmin. I'm insisting that the Dragon make a few special cases."

Silence was almost motionless now, in her features and her expressions. She'd turned off everything. Despite that, Avyi was not discouraged by having her newly revealed sister turn into a stony-faced warrior. Maybe that was because Silence was a Dragon-damned impressive warrior. Even there in the airport, she radiated violence and the confidence of a woman ready to rip off limbs.

"To Battersea," Mal said firmly.

Avyi tilted her head. "Not the Townsend complex?"

"We're taking the offensive. I happen to know that the Townsends have already encamped their Cage warriors in cells beneath Battersea."

His fey, raven-haired woman smiled like a conspirator.

His woman? *Dragon save us both.*

"You 'happen to know'?"

Mal smiled without mirth. "It's good to be Giva."

"That's new."

They crossed town in a limo and found a hotel near the power station, which was now defunct and crumbling, held aloft by various investors and its status as a protected monument. Mal unpacked their weapons. They'd wait until night, only a few hours off. Silence seemed on edge, despite her composed nature. The energy shimmering out from her skin was practically strong enough to fuel Mal's gift. She was lit dynamite.

"Can you tell us anything?" Avyi asked, while they stood looking out the suite's window toward Battersea. "Find a telepath? Anything?"

"No, but I plan to." It was the first she'd spoken since leaving Florence. "You two rest or . . ." She shook her head. "Stay here. I'm going for a walk. If there are Dragon Kings in cells, I'll know. I'll find out how many, which clans, how strong—the recon we need before suiting up for nightfall."

Mal caught up as she walked away. She flicked her gaze down to where his hand enveloped her upper arm. "Just recon. Not engagement. We have enough to do without needing to rescue you, too."

Orla became Silence once again, with a single smile. It was a cold smile, one made of the hunger for blood and revenge. "Who says I'll need rescuing?"

In clothing that nearly matched Avyi's militaristic style, they looked more alike than ever—lithe, pale, graceful. Silence was tall and so very blond, while Avyi was petite with that trademark raven-dark hair. But the

resemblance between the half sisters was otherwise remarkable. Mal wondered why no one had ever made
the connection before.

"Silence," he called to the departing woman. "Stay
true to that name. Think like a warrior, not a lover. Information first, then action. Hark is dead or he's not.
Don't make the mistake of taking on anyone by yourself.
You came for us in Florence for a reason."

The woman paled. Then she swallowed and nodded.
"Yes, Giva."

She'd used the title dismissively before. Now, the
word was infused with respect. He fed off the surprising
shift in tone and knew she would obey his instructions.

She bid her shorter sister good-bye with a swift kiss
to Avyi's crown. She was dressed in black, weaponless,
and fierce. Then she was gone, with the door closed
behind her.

Silence had called him *Giva* and had meant it. But
to become the leader they all needed, he had to tell Avyi
the secret that plagued him. If she still chose to follow
him after learning the truth, then he was the man worth
claiming the mantle of the Honorable Giva.

"Avyi."

He opened his arms and enveloped her in an embrace that stabbed unexpected pain in his chest. He'd
never felt compelled to open himself so fully. Now he
risked losing her forever, when her esteem was the most
important thing he'd come to value. But he deserved no
one's respect or affection if he lied for the rest of his life,
even by omission. And he very much wanted the respect
and affection she seemed eager to bestow—a lost girl
grown into a woman who craved love. He didn't believe

in love enough to give her what she needed, but at least he could be strong enough to admit his wrongs.

"There's something I need to tell you."

Avyi's heart tightened on a stuttering rhythm, then picked up at double speed. She couldn't breathe, although she couldn't say why. Orla would be fine. She was too skilled and clever not to be. She'd return in a few hours with information vital to any rescue attempt. The source of her consternation wasn't her sister but the man who held her. He was so tense, so distant—and all so suddenly. Whatever had come over him was a swift-moving storm that rivaled his gift in its power.

As if she might find answers before he spoke, she searched her visions and predictions for anything that hinted at this moment. Mal was holding her, and he was at war with himself. Was this the new beginning he'd offered her by name, or some terror yet to be unleashed?

She stepped away. Dr. Aster's occasional embrace had made her feel equally wary. That she could find anything comparable between Mal and the doctor added another dose of nausea to her roiling stomach.

"Then tell me," she said simply.

Mal turned away, with his blue eyes on the power station that loomed outside their hotel window. So near, yet with so many unknowns. Just like Mal. There was no stopping this version of him. Whatever decision he'd made was what he would do.

For good or for ill.

"I told you about the Tigony tradition, when a young person climbs to the top of what the humans mythologized as Mount Olympus."

"Yes," Avyi said, edging back until she sat on a desk chair. "You stayed up there so long."

"Four years. My parents were power hungry and vicious politicians. My grandfather was the worst. Nothing got past him. I hated the old bastard." Mal crossed his arms. The leather jacket he wore accentuated the breadth of power across his wide back and muscled chest. "I did everything I could to counter him, vex him, make him know that I wouldn't grow up to be a manipulating ass just like him."

His jagged laugh cut through his words.

"I had big ideas and no clue what sort of perverted will I was up against. I was still young and believed there were rules." He lifted his eyes to hers, shook his head. "There are no rules in the quest for power. That's all politics is. We like to think the Honorable Giva is somehow above that fray, but really, he's at the center of the tempest. Struggles among the clans, egos, rivalries. It's the headiest thrill to always be right, never questioned or contradicted." A pause. A rueful smile. "You knew that from the beginning. Sometimes it's just about being right. It's made me complacent, even selfish. I think that's what must've happened to my parents and grandfather. Who demanded anything of them? Who denied them anything?"

Avyi watched him, particularly the torturous recrimination that turned his features from handsome to haunted. She needed to touch him, or at least try, even if he pushed her away. Were they at the point where he could still push her away?

Yes.

They were still so tenuous.

She crossed to where he stood, took his hand, and pulled him to the bed. "Lie down with me. We've been traveling for hours. Tell me here."

He hesitated. Unbearable stiffness turned his limbs to heavy wood in her hands. Finally he acquiesced by taking off his jacket and tie. Then he kicked off his shoes and unfastened the top two buttons of his dress shirt. He lay beside her, where the darkness enveloped them in a place of safety. If not forever, they could at least be safe enough for Mal to reveal whatever he needed to free from his chest and his soul.

Avyi didn't want to know.

But it was her responsibility to hear as much as it was his to tell.

"I thought I would best him," he began again. "I would stay on the mountain longer than anyone. I wouldn't come down until I knew every aspect of my gift, as if I'd memorized the exact placement of a thousand blades of grass. I would not be a Tigony who lost control and used his powers when an argument was lost. That's what we do. We're Tricksters. We talk and cajole. But at the end, we're no more than spoiled children who lose our tempers."

"I've seen your temper." She touched his silky hair, where it shone in the near-darkness. If they were going to make love that night, it would all be by touch. And if they were going into battle before dawn, they were definitely going to make love. "But I've seen you changing, too."

"You don't live in my head. I throw tantrums every other minute."

"That doesn't count," she said. "What counts is what

you do to push those selfish voices down and make the most of a moment."

"Who *are* you?"

"What do you mean?"

He slipped his hands around her waist and nestled her head beneath his chin. She liked that far too much, because it felt perfect. She wasn't a woman who was used to perfect. Then again, the circumstances were anything but ideal. Maybe this was a compromise she could believe in—just enough mythology, and just enough reality.

"You grew up under horrific circumstances, and you grew into womanhood as the sentient possession of a madman. Yet here you are telling me that I can make the most of a moment. How?"

"To do otherwise would be to become something unholy. Imagine what sort of evil I could do in this world, if I unleashed all my bitterness and rage." She shivered against the picture she created. "I live in fear of taking the wrong side again. Do you know that? I stayed with the doctor because I thought I was doing some good. I hated him, but part of me knew that without the myths he spun about his own brilliance, those children wouldn't be conceived, wouldn't have been born. He was sick. He was the person who kept me chained from the age of twelve. But he lured all those Cage warriors into battle on the promise of something beautiful."

"Even if you were the element necessary to make it all work?"

"Who was I to take credit? I got the privilege of seeing each child, feeling their love, and touching a small part of their lives. A hundred loves. So maybe I stayed too long and perpetuated the wrong ideas, because I wanted those touches of love more than I wanted justice or truth." She exhaled and nuzzled where his shirt parted to reveal the smooth, hot skin of his upper chest. "I'm always on the lookout for doing something for the wrong reasons."

"Why are you with me?"

"Because I want to be," she said plainly. "Now tell me what terrible thing you did after you came down from the mountain. Because it was terrible, Mal, wasn't it? You didn't want it to be, but it's kept you small."

"Avyi."

Her name was a warning—a warning she didn't heed. She never did when he said it with such menace.

"It's kept you small, my Giva, when you are a man meant to stand taller than giants."

❧ CHAPTER ❧
TWENTY

When the Tigony come down from the mountain, confident in their mastery, they're given a reward. I had no idea. No one ever talked about it." The tightness in his chest was cutting off his air. For every breath he struggled to catch, he reminded himself that Avyi was in his arms. For the future to matter, he needed to exorcise the crimes of his past.

"I was given a small home in a village called Bakkhos. The word is what the Romans would eventually transform into *bacchanalia* in honor of one of their gods."

"A wild party. With sexual overtones of excess and wanton greed."

Mal nodded. He arched his neck toward the darkened ceiling but found no answers, only images of blood. "The village was the reward. Dragon King priests or priestesses were given to the young Tigony women and men who survived their arduous task. We were adored. We were introduced to sex in all its forms, tutored, treasured, pampered, and frustrated beyond reason until release was overwhelming and total. I wanted for nothing for two years. My priestess was named Pollakioh."

Avyi gasped. "The name you would whisper if you were murdered in Greece."

"That's when I first started to give your predictions credence. There was no way you could have known her name without some sort of otherworldly gift."

He exhaled heavily. "She was astonishingly beautiful and easy to talk to. I think that's why they were chosen, because of those exceptional traits."

"So she tempted the spoiled only child of the Tigony ruling house with even more unmerited admiration?"

"I forgot how blunt you can be."

"Only supplying what you know but might not say."

"Yes," he said, with a heavy weight to the word. "That's what it was. I was a young god. Invincible and in love with a seemingly untouchable goddess who did more than let me touch her. She was quick-witted but never contradicted me. She brought me everything I wanted, even in anticipation of my wishes. But I never saw any of it, not until later in hindsight. I was so caught up in myself that the way she treated me—practically reverentially—was, to me, just how things should be."

"That doesn't sound real." Avyi's words were hushed and warm against his skin. "Like a dream of paradise."

"And what does it say about me that I didn't recognize it as such? No one in my position in the village did."

"It says the system was ancient and very well practiced."

He petted up her ribs, under her T-shirt, gratified when she leaned closer to give him better access. "There were humans in the village, too. They must've been selected with equal care. They served the priests and priestesses, kept the village in good repair and working order, but otherwise, we had nothing to do with them. What I didn't realize was that each one, male or female, was a virgin. Even had I known, they were so far below us as to be invisible."

The next breath would be the one when he revealed what he'd done, so he took extra care, taking in the scent of Avyi's hair where he nuzzled her temple. Had he truly been able to give himself over to his belief in the Dragon, he would've prayed that these wouldn't be the last seconds he held her.

"Two years to the day after my arrival," he said roughly, "Pollakioh ushered me into a temple. It was a temple no one ever seemed to use. We had another for the regular worship of the Tigony dragon. I was curious, not apprehensive. What cause did I have to be apprehensive? But waiting on an altar at the far end of the temple was the virgin girl who tended my household. She helped with the cleaning, the cooking, and other menial tasks." He swallowed. "She was bound, gagged, and naked."

"*Bathatéi*," Avyi whispered—the curse made almost musical, but no less intense.

"Pollakioh was joined by my grandfather. I'd never been so surprised. He went about stripping and binding Pollakioh in the same manner. She knelt on the altar beside the serving girl. I was handed the family's Dragon-forged sword and a ceremonial knife with the Dragon carved in the hilt. Grandfather gave me a choice. I could take the serving girl's virginity before slitting her throat, or I could behead my lover of two years."

Mal needed to sit up. His stomach roiled with the need to burst free of his body. He clenched his muscles tight. His body would hold everything in, just as his mind had for years. Avyi joined him, with her torso draped across his back. She rested her cheek between his shoulder blades. "It had all been a trick," she whispered. "A test."

"An initiation, yes. I could either become culpable in the Tigony's secret, long-standing tradition of human sacrifice, or I could kill a fellow Dragon King who'd been my constant companion. She'd tended every need and had done her job so very well. I looked at her and I loved her. I looked at the girl and felt nothing but pity . . . and rage. Not at her, but at a system designed to bind my clan in a practice so old, barbaric, and sick that no one ever spoke of it. And no one ever refused to participate. Everyone was bound to its secrecy."

He wiped his face with his hands, then held where Avyi was holding him around his waist. "I killed Grandfather first. I killed Pollakioh next. I could tell from their expressions that neither had expected it. The way of things was to choose the girl whose name I didn't even know. Who was she but a human? Defile her and sacrifice her. How easy it could've been. But I didn't act out of righteousness. I acted because I was embarrassed and ashamed. I'd been taken for a fool, tricked into falling in love with the equivalent of a Tigony goddess who'd never thought me anything but a chore. I was just another young man to bring into the secret fold."

"You did the right thing."

"No, I didn't. Because the girl knew as well." He shuddered. "I removed her gag and she smiled. 'No one has ever chosen to spare the human,' she'd said. Even the humans in the village knew. They all did. They believed that to be given their first, only, and *extraordinary* sexual pleasure by a Dragon King, and to die in the throes of that ecstasy, was the ultimate blessing from the gods. I could practically hear two years' worth of laughter. The snickering and talking behind my back. 'Look, the great Malnefoley has fallen for his priestess. Exactly as was planned.'"

"You . . ."

"I killed her, too. Not with the knife. With a shock of lightning so strong and powerful that, later, I could almost convince myself it had been natural—from the heavens, not from me. I'd mastered my gift. *Four years*. That couldn't have been me." His voice tightened. He hated its tone, so rough and tinted with sick sadness, but it was how he deserved to sound in the midst of his gory tale. "It was me. It was me when I beheaded four priestesses and two priests, and when a storm of lightning like a living hurricane shot through the bodies of fourteen human servants. By the time I was finished, Bakkhos was smoldering and charred. I spared . . . Avyi, I spared nothing and no one."

She backed away from him, leaving Mal colder than he'd ever been. A void he hadn't known possible opened in his soul. It was deeper and blacker than the place where he'd stored that shameful crime. Avyi was gone. He'd been a fool to think otherwise, just as he should've known that Bakkhos was unnatural—a paradise no sensible person could believe real.

"And after?" Her words were thin and soft, like tissue.

"I was hailed a hero," he said with a deranged laugh. "Finally! Someone strong enough to expose the horrors of the secret Tigony practice of human sacrifice. I'd torn the system down. I'd ended the shame. Even the Leadership hailed me a conquering visionary. Dragon damn, I hated myself, but I hated them worse. I was a murderer. Each of us was, yet they'd colluded all that time, having taken human lives. Then they sent their Tigony children up the mountain and down into Bakkhos, expecting the same results. That hypocrisy . . ."

He coughed into his fist. "It scarred me. Ancient ways. Power and influence. What did it matter, when so much death and deception rested at the heart of leadership?" He cracked his knuckles, hoping Avyi might touch him. He was shivering with cold and a resurgence of anger that sparked off his fingertips. "In honor of the service I'd done for our people, I was named head of the clan to take my grandfather's place. A half-grown kid who'd just committed mass murder. *I* was the best of the Tigony? The wrongness makes me ill, even now."

"And then to be chosen Giva . . ."

Mal kept his movements as calm as possible, but he felt as if his skin were stretching away from her. From the stark quality of her simple sentence. It was the condemnation he'd always heaped on himself for twenty years. "Yes. And then Giva."

"I think I'd known it," she whispered. "Forget prophecy. You resent everything about our heritage, from Bakkhos until now. Simple logic is enough to see why you've lost faith in the Dragon . . . and in yourself. Malnefoley, there is no shame in what you did."

But there was shame.

He whipped out of bed and whirled on her. She would leave him now, if he didn't protect himself first. If she had a tiny fraction of his loathing, she would see that their entire journey was an exercise in hopeless fumbling. She was the Pet. That he had trusted her with his deepest hurts and fledgling optimism was nauseating, while she looked at him with a calm expression that Mal interpreted as nothing better than smug. He would not be tricked again. His path was his to determine, for good or for life-altering ill, and was not subject to the wide-eyed whispers of a false prophet.

He was furious with himself and all he couldn't control or change or accept. He was furious with Avyi for peeling back his defenses until he was a trembling young man with the scent of a burning village in his nostrils. He needed to be free of a woman who believed in him so strongly, with or without her gift. He would never be himself again.

That meant severing the connection between them—no matter what it was or what it could've been.

"Is this how you get off? Playing hide-and-seek with information and sanity?" He vented his anger even as her brows lifted in obvious confusion. "Your real gift is having become the most practiced manipulator I've ever met. Not even Pollakioh held me in her spell as well as you. Was that one of the skills the doctor taught you?"

Avyi jumped from the bed and slapped him full across the cheek. She kicked his shin, and used momentum to push him back. Stance wide and loose, she was ready to fight. *Really* fight. "You piece of shit," she snarled.

"Tell me otherwise."

"I saw first words and midnight feedings and, yes, hide-and-seek. Each baby had a future I envied, even the ones I knew would die early. They were *precious*. They would be adored no matter the course of their lives. I learned what that could feel like from the souls of unborn children." She glared at him, heart throbbing in her chest, and blinked back a sheen of tears. "You tell me, Giva—who taught you what that sort of pure, unblemished love feels like? I don't think you learned it. Ever."

"You shouldn't exist."

"And neither should you, *Giva*."

One year away from Dr. Aster's influence, and she'd done it again. She'd chosen the wrong side.

She'd held on to her respect for Mal as long as she could. However, his betrayal of her trust—simple words that could never be taken back—ripped that respect to shreds. She could understand killing his grandfather and the woman who'd seduced him. She didn't blame him for those acts of violence. After all, in Avyi's heart, she'd already killed Dr. Aster.

"You said you believed me." Her throat was choked with raw pain and the hot flush of disappointment. "You held me as I cried and thanked you because I'd finally found someone who actually *believed me*."

"I was mistaken."

"How could you stoop so low as to compare me to Dr. Aster? I've revealed only pieces of what he did to me. Would you like to know about how, when the mood struck him, he fed me by a tube through the bars of my cage? Or the fact that every day, *every* day, he was the one to zip me into that latex suit? I could go on and on, because I have twenty-five years' worth of memories I'll never bear. You have *one*."

Mal stared her down. "You used Pollakioh's name to string me along."

"She was just that! A name. A feeling. You wouldn't have taken me seriously anyway, no matter what I saw."

"What else are you keeping from me?"

That you're breaking my heart.

She pushed down the urge to knock his face in, instead shoving her belongings into her backpack. "I was twelve, in the service of a madman. Those brainwashed human virgins—how could they have truly understood the sick world they'd been drawn into? Sometimes a choice isn't a choice at all. All the while, you've dwelled on your pain and anger so long that it's actually numbed you. It's easier to make decisions from on high than to consider how your actions affect individuals."

She turned to face him, summoning all her courage to do so. But she couldn't stop her tears. "You compared me to . . . *him*. Now it's my turn. I never had any faith in Dr. Aster. I had faith in you."

"Had."

"You heard me."

Their conversation ended abruptly, with Avyi's bitter pronouncement hanging in the air. There was nothing more to say.

She joined him in silent preparation. Any hope she'd maintained that they would make love again before entering the lion's den of the Grievance was burned to cinders. Could they even be allies now? With Mal behind her, she'd need to tie up one eye just to watch her own back. His goal was to find his would-be assassin. Hers had always been to find Cadmin, and more recently, to live out the extent of her destiny with Mal. Together. That was no longer possible. Now, there was Orla and Hark and the shadow of a dragon. What Mal intended to do as Giva, or as a man, was not her business—unless it interfered with hers.

She had family.

She had *family*.

They came first. The question of conception and the future of the Dragon Kings could wait these next few hours while she saved the first people in her life capable of returning the love she wanted to give.

Mal wasn't one of them. She choked back a sob. He wouldn't hear another whisper of weakness from her.

She strapped on her backpack. She felt stronger wearing her boots. Donning her brass knuckles. Stowing her switchblade. They were hard accessories for hard decisions and even harder fights. Then she ran her fingers through her hair, spiking it into the mad tease of strands she never should've been so concerned with taming. For him. To look pretty for him.

He stood by the door, wearing his casual clothes topped with a light overcoat that trailed down to his calves. His was a picture of power, only of a different sort than she'd wrapped around herself. When he battled the cartels, he would do so from the inside, using Tricksters' words and the language of men of influence.

Avyi walked to him until they were toe to toe. She needed to stretch her neck to meet his eyes, but she didn't feel diminished. No matter the mantle of authority he'd assumed through clothing, posture, and expression, he could not hide his eyes from her. Even shadowed and half hidden, with that vibrant blue obscured, she saw self-recrimination. She didn't have the time or energy to sort through how that affected her.

"You never took issue with the insult they leveled at you. *Usurper*. It never bothered you because it wasn't true. A usurper needs to want to control before he plots to take control. Tallis is known as the Heretic because of his past crimes. That name should've been reserved for you. You live a lie every day. Not because of what happened at Bakkhos, but because you make decisions with no trust, no faith, no love." She eyed him up and down, ignoring the longing that pounded in her chest. "I feel sorry for you."

The muscles along his jaw flexed into hard knots. "Where are you going?"

"Battersea."

"You're not going without me." Mal grabbed both of Avyi's arms. "I am still the Honorable Giva. We do this together."

"Let me go before we tear this building down. I can provoke you to that and we know it."

"I will not let Battersea and this Grievance become another of my failures," he said. "You're right. I've stood in the shadows of my own hatred for too long." He released one arm so as to stroke the underside of Avyi's chin. "You said I could stand with giants."

Avyi's blood beat too quickly. "You really are a Trickster. Words are your true weapon."

"I have my gift and a Dragon-forged sword. I will use both if our people are in danger." He shook his head, which scattered a straight, golden shimmer of hair across his forehead. "And they are. They have been for as long as I've claimed the title of Giva, but for much longer than I've committed myself to protecting them."

The tightness around his mouth eased in a way that made Avyi soften. She wanted more of that. A man with a calm, composed face was one ready to do battle with confidence in his soul. And perhaps with the righteousness they needed for such a tremendous undertaking.

He kissed her, swiftly and with a powerful echo of how they'd made love. That strength and vigor and daring. They'd never had the opportunity to explore each other with tenderness. Slowly. Deliberately. Feasting on one another. Instead, they'd gorged. His kiss was a reminder of that quick feast, while sparking to life the hopes Avyi wanted so much to banish.

But couldn't.

The hurt he'd caused her . . . How could she trust herself to a man who flung his own hurt with such cruel accuracy? How could any of their people?

She backed away from him, one step, then another. Although she was shattered, she'd known for some time that Malnefoley would be part of this final scene. The only question now was what part he would play.

❧ CHAPTER ❧
TWENTY-ONE

They stepped outside the small hotel to find Orla waiting for them crouched and hidden among the foliage.

Avyi had no trouble locating her, homing in as if they were Indranan twins who'd managed to resist the clan's forceful, almost overwhelming imperative to kill one's sibling. All for the promise of greater power. Everything in Mal's experience was about power.

I feel sorry for you.

As if they'd always known the depth of their connection, the women embraced.

"What did you learn?" Avyi asked.

Orla frowned in the near-darkness. Only a light above the courtyard's wrought-iron gate illuminated the scene. She smoothed a finger along the deep line between Avyi's eyebrows, then flicked a censorious scowl toward Mal. "Seems I should ask you the same question."

"No time."

"I met with Grandio, the rebel Indranan I mentioned, and borrowed his gift of telepathy. For years I wore the damping collars while in the service of the

Asters. Without that restriction of my gift, it's become much easier to share and amplify rather than to steal. We were able to find a large body of Dragon Kings in three underground tunnels beneath the power station."

"The three cartels' warriors, perhaps," Mal said.

"Our thoughts, yes. I was able to identify an Aster . . . possession . . . named Hellix among those in the tunnels."

"Possession?" Avyi's voice shook with indignation.

"Calm yourself." Silence took her hand. The woman's other arm was protected by the shield that was certainly not a mere defensive weapon. "He's a rapist, a liar, and a refugee from the dismantled labs who deserves no pity. He's . . . repulsive. And he would kill me on sight. I won't give him the opportunity."

Mal crossed his arms, glad for the coat in the chilly evening London air. "What did you do to him?"

Smiling like a cat with a secret—as all cats did—she said, "I sided with your cousin Nynn's partner, Leto of Garnis. Leto and Hellix didn't get along. At all. To see one's mate whipped by a soulless animal tends to anger a man beyond reparation."

"Leto seemed like a good man," Mal said, pleased when Avyi nodded in agreement. It was the first time she'd truly acknowledged him since their argument. "He would be a useful ally to discover here."

Orla shook her head. "Grandio and I couldn't locate him or Nynn. We're on our own. Any allies will be ours to secure by their liberation. Now that I've repaired the dragon idol, it will serve that purpose, unfastening the damping collars."

Avyi cupped her sister's cheek. "And Hark?"

"No trace." Her voice was a dead, flat calm, like a lake that hadn't thawed in centuries.

The woman turned away from the hotel, leading Mal and Avyi into the night streets.

"It would make sense to send Hark into one of the initial Grievance rounds," Mal said. "The last I witnessed was preceded by executions. Humans and Dragon Kings alike. They weren't there to fight, only to pay their debts in blood. A grim opening act."

"That has been the way of it," Avyi said. "But which cartel would have him?"

Orla's pace had increased, perhaps without her realizing. "The Asters, for having helped demolish the lab. They will have paid the Townsends or the Kawashimas any price for the right to execute him how they choose. They'd find no joy in leaving the possibility of a quick death at the hands of another crime family."

Mal knew she'd once been called Silence, but Orla's quick thoughts and quicker tongue bespoke deep secrets kept hidden for years. The same could be said for him and Avyi. How many of their kind concealed shames, ambitions, and clandestine hopes? He couldn't help looking to his right, where Avyi kept an even, graceful pace with his strides. Her jaw was set, her lips turned down at the corners, and her eyes narrowed—sharp and observant.

Clandestine hopes.

He'd never had any before meeting her.

"What about a young Cage warrior named Cadmin?" he asked. "A woman. Did you find any hint of that name?"

Avyi shot him a look of surprise. If he was going to

repair the damage he'd done during their fight, he needed to start with the basics. That meant proving to Avyi that he was sorry for the cruel things he'd said, all of which had been born of his own years-long guilt. Maybe even his self-doubt. He would not lose her. That meant proving he was the man she had believed him capable of becoming.

"Describe her," said Silence.

"About eighteen now," Avyi said. "Taller than you. Muscular but graceful and beautiful. Red hair like a Pendray, although she was crossbred with Tigony."

Mal frowned. "Like Nynn. I wonder if their powers are similar. Is that enough to go on, Orla?"

"Perhaps with Grandio's aid," she said. "This way."

Within minutes they'd crept beneath the shadow of the abandoned power station. It looked out over the Thames, where the river's current had once turned massive turbines to supply electrical power to a substantial portion of London. In the years since the nineteenth century, when the station had been the height of engineering prowess, it had been replaced by more advanced technology. Decades of disrepair had transformed it from vital to decrepit.

"Can you believe developers wanted to turn this monster into condos?" Orla asked. "Human ambition sometimes outstrips their means. The Kawashimas own it now, although I doubt their intentions involve human housing."

"You've been studying," Mal said with a note of appreciation. The rebel forces forged in the ashes of the Asters' labs had become substantial. The Council, so divided along clan lines, sat like overfed hogs by comparison. He didn't like knowing how much stock he'd placed in winning their consensus when the real work had been taking place out here, in the field, at the level where battles meant freedom—and where antiquated clan allegiances were debilitating.

He'd had it wrong for too long. No Dragon King brought into this world would be truly free if the cartels still tempted the unwary and desperate into the Cages.

Freedom first. Then the question of conception.

"We've needed to study," Orla said. "The cartels are a virus. The three that we know of, at least. Rivalries and differences have split them into smaller factions." She arched a blond brow at Mal. "Sound familiar, Giva?"

"The Council? Too familiar. And none too admirable."

The building glowed a sandy color, sprinkled by bright streetlights and the windows of houses and businesses. Four towering smokestacks cast long, long shadows that warped when they stretched over road signs and rooftops.

"What about underground?" Avyi asked. "What are we dealing with?"

"Ancient hovels from back to Roman times. Britannia, aided by the Tigony. More recently they've been expanded by Underground tunnels, most of which were never completed or left defunct after World War II. Without Grandio, I'd have already been lost a half dozen times among the winding train tracks."

Avyi's mouth went slack. "A half dozen?"

As if ashamed, Orla looked away. "I tried to find Hark myself. Even after the other rebels were captured and I escaped." Tension warped the graceful line of her shoulders. "Maybe I was wrong. Maybe I should've sought your help right away. If our comrades have been killed since because of my delay . . . I may get Hark back, but I'll have done so at the expense of good men and women."

Avyi took Mal's hand. Although she said nothing and didn't look at him, she offered something he'd thought lost. Reassurance. Maybe even quiet absolution, although he wouldn't give himself that gift until all of this madness was over, if ever.

She offered the same reassurance to her sister. "Hark is your husband. I would've done the same. We will do what we must."

Mal caught Avyi's eye, where green and gold gleamed in the acidic evening lights. Had he been Indranan, he would've asked her the question she probably read on his face. *What about your prediction that the rebels would be killed?*

Avyi only closed her troubled eyes and gave his hand a squeeze. It was a start on their road back.

"Here," Orla whispered. "Grandio."

"No need to speak, Silence. You should know that much." A middle-aged Dragon King of modest stature stepped out from a shadow Mal wouldn't have even recognized as a shadow, let alone as a hiding place. It was that slender and tucked away. Then again, the Tigony lacked skills of observation that Garnis, Indranan, and even the berserker Pendray could claim. The Tigony were either vicious or sleek-tongued. Little room for middle ground.

Orla shook hands with the man. "This is Grandio. A Southern Indranan, if we want to be specific."

"Which we don't," he said. "Those distinctions are ripping us apart. Tonight is a night for unity." He dipped a slight nod toward Mal. "Giva. My privilege."

Mal clasped the man's shoulder. "Those distinctions are ripping us apart," he repeated, firmly believing the words. His people needed a leader, not someone who received deference based on title rather than action. "And this is Avyi. She's like you." He grinned. "No clan either."

"She's also my sister," Orla said.

Grandio's shock was apparent, with wide, dark eyes and a shake of his head, which was wrapped with the bindings of a human Sikh.

"Silence, "Gradio said, "sometimes I believe you say things just to shock me."

"It's true."

True, but madness as well. The circles. The idea that threads were being woven together or, more ominously, that a noose was being tightened. All Mal could do was start with the person closest to him. Avyi. Start with her, and work his way out toward the people he couldn't see and didn't know. She was . . .

She was his touchstone. She was the person who made his responsibilities real, when every other attempt to lead had been met with grandiose, overwhelming, and ultimately ineffective results. How could he lead the Dragon Kings if he didn't know what it was to care deeply for one of them?

Because now he did. He cared for Avyi. He wasn't going to let the next few hours' events take her from him. He would make sure of it.

"She's looking for a crossbred Tigony-Pendray

named Cadmin," Silence said. "About eighteen. Set to participate in her first Grievance. Can you help?"

"You're a very polite Thief for asking." Grandio had recovered from his momentary shock, replacing it with a teasing smile. "Just don't dig around too deeply." The man glanced at Avyi, and pointedly at Mal. Mal felt a gentle *tap-tap* in his brain, as the telepath touched his surface consciousness. "We all have dark corners we'd rather not see revealed."

A full hour of mental exertion passed, during which Orla and Grandio worked together to map the souls of imprisoned Dragon Kings and their human captors. Still no sign of Hark or Cadmin. Orla broke the connection with a gasp and a frustrated growl, then slumped to the damp pavement. Avyi's heart burned for the half sister she'd never known was hers to claim.

She knelt and touched Orla's trembling forearm. The dim lighting didn't prevent Avyi from realizing what her fingers brushed against: the Thorn of the Sath mating ritual. Embedded just beneath the skin, the crescent-shaped needles symbolized a permanent commitment between two Sath. "I'm glad you married him," she said softly. "Hark. I knew you would. I just didn't know when."

Orla only nodded. Sweat had beaded along the line of her white-pale hair. "Best man I've ever known." Her words were tight. "And the most infuriating."

Avyi risked a quick glance up toward Mal, where he leaned against the decades-old exterior of the power station. "Perhaps in some men, the two qualities are inextricably paired."

"Is he worth it?"

"Has Hark been worth it?"

Although Orla looked away, Avyi caught sight of shimmering moisture in the woman's black eyes. "Yes. Even now." She straightened her shoulders and returned her sharp gaze to Avyi. "But you didn't answer my question. Is *he* worth it? Worth the way you look at him? I didn't need a piece of Grandio's telepathy to feel what snaps between you both."

Avyi swallowed. She wanted to be small. She wanted to find a place where she would be as mindless and unaccountable as she'd been as Aster's Pet. The joys of freedom were tempered by the extreme responsibility of making one's own way in life. "I fear what I'd do for him. That's not something I ever wanted to feel about another person. Not . . . again."

"Aster."

"Yes. He created what it was for me to understand devotion. Just a trick of the mind? A craving from the soul? I don't trust myself any more than I trust Mal."

That raised Orla's brows. "You don't trust him?"

"I don't trust that our goals align. When the moment comes, he'll choose what suits his purposes—which may be noble, I grant you. He's the Giva, after all. But would you believe him capable of putting Hark's life above the concerns of a hundred Dragon Kings in need?"

"No," Orla said quickly, quietly. "You're right. His priorities may not align with mine, not at the moment of choice. I don't know what to tell you, sister. Only that he looks at you the same way you look at him."

"What way is that?"

"Like he won't be able to take another breath without you."

Grandio grunted. His skull smacked back against the wall with a sickening thud. He grabbed his head with both hands and applied what appeared to be a terrifying amount of pressure. He grunted again, this time with a word that resembled *Silence*.

Orla shot to her feet and stood face to face with the pained man. She threaded her fingers with his on either side of his temples and pressed their foreheads together. "Show me."

"Another . . . By the Dragon and the Chasm, she's unnatural. Indranan witch. Thrice cursed."

Avyi shuddered. Most Dragon Kings believed the thrice-cursed Indranan a myth. She knew differently. Although most Indranan were born as twins, some were birthed as one of three. Triplets. And some of those triplets killed both siblings to assume untold telepathic powers. They also assumed the screaming minds of their wronged brothers and sisters. The thrice-cursed were abominations—exceedingly powerful and completely mad.

Avyi had only ever known one such woman.

"Ulia," she said. "Aster's telepath."

Silence mumbled an affirmative, then cried out. She and Grandio were caught. They were fighting an unseen battle.

Mal took position at Avyi's side, his hand threaded with hers. "Helpless. Dragon damn it."

"You?"

"Yes. I hate it."

"Our time will come. Every attack has multiple assaults. Yours, Malnefoley, will be of the explosive variety. This . . ." She shook her head, watching her sister and the Indranan man physically bound as they fought a mental battle. "This is not our domain."

"The rebels will still die? Do you know it, Avyi? A fixed point?"

She mashed her lips together. "No. I don't know for sure. I thought I did. It's all coming together too quickly. Nothing makes sense anymore." Embarrassed, scared, she glanced at him, where he stared her down with piercing eyes. "Maybe that's why I've needed you all along," she said softly.

"Hark," Orla whispered, sounding strangled by an unseen hand. "And that girl."

"Cadmin?"

"Yes. Dragon be merciful—yes." She shook free of Grandio's hold. The man collapsed onto the sidewalk. "I couldn't— The witch— It was let him go or be erased along with him. Oh, Dragon forgive me."

Mal knelt beside Grandio's fallen body. He felt the man's neck, twisted his pinkie finger, pulled his eyelids apart. "Nothing. Not a thing. Ulia did this?"

Orla swayed on her feet. Avyi supported the taller woman, who replied, "Yes. Like flipping a switch. We can't search again. She could find us, but the cover of so many Dragon Kings may give us time. We have to get to the holding cells."

"You found Hark?" Avyi asked, hoping as she'd never hoped.

"He's in chains. Alone in a . . . a tunnel? Human guards surrounded him. He . . ." She broke off and hefted her shield. A murderous expression turned her sharp but beautiful features into those of an unearthly avenger. "He's not suffering another moment that can be helped. Do you believe I can find our way?"

"We have no choice," Mal said.

"What about Grandio?" Avyi knelt next to the fallen man and stroked sweaty hair back from his face. He didn't respond in any way. Had it been so simple for Ulia to turn him from man to meat? "We can't leave him here. Are we sure he won't recover?"

Orla shook her head, leaving Avyi with a wellspring in her stomach where sickness and fear bubbled up. " There's nothing left of him now. I was lucky to escape with my own mind intact. The Indranan can only focus on one individual at a time. That mind witch got to him first."

"I'm glad you're safe. But we can get him out of sight. And we can . . ." She flicked her eyes to the sword Mal held.

"I'll do right by him." Although Mal's face was etched with dreadful tension, he moved Grandio so that his body lay horizontally on the sidewalk and his head dropped back into the gutter. His chest cinched tight. "Great Dragon," he said, echoing Avyi's words back in the labyrinth, "he is yours."

He swung the sword in a sure arc, beheading Grandio with a single blow. Without speaking, Avyi and Orla moved his body back into the shadow and aligned his head with his torso. They each whispered, before touching his forehead and standing.

"No more," Avyi rasped. "Not another one of our kind."

❦ CHAPTER ❦
TWENTY-TWO

Avyi ran, with Mal on her heels.

Orla raced up the street and veered into a narrow shaft that connected two segments of the Battersea. "This may get tight," she called over her shoulder.

The shaft was hot and shot steam up from slats low along the wall. "Some sort of release valves if the turbines overheat," Mal said. "A way of venting excess energy."

Avyi smiled despite the throbbing in her chest, as anger, grief, and their fast pace tightened her lungs. "You could do with some of that."

A quick glance backward revealed Mal's grim smile. The expression in his eyes was a combination of mirth and teasing that made Avyi's heart pinch.

"Right now I'm trying not to lose my legs to bursts of steam."

The shaft narrowed as Orla had warned, until Avyi was forced to shuffle sideways. Mal shed his lightweight overcoat. He had gained a wildness that appealed to Avyi on a deep, inexplicable level. The heads of the cartels bought and sold and negotiated. She would rather place her faith in Mal's ability to lose control than his

fallback penchant for trying to keep matte▯
on an even keel.

She might even put her trust in him after▯
words they'd said. She didn't want their argum▯ ▯▯ be
the final, overwhelming sentiment they exchanged.

The grim set of his mouth, the tense readiness that
radiated from his chest to his shoulders to his arms, and
the dusty, ruffled hair of a true fighter made him more
handsome than she'd ever seen. He shuffled beside her,
taking up the rear of their trio, and she felt calm. Suddenly calm. Orla and Mal. She wasn't alone anymore.
She *had* chosen the right side, without the need to explain to herself, over and over, how the ends justified
the means.

She was a woman at home in her body and in her
life, even on the verge of battle and the potential for the
bloodshed she'd foretold. She would be a part of it, but
on the side of her people. So when Orla stole a burst of
Mal's kinetic energy, blazing light into a hollow space at
the end of the tunnel, Avyi was ready.

Ready to face the most deformed Dragon King she'd
ever seen.

"Hellix," Orla said coldly. "You here to die in the
Grievance or die right now?"

"You always were a cold-ass bitch. Where's that jester
freak of yours?" He smiled in a way that bunched the
lines on his forehead. There, the brand of a knife warped
into garish folds of scarred skin on skin. "Maybe I could
help you find him."

Orla sneered. "Maybe you gave him up."

"That's a possibility, too."

Avyi felt a tickle of awareness along her nape before

the actual strike. It wasn't premonition so much as simply knowing the two warriors who fought at her side. She dropped to her stomach. Mal crackled with energy, which Orla concentrated in the metal of her fiercely serrated shield. Sparks like a hundred bolts of lightning shot from its knife-point edges.

Hellix was fast, and he was well trained. That probably explained why his deformities included more than just his brand. He looked like he'd been caught in a fire and burned and burned. Part of his left forearm was twisted down to the bone. Yet he was still able to deflect the energy bursts when he spun into the ferocious berserker rage of Clan Pendray. He tore through the pipes until steam concealed him, and the heated vapor was nearly suffocating. Orla fell to her knees, with her hands around her throat.

Mal leapt over Avyi and her downed sister. His body was a living electrical current. Each microscopic droplet in the steam glowed, supercharged all the way to their neutrons. Steam became living light that he swirled—an in-person view of how he manipulated the skies and brought lightning down at will.

Briefly, Hellix's spinning, furious, malformed limbs could be seen silhouetted in the bright vapor. Avyi didn't expect her sister to recover so quickly. Then again, the woman known as Silence would not have survived more than five years in the Cages, and her entire life on the run from Clan Sath, had she been any less resilient. Or any less deadly. In the time it took for Mal to reveal Hellix's location, Orla pounced. She used the shield first as a slicing weapon, then as a blunt battering ram.

She landed atop it, square on Hellix's chest. From where she lay flat on the ground, Avyi almost smiled at that familiar crouching stance. She'd used it herself countless times. Cut off an enemy's air. Squeeze his heart. Loom above him with the ability to leap away if needed. They were sisters in combat, as well as by blood.

"Where is Hark?" Orla asked, her voice deadly quiet.

"Fuck off."

"Giva? Do you mind?"

"Not at all," Mal replied, equally cold and deadly.

Orla balanced on the toes of her boots and spread her palms on either side of Hellix's head. Her fingers already glowed with the power she borrowed from Malnefoley. The zaps made Hellix's legs twitch. His arms splayed out to the sides, useless. "I won't kill you," she said. "I'll paralyze you, with your mental functions still intact. Nod."

The man did.

Avyi crawled to her knees, crouching, ready to aid Orla however she could. In the face of such skill and power, however, Avyi's street-fighting techniques and man-made weapons seemed like barbarian clubs.

Hellix's eyes were wide, although it didn't appear as if he did it on purpose. Orla was in control of the man's mind, right down to how his body functioned.

"Then I'll leave you here in the steam, until you suffer even worse than when you burned in the rubble of Aster's labs. I'll press you against the furnace pipes. You'll sizzle, feeling every second, but you won't be lucky enough to die. The Giva carries a Dragon-forged sword, but I doubt he'll do you the mercy of a behead-ing." She smiled, seeming half crazed. "I'll kill him with it before he tries. Nod."

Hellix was losing consciousness. His eyes rolled back. But he still managed a scant acknowledgment.

"Now," she said calmly. "Where is Hark?"

"Asters."

"I know that, you *bathatéi* shit. *Where*?"

"East of here. One level below. With humans."

"He wouldn't be able to use his powers," Avyi said. "Trapped with humans, with no Dragon King gifts to borrow."

"I bet we'll find all of the Sath in similar confine-ments," Mal added.

Orla hopped away from Hellix, who gasped and smacked at his head as if it were on fire. "Bitch," he growled.

"Help me, Avyi?"

Avyi stood and grabbed a foot and hand, as Orla did. They pulled Hellix to one side, carefully avoiding the steaming-hot pipes as they positioned his body flush against one. The man screamed. "Mal," Avyi said. "We have no rope. What can you do?"

"Something terrible." His face closed down. She read nothing in his expression, much like when he'd related the tale of his destruction of Bakkhos. "Go. I'll follow."

Orla took hold of her, just as Avyi saw the flash vision of Hellix's future. Mal was going to . . . .

Hellix screamed again, a sound that promised to be never-ending.

No wonder, with his skin cauterized to the pipe.

"We'll come back for him and finish the job," Orla said. "If what he claimed about Hark is true."

Avyi turned in time to see Mal stride through the hot mist, which swirled around his body. His chin was lowered, with his bleak, soulless eyes looking forward. He met her gaze without apology. Avyi found that she didn't need one. He was a leader, and that meant taking on terrible deeds himself. Avyi had only known Hellix by reputation until the day the man had gleefully carried out Old Man Aster's order to have Nynn of Tigony flogged to the point of unconsciousness. The smile on Hellix's warped face had been almost sexually charged. He was guilty of too many crimes to list, mostly against human women the Asters considered expendable rewards for victorious Cage warriors. None of Hellix's female offerings lived to see the dawn.

Not every Dragon King deserved to live.

Mal had determined Hellix's fate. Nothing about his posture or assured stride showed the least bit of regret.

She'd known it all along. He was the leader they needed. Apparently one of his first acts as an unrepentant Giva was to dispatch a heinous Dragon King. Leading their people by intending to kill one seemed counterintuitive, but it was what needed to be done.

"East is this way." She led her two companions on a twisting course through pipes, low-hanging metal ventilation ducts, and solid I-beams. They came to a flight of stairs. The concrete was crumbling, which spoke to Orla's account of how old Battersea was, with its crumbling underground structures.

"That looks remarkably unsafe," Mal said with a dark edge of humor. "Care to go first, Avyi?"

"Not at all. My gift has left me in the dark like a woman without eyes. Light the way for us, Giva. We have your back."

Malnefoley regretted the innocent lives he had taken at Bakkhos as he and the sisters at his back forged through the tunnels beneath Battersea. He regretted them in a deep place, where he wished the world could be a different place, a softer place. He'd experienced a glimpse of that softness in Avyi's arms. Yet that alone should've told him what a rare and impossible wish it was. He had never felt anything that intense and full of trust before. Unless he protected her now, he never would again.

That meant the armored men who stood between him and the enclosures that held human and Dragon King alike became his victims. They were unfortunates who had chosen to work for the cartels, seduced by the promise of power or wealth.

They were in his way.

But unlike the burdens he had carried since Bakkhos, his conscience was clear as he used his gift to light the deep tunnels and fell the men who stood ready with plasma guns and Tasers that temporarily stripped Dragon Kings' powers. These people would not hurt Avyi. They would not hurt Orla. And they would not keep him from freeing his imprisoned Dragon Kings. He was the Honorable Giva, and he was the Great Dragon's representative on this mortal plane.

He twisted through two pipes. The bow jostled off

his shoulder. Avyi snatched it up and threw it over her shoulder where the quiver of arrows was strapped to her back. The two weapons, reunited for the first time, snapped with red fire.

Avyi skidded to a stop and dropped behind a half-rusted beam that appeared sunken and tired of its century-long burdens. She held her head, shook it, stomped her feet. Mal was by her side in a second, while Orla kept watch.

"Avyi," he said, both of her forearms in his hands. "Avyi, answer me!"

"*No.* No, no, no . . ."

"Tell me."

Haunted golden-green eyes were made sickly dark by the underground shadows. He wanted to see them in daylight. He wanted to see them eager and happy and satisfied—all of the emotions he had never expected of the woman formerly known only as the Pet.

She thrust the bow into his hands. "I can't. Do you understand me? I *can't*. And I . . . Mal . . ."

Two tears streaked down her cheeks. Mal wiped them away as if he could just as easily wipe away her distress. "You can't trust me with this?"

"I can't tell you, because it can't be changed. And I hate the Dragon for showing me what can't be changed." She shook her head, meeting his gaze with startling hatred.

"You don't mean that. You believe."

"Yes, I believe in our creator, but I can hate it, too."

"Time to go," Orla said tersely. "No time for this. It happens or it doesn't. Avyi, you've never steered me wrong. For your sake, for whatever you've seen, I hope you're wrong. But Hark needs me. I have to go, and I need your help."

Mal hoisted Avyi to her feet, which were surprisingly steady. She was wearing her brass knuckles and holding her open switchblade, although he couldn't say when she had donned the weapons.

"One last time. Tell me."

Her features, at times so impish and mocking and stealthy, were made of stone. "No."

She raced after Orla, with Mal to follow them both. The caverns below Battersea shrank and became more narrow, reminding Mal of the crypt where they'd found the bow. Cadmin's bow. He couldn't think of it any other way now. He couldn't think of any of Avyi's predictions with doubt anymore. Which was why her sudden premonition—the one she refused to share—was so distressing. Something about Orla, Hark, Cadmin.

Or herself.

She wouldn't tell him if the prediction was a fixed point that ensured her death. That fact, which he knew with utter certainty, knotted in his stomach like a coiling snake. But what was worse? This frustration, or knowing the moment she would be taken from him? She could be taken from him when he envisioned more for their future than this desperate mission.

His wasn't a prediction. His was a wish.

Knowing would be better. At least then he could fight, no matter how useless. At least then he could say what was bottled inside him, too strong to put into words.

They reached what appeared to be a dead end. Orla kicked the dirt wall and slashed at it with her shield. She railed, cursing Hellix. Mal had to restrain her from taking hold of his sword. The determination on her face said that Hellix was a dead man—sooner rather than later—for having led them on this wild-goose chase.

"Wait," Avyi said. "Orla, calm yourself."

Orla was a snarling beast of a woman. Mal cut the leather strap that held her shield in place, then kicked it away. He grabbed Orla around the waist and spread his palm at the base of her skull. "I won't hurt you," he said against her ear. "But I can make it so that your place in this fight ends here. Do you want to be unconscious while Hark needs you?"

"No," she growled.

"Then listen to your sister." He swallowed, meeting Avyi's eyes over Orla's blond-on-blond crown. "Tell us."

"That's just it. Orla, use your gift. Try to find something. Anything. Reach deep, sister. Find a Dragon King who can tell us the way."

"That deformed prick said Hark was trapped with humans."

Avyi smiled softly. "And you trust him?"

A vicious smile, completely opposite in emotion, transformed her face. Mal was surprised. As the warrior named Silence became more ferocious, her features became more starkly beautiful. "Not enough to stop trying," Orla said. "You can let go, Giva. Hark has always insisted that my name should be Patience. I don't feel patient, but I can behave."

"You two are some pair," Mal said, releasing Orla and stepping back, his sword out of reach.

"I'll take that as a compliment." Avyi's words were stripped of emotion, but she caught Mal's eye with a brief twinkle of sharp humor. Then she took Orla's hands in hers. "Look. Use my gift. See what I see. No one has ever been able to read me as clearly as you." She smiled, almost sadly. "Now we know why."

Orla nodded. The sisters pressed their foreheads together, their fingers clasped. Concentration shaped their features until only their difference in height and their hair color differentiated them. "There," Orla whispered. "Dragon be, a Garnis. That's not the present, is it?"

"No. It's hours from now. But now you know where he is. Use him. Use his senses to find Hark."

Because the Sath could only borrow the powers of one Dragon King at a time, Orla let go of Avyi's hands and backed away, until she was flush against the crumbling dirt wall. Maybe a century ago, humans had intended these tunnels to be an extension of the Underground, or even bomb shelters. Now they were forgotten ruins, propping Orla up as she fought to find one of the Lost among so many warped paths.

Another damned labyrinth.

Avyi took Mal's hand. "There. She has it. Look."

Orla grimaced. "Giva, I need a little help."

"Name it."

She seemed to shake out of a trance, which must be what every Sath felt like when they released another Dragon King's powers. "This dirt blockage is roughly ten meters thick. I can hear the Garnis on the other side. He's in chains. He won't be for long, if Avyi's vision is right. But for now, he's my eyes and ears. The human cage is beyond that. I saw Hark."

"Then why isn't he using the Garnis's powers?" Avyi asked.

"He's collared," Orla answered. "And unconscious. I hope."

Mal wasted no time. He stood before the dirt barrier and closed his eyes. They were away from strong sources of energy. Avyi rubbed her hands together. Orla took the ends of her shirt and scrubbed the fabric until pieces fell away. But friction was only so useful. It took time. Mal dug deeper within himself than he'd ever tried, even during those four isolated years on a distant Greek mountaintop. He focused on the pulsing of the women's hearts, and how their blood sped through their veins. Their energy was enough for him to work on an even deeper level, as the turbine of his gift amped up.

He grounded himself on the dirt floor. The earth itself became his wellspring of energy. Why hadn't he ever noticed before? Perhaps because, like most of his life, resources were usually plentiful. Now, he dragged energy from miles-deep wellsprings of water and lava. He harnessed those flowing currents until they were bolts of electricity warping the air around him. He couldn't see Avyi or Orla. He could only hope they knew to take cover.

In the moments before he released the most potent expression of his gift he'd ever experienced, he thought about his cousin. About Nynn. She was half Pendray. That meant half berserker. Her power had been enough to explode buildings, and was so feared that she had been banished by the Council—at a time when Mal hadn't been courageous enough to stand up to those ten influential figures.

He was the Giva. He should've protected his cousin. He'd known that for a long time, but as unimaginable power surged through his blood, through the whole of his being, he sympathized with her. He admired her. Because he, too, knew what it was to explode.

❧ CHAPTER ❧
TWENTY-THREE

The wind was knocked out of Avyi's lungs when Orla grabbed her and they landed in a pile on the hard-packed ground. Orla's shield covered them both when Mal's energy burst from him with the force of a cannon. The sound of his raging bellow was even louder than the shock of lightning meeting rock that had been buried underground for hundreds of years. She and Orla huddled together. She clutched her eyelids shut when the light became too, too, too bright. Briefly, she was glad that she didn't have the power of a Garnis. Those ultra-keen senses might've been shattered beyond repair in the wake of such power.

The rock crumbled; she heard it give way. Then it was a shower, beating down on Orla's shield.

"It's going to collapse," she shouted to her sister.

They had to take the chance that Mal would see the danger, too. Avyi knew neither of them would die in that tunnel.

Mal.

All she could see was blood. *His* blood. He clutched his slit throat as red gushed from a wound. Only when she united the bow and arrows had she been able to see the clearest prediction of her life.

Mal would die at the Grievance.

She refused to share it with him because she refused to believe it.

She wouldn't let Mal die. She would rip apart the fabric of time if it meant keeping him safe. There was no power short of the Dragon himself to keep her from trying to her last breath.

But she hadn't seen anything about Orla. Her sister, so new and precious, could die in those caverns without warning. That was the burden of Avyi's life: to see the unwanted and to fear the unknown. She choked back the flash flood of grief that threatened to drown her, just when she needed a clear head and even faster limbs.

Avyi and Orla scrambled on all fours toward where the jut of Mal's energy blast was beginning to taper. The hole he left in the earth was considerable where it began, and then narrowed to the width of a body doing a belly crawl. But he had cleared what needed to be cleared.

As soon as he finished with another shout that sounded nearly painful, Orla ditched her shield and began the long crawl. There was no way to get the wide circle of metal through that last meter at the end of the tunnel. Avyi was about to follow her sister, but she caught sight of Mal. He'd dropped to one knee. Something like smoke—no, steam—lifted from his back and shoulders. He was as hot as cinders.

She rushed to his side but hesitated to touch his skin. He was pulsing, vibrating, shimmering with what remained of his gift's powerful explosion. "Mal, talk to me."

"Hi."

"Idiot man."

He lifted his head. She should've seen a charred face, hairless, with nothing but bone remaining, but he was just as handsome as ever. In fact, the extreme usage of his gift added a sheen of otherworldliness that couldn't be defined. Every feature was sharper and even more dramatic. His eyes burned crystal blue, even in the dim light of the tunnel. High, aristocratic cheekbones added refinement to rugged looks made wild by the power that still hummed from his golden skin. The man who'd let loose on that distant labyrinth in Crete was a weakling compared to this living, wildly smiling god.

"You had a vision that terrified you. You've seen most of what happens to Cadmin." He pushed to his feet, speaking as though continuing a thought that had been interrupted mid-sentence, standing stronger and taller than she would've expected from a man who'd just burst apart. "If it was about Orla or Hark . . . No. You would've confided in me. That means what you saw was about you or me. One of our futures. Tell me I'm wrong."

Avyi's chest burned. "You're not wrong."

"Then I did the right thing. This wasn't the time to die, or you'd have tried to stop me. Fixed point or not, you'd have tried."

He grabbed her wrist with one hand and picked up the Dragon-forged sword with the other. With more power than grace, he shoved her toward the tunnel.

"Go," he said. "Orla will need us."

Avyi wanted to protest. She wanted to process. She wanted to hold him while he still lived and thrived. Instead, she crawled, the terror of her vision refusing to leave her alone.

How could both be fixed points?

She'd seen them lying together, lovers, but more than that—two people in love. The feeling was just as important as the moment. More so, even, because they'd already experienced the carnal satisfaction of taking each other to the very limits of physical pleasure.

But she'd also seen Mal consumed by fire. *Consumed*. Nothing left. She'd heard his dying scream. It was nothing like the bellow of raging power he'd expelled when burning the earth. It was absolute pain . . . in the center of the Grievance arena.

They were going to lie together, open and vulnerable to one another—when? How could what she saw of their love affair take place before the vision of his fiery death came to pass?

She was already in love with him. That sudden, almost easy realization—how could it be otherwise?—contrasted so severely with his fate that she retched as she crawled. She only hoped Mal wouldn't hear or see her misery, because he already knew too much about her, and about what would terrify her so much.

She crawled the last two meters with caution, softly calling to Orla.

"Here," came her sister's quiet reply. "The way is clear."

Avyi scampered out and to the left, which allowed Mal to jump clear with his sword at the ready.

"Meet Jorvaki," Orla said. "He's the Garnis I found. Would you mind, Giva?"

Jorvaki was chained to the wall of what appeared to

be a concrete dungeon. It was large enough that Avyi could see the other side, but barely. Along the walls, another dozen Dragon Kings, women and men in various states of undress, were bound at the wrists and ankles, completely vulnerable. Some faced forward, with cuts and slashes across their chests and thighs. Others faced the concrete and bore the stripes of whip marks across their backs. Only three were so devastated that they wore no damping collars. Jorvaki was one, his body abused to the point that his captors must not have thought a collar worth the trouble.

"Why are you here?" Malnefoley asked the wounded man.

"I killed two Kawashima guards in an attempt to escape. I won't fight tonight. I'll be executed as punishment."

"As will everyone here," Orla said. "Enemies of the cartels are the opening acts. The fit and ferocious Cage warriors fight last, on a stage already soaked with blood."

Mal growled in his throat, his eyes fiercely charged with flaming blue purpose. He used the Dragon-forged sword to clip through chains as easily as scissors through paper. Orla grabbed the onyx dragon idol and began to snap collars off callused necks. Gasps and even shrieks followed her progress around the room as she freed each man and woman. The rapture of having their gifts restored was too great to contain.

Avyi watched in stunned wonder. She was overwhelmed by the moment, when her sister and the man she loved did so much to save Dragon Kings who'd been left to rot, or left to be used as fodder for the entertainment of the cartels and their guests. These were powerful beings laid low, but they wouldn't be forever. They would heal. And they would have their revenge.

Orla was anxious. She asked every Dragon King she freed if they had seen Hark, or even where groups of humans were trapped—more entertainment for the bloodthirsty crowd.

"Keep going through there," said one woman. Her flame-red hair suggested she was Pendray. "I was blindfolded, but it slipped when I was dragged down here. There's a pen. The humans smell different."

"They do," added Jorvaki. "Your man might be with them."

Mal was quick to appoint the strongest of the freed to attend the rest. He used the sword to cut pipes and rebar to act as crude weapons. "Put aside what differences we have as clans. Work together, or we'll all die today."

"Who are you to tell us what to do?" asked a halfstripped man whose flesh had been branded up and down his thighs.

"I'm Malnefoley of Tigony. You may call me the Honorable Giva or the Usurper. Right now, I don't care. Right now, I'm the man who helped set you free. Repay that kindness by using your Dragon-damned heads. The cartels are better organized, and when the moment comes, they'll band together as humans against us even more readily than our clans would against them."

He surveyed the concrete fortress with all the bearing of his station, and with the arrogance only a man of his authority could bring to bear. Avyi's heart lurched with admiration, love, and abject fear. What could bring down such a being? She looked at him and saw indestructible power. But she'd once thought the same of Dr. Aster, that he was so overwhelming and influential that no one would ever rebel against his sick authority. Men were laid low all the time. Malnefoley could become one of many.

If Dr. Aster was the one who killed Mal, her Giva, then one of her oldest predictions was easy to imagine. She would fight her old master, but instead of worrying about its outcome, she knew the contest would be hers to win.

Mal flexed his arms and upper back with a long, strong exhale. He felt more powerful than he had during any time short of those brief, beautiful moments when he and Avyi had collapsed in breathtaking mutual pleasure. This was a different sort of power. This was the measure of a man coming completely into his own.

This moment made his four years on that distant mountaintop feel like he'd been a child just beginning to walk.

Although any number of those freed could've looked on him with derisive contempt—was being freed by the Usurper something to truly celebrate?—they stared at him with awe. A few touched his sleeves as he passed. They thanked him in quiet tones. A shiver shot up his spine.

This was power . . . and it was something he needed to protect, something that could easily be abused. He knew that lesson well. It was time to learn another lesson, one born of humility and temperance.

"Orla," he called. "Grab something metal and be ready to fight."

She already held a length of rebar about a meter long. If swung with the precision he didn't doubt her ability to muster, the metal girding could take off a human head. A Dragon King might suffer a debilitating skull fracture or a crippled spine. The energy coming off her was potent, and growing stronger with every second. He would feel the same way, too, if Avyi were in jeopardy.

"And if any of the rest of you feel fit enough to fight with us, gear up."

With a quick glance at Avyi, whose golden-green eyes were shadowed by futures yet to come, he exhaled again and let go of his doubts. This was happening. It was the present. The future as Avyi saw it would happen. That didn't mean he would keep from doing his damned-est to bring down the whole fucking complex and every cartel bastard in it.

Orla took point, followed quickly by other men and women who seemed to have been trained for Cage fighting. Some bore the distinctive seven-pointed star of the Kawashima cartel, branded into the skin of their left shoulders. Few of the others bore such distinctive markings.

As a Sath, Orla was the ideal woman to lead them through the two-story tunnels that waited on the other side of the concrete dungeon's exit. She had long experience without her collar, and knew how to skillfully borrow other Dragon Kings' gifts without being overwhelmed by them. She was also a woman with purpose. Mal looked around to find Avyi beside him, and the rest of the freed captives taking up the rear. It seemed . . . intentional.

"They're protecting you," Avyi whispered. "Their Giva."

"I don't need protecting."

"As a man? Perhaps not. But as an institution, as a symbol, you mean everything to us." She took a shallow series of breaths. "And whoever tried to have you killed before will not give up."

"These newly freed can't know of the assassination attempt."

She smiled up at him, with more awe in her eyes than he was used to seeing. She almost appeared as bowled over as the rest of those he led. "They don't need to. They're willing to die for you. That's real power, Malnefoley. Forget the Council. Forget our gifts. You're the Giva we've been waiting for."

He kissed her swiftly, with all the promise and hope that surged in his veins. "I don't need another supplicant. I need Avyi. My new beginning and my partner, my equal and my Dragon-damned pain in the ass." He caught her gaze and wouldn't let go. "Forget gifts and visions. Tell me what you *know*."

"I know I love you. Past, present, future—I love you, Malnefoley."

He exhaled heavily, accepting her words into the darkest parts of his soul. "Then we do this."

"Here!"

Orla's shout prompted the Dragon Kings to surge forward. These Garnis were practiced Cage warriors, which meant Mal had been more lucky than not in besting the pair in Florence. These men and women were fast—almost too fast to be seen, with supreme reflexes and speed. Mal managed to count four before he lost track of the contrails of their bodies. The Pendray were next, roiling and raging as they succumbed to berserker furies. Their conscious minds hid beneath layers of animal instinct, like the legends of werewolves they had inspired so long ago in the Scottish Highlands.

His own Tigony fed off that energy until four sparking, shining individuals arced energy between them like children tossing a ball. Every so often Mal would feel the *tap-tap* of an Indranan mind, before that telepathic touch backed off. But the connection they forged helped organize the attack. And through the melee, the Sath borrowed here and there, filling in gaps in the phalanx they created.

The Five Clans. Acting as one.

Mal, at the center, had never seen anything so breathtaking. It was as the Dragon would've wanted.

The thought shocked him, because he'd long thought himself beyond feeling any genuine belief in their creator. But this . . . this was right. Their phalanx of roughly sixteen emerged into a huge domed room that looked as if a large bomb had hollowed out the earth. A practice Cage stood at its center, only the octagonal frame was not empty and tempting, ready for the strongest Cage warriors to step forward in deathly combat. It was filled with human beings like a cattle car. Perhaps they were enemies of the cartels, or simply hapless captives, but all were destined to be executed in the opening rounds of the Grievance.

Those who had been silent or even whimpering began to scream with the approach of so many buzzing, eager Dragon Kings. Mal sympathized. It would be like seeing every mythical creature made real.

All the myths are true.

Avyi was smiling up at him. "Told you."

"Quit it," he said without malice. "You can't read minds."

"No, but I can read your expressions. You know what they're thinking, all these terrified people. We are their religions and demons and legends made flesh—and coming for them." She crossed her arms, where her brass knuckles flashed in the light of the eight lamps atop the octagonal posts. "I'd be scared of us, too."

"Hark!" Orla climbed the wire frame of the cage like a monkey up a tree. "Hark, where are you? You Dragon-damned fool, talk to me!"

An Indranan to Avyi's left fell to her knees and clutched her head. Avyi quickly knelt beside the woman, with an arm around her shoulders.

"That Sath bitch is in my head. I can't—she's so furious." The woman's neck bore the heavy ringed callus of one who'd served a long, long time as a Cage warrior. Her accent was English—perhaps property of the Townsends.

"Try to relax." Avyi gave her a squeeze, and brushed matted hair back from her forehead. "She's my sister. I know her. She's terrified for her husband. Please, let her borrow your gift. Help her find him."

"There," the woman said on a whisper. "There he is."

Mal and Avyi exchanged glances. "Is he alive?" Avyi asked, sounding reluctant.

The Indranan woman gasped, then fell forward. She would've hit the ground had Avyi not been there to support her weakened body. "She let me go—your sister. She found him."

Avyi quickly thanked the woman, then handed her into the care of another nearby Indranan. Mal could only assume the two were speaking to each other telepathically, foreheads together, eyes closed. He chased after Avyi, to where the humans were caught like terrified fish in a huge net. Frightened down to their basest impulses, they were frantically clawing at the wire mesh of the Cage and trying to climb over one another. In their blind terror, they made even the berserkers seem lucid.

Avyi flinched back from the throbbing mob, her face dotted with sweat and panic in her eyes, but Mal watched as she visibly shoved her old fears aside. "They need us."

"Sath and Indranan," Mal called from a high set of metal steps. "Calm them! They're terrified! Calm them before they kill one another!"

Slowly, he felt an eerie wave build and pulse across the domed, hollowed-out cavern. The touches of telepathy weren't aimed at him, but he felt the brush nonetheless, like what humans believed to be ghosts—that sense of unease, of being watched. The humans began to quiet.

When he believed them calm enough to exit without a mass stampede, he gestured for two Garnis to open the Cage. They would be fast enough to quell the humans should panic arise again. He was giving commands to a pair who obeyed without hesitation.

Avyi did as her sister had, clambering over the wire mesh with superhuman agility. It was the Garnis in her, those reflexes and the gift of senses so deep . . . He blinked. Senses so deep that she could extrapolate events, sorting through a hundred thousand possibilities until she found the most likely outcome. Perhaps that was how she made her predictions. He had thought her gift unique and separate, but he had been looking at the end result rather than the process. Her mind was as agile as a Garnis's extraordinary physical prowess. She wasn't predicting the future so much as running through countless scenarios, using bits of clues and nuances hidden to everyone else, until she found the most likely path. They were probabilities that played out over and over too often to be considered probabilities any longer.

She jumped into the fray as the last of the humans cleared out. Mal rushed down the metal steps and through the Cage door. At its center lay Hark, with his head in Orla's lap. Avyi knelt beside them. Hark was bloodied. His leg was twisted at an odd angle. His blond hair had been shaved. The Asters' serpent tattoo wrapped around the back of his skull, with the head at one temple and the tail at the other. It was the ultimate symbol of possession.

Weeping without sound, Orla held his right forearm to the glaring lights. The Thorn that had been the symbol of their union had been torn out. A nasty gash remained in its place—a wound they would both bear.

Hark, however, remained the strangely optimistic, jesterlike man Mal had met briefly in the ruins of the Asters' detonated labs. "Hey, Giva. Mind getting the women off me? I have some serious retribution to attend to." He looked up at Orla. "And you, quit that bullshit. Crying over me? You're tougher than that."

"I am," Orla said, her throat tight with obvious emotion. "But now I'll have to support your lazy hide."

Mal and Avyi helped Orla get her husband on his feet. "You two aren't going anywhere," Mal said. "That's an order. We have to find a young Cage warrior named Cadmin, and I can't have Avyi distracted. This is Cadmin's first Grievance. She fights tonight, during the first round."

Hark's expression sobered. "Pendray, yeah? Young, sorta stout but with sharp features?"

Avyi nodded. Mal saw the pale gold of her skin leech of color. "Yes."

"I'm sorry. Other than to save my Dragon-damned soul, you've come a long way for nothing." Hark looked at each of them in turn. "I saw her fall. She's dead."

⚡ CHAPTER ⚡
TWENTY-FOUR

Avyi's knees sagged until she thought even the sturdy, wide soles of her boots wouldn't hold her upright. But instead of falling, she channeled her disbelief into anger. "No," she said pointing at Hark. "You're injured. You've been abused. That can't be true. She's *alive*."

Orla's face was edged with sympathy, but she was too concerned about Hark to offer the reassurance Avyi needed. She turned instead to Mal. His lovely mouth was pinched into a frown that deepened to encompass his entire face. "When have you ever been wrong?" he asked quietly.

"About something this important? Never."

"And there's no chance something we've done could've changed what you've seen for so many years?"

Avyi shook her head. She didn't want to consider it, even though her contradictory visions about Mal's future made her less than certain. *What special sort of hell is this gift?* She couldn't trust anything that had once been true. The only thing she knew to do was to keep looking. Her faith in the Dragon had sustained her through decades of suffering. Without that faith, she had nothing else.

"Orla, get him to what safety you can." She glanced at Mal, her heart uneasy. "Are you coming with me still?"

They stared at one another for what seemed to be an eternity. They were motionless. No electrical current passed between them, but a deeper, less distinct jolt of pure emotion. If one person in this world was to believe her crazy, frustrating gift, it was Mal.

"Yes," he said soberly. "Lead the way. I have your back this time."

Only instinct now. No direction in mind. Some of the other Dragon Kings followed, likely because of Mal. She'd guess that none of them identified her as the Pet, because her appearance and demeanor had been so changed. That is, unless she'd once touched their minds. Any warrior from the Aster cartel could suspect her. They were only temporary allies, if that. She was in as much danger as Mal.

Mal . . . burned alive.

She shoved the vision away, reached back, and was gratified when he grabbed her hand. They ran together through the underground tunnels.

"Wait," came Jorvaki's voice. "Listen."

Avyi stopped cold. She strained the limit of her senses but heard nothing.

A Sath and another Garnis nodded. Jorvaki looked gravely between Avyi and Mal. "People. Thousands of people. I can hear their voices and footsteps, far above us. It must be nearing time for the games."

"How long have we been down here?" Avyi asked in frustration. "I thought we'd have more time!"

"Apparently not," Mal said. His voice was calm and

authoritative, but she knew his face so well now. He was as anxious as she. "Let's go."

Another winding corridor turned into a long, straight tunnel that had been hollowed out by what must've been an industrial drill. Twirling scrapes created a dizzying, circling effect all around. Avyi reached back into the quiver and withdrew the Pendray arrow on the first try. It had simply felt right—dangerous and crazy. She looked at their fat, happy fertility goddess impression of the Dragon and . . . saw.

"Cadmin," she whispered.

She bolted down the tunnel, with Mal's angered voice at her back. She didn't stop, not even when running the length of the tunnel stole the air from her lungs.

At its end she found darkness. There was no light, but there were voices. Whispers from some. Vocal boasts from others. She remembered the Asters' technique of transporting their blindfolded Cage warriors by bus to each combat arena. It was to protect eyes used to artificial underground lights, until they could be slowly acclimated to the brightness of the Cages. This would be even more extreme, with Battersea turned into an arena, lit like a football stadium to contrast against the deep black of the night sky.

Mal snapped his fingers. He might as well have been holding a match, so quiet was the flame. Some in the room hissed. He increased the flame until it illuminated the whole space, which was cordoned off into three holding pens.

Like animals.

They were warriors from each cartel. The ones she,

Mal, and Orla had rescued had been marked for death. These Dragon Kings were prime, fit, gorgeous specimens. But, as with the partner of Mal's cousin, Nynn—a man named Leto, who was arguably the most triumphant warrior of all time—these men and women were likely brainwashed. They had fought through individual cartel tournaments to reach this moment, when success in the Grievance would ensure the ultimate reward.

The chance at conception.

It could also mean the ultimate sacrifice. As opposed to cartel matches, which were bloody but nonlethal, these warriors would fight with Dragon-forged swords. To the death.

"Cadmin!" she shouted. "Cadmin of Pendray! I am here for you. I need you to come forward and take the weapons the Dragon has provided for your first Grievance." No answer. "Cadmin!"

Mal burned brighter, and each Dragon King in their company searched the cartel pens. Some greeted each other with surprised relief, while others snarled insults and damned one another to a lingering death. Mal climbed atop one of the pens. He looked half animal now, with a ragged T-shirt open at the neck. His blond hair was wild. His expression was as feral as it was completely, calmly, forever in control.

Avyi's heart burned with admiration for the man she'd unknowingly chosen to love.

"Quiet! Everyone!" He circled so that everyone in the pens could see his face. "Do you know who I am? I am Malnefoley of Tigony, your Honorable Giva. You may want to fight today, but you will not fight one another. Our people are on the brink of extinction. I forbid you to kill any of our fellow Dragon Kings. Is this understood? Our enemies are the humans who would profit from the strength of our backs and the mysteries of our gifts."

"Usurper!" came a shout from the masses.

Mal, as if he had a Garnis's refined senses, shone a light on the man who'd cried out the insult. Sath, perhaps? Maybe Indranan? The light Mal flared across the naysayer's face also glinted off the damping collar practically fused to his neck. He may have been wearing it for decades. "There has never been any Giva in the history of the Dragon Kings like me. You take it as a sign of weakness or trickery." Grinning tightly, he said what was on everyone's mind. "The Tigony. Tricksters. I know what you think. But being chosen as your Giva is a sign from the Dragon. We are dying. Our ways are being thrown to the winds of chaos. The humans are marching us over a cliff, while lining their pockets as long as they can." Again he shone that flaring light on the man who'd protested. "Do you wish to be a slave forever?"

"No, but I would see my wife bear a child. How do we fulfill the basic needs of our people if we don't fight?"

"Because none of the cartels hold the key to conception," came a quiet, gurgling female voice.

Avyi ran toward the sound. She experienced the same unmooring sensation she always did when coming face to face with a prediction made real. "Cadmin," she whispered. "You're here. I thought you were dead."

"Nearly." She glared toward some of the warriors in her pen. "Seems a few here feared my abilities even before we stepped into the arena."

She was just as Avyi had envisioned, but her face was bruised and she lay beaten on the ground. Only her fingers, clutching the wire frame of the pen, were strong enough to lift her upper body and head a few inches off the ground.

"Tell me who," Avyi said with deadly purpose.

"No. Their time will come."

Mal seared open the pen, then sealed it again after Avyi and another freed Dragon King pulled the young woman loose. She lay across Avyi's lap, where Mal's gift revealed a gash across her forehead and a deep cut in her left arm. She wouldn't be able to hold a shield.

"I remember you," she whispered to Avyi. "My mother before my mother."

Tears gathered in Avyi's eyes as she stroked bloodied red hair back from Cadmin's face. "Tell them. Please."

With Mal to help Avyi lift the girl, Cadmin faced the three cartel pens. "Many of you are my age, or even younger. Think back. Feel with your heart. Do you remember this woman? Do you remember how she touched you with the softest touch, so that you knew safety and love even before your real mother held you for the first time? Do you remember feeling destined for greatness before you knew the definition of the word?"

Murmurs of agreement and some of disbelief filled the tight room, which reminded Avyi of an abattoir just before cattle were herded in for slaughter.

"Can you feel her? Do you?" The calls of fellow Aster warriors bolstered Cadmin's strength, until she was better able to hold her own weight. Her face revealed awe and something akin to love.

Avyi held her closer, rocking, unable to say what that expression did to fill her with joy. Cadmin remembered her. None of what she'd done was purely in the service of the Asters. The ends had justified the means. She had not chosen the wrong side, not when she'd given such an unexpected gift to so many Dragon Kings she would never know by name.

"This woman helped our mothers and fathers give birth," Cadmin said, her rough Scots voice unrelenting now. "Listen to the Giva. Listen to me, although few of you trust him and few of you know me. If we fight today, we will live or die. But we will not be rewarded with the prize we desperately want."

"Then what do we do?"

"Who speaks for us?"

"There's no guarantee what you say is true!"

Avyi lay Cadmin gently on the concrete floor. She took Mal's hand and stood by his side. "I am Avyi. I am crossbred of Sath and Garnis. Today, we will not shed the blood of our kind. The Great Dragon would weep when looking down at our fear and subservience. This is the time to overturn the corrupt system that has made mighty lions whimper and crawl beneath ants." She inhaled. She pushed away fear. She trusted in all she ever believed to be true. "Today, we take back our lives and our futures . . . at any cost."

Those already freed stood in preparation. Mal and a select few waited for human guards to come for the first combatants.

"Please, Mal," Avyi begged. "Let them take Cadmin. It has to happen this way."

"What happened to choice? What if we simply fight back?"

She shook her head. Unlike the speech she'd delivered to the captured of their kind, she showed no such assurance now. "I can't say."

"Then let me do what I know."

Standing tall on her tiptoes, she hooked her forearms around his neck and kissed him. The kiss was possessive and strong, fearful and yearning. If anyone saw, they said nothing—not that Mal would've cared. He held Avyi in his arms, tasting her and touching her as if this would be the last time. Who could tell what went on in that tipped-over mind of hers? She might very well know that this was the last time. She'd never tell him. That thought made him tighten his arms around her lower back, holding her flush against him, unyielding.

No matter what happened in the next few hours, he would not lose this woman. His feelings were too strong. She was too precious. And they would never be as powerful separately as they were together. With a final sweep of his tongue over hers, he gently pushed her shoulders until she returned to the firm footing of her sturdy boots. Armed and fierce, she was the warrior with the most unpredictable gift, least useful for combat, but with skills and determination he doubted could be matched.

"Yes," she whispered against his mouth. She stole one more quick kiss. "Lead us, Giva. It's your right and your duty."

When the guards entered the holding pen, he and another pair of Tigony built on one another's gifts until the pens disintegrated. Not melted. Simply . . . evaporated under the strike of so much potent energy. Human guards in SWAT-style armor, bearing their napalm rifles and Tasers, stood in stunned awe for the few seconds the Dragon Kings needed. Avyi had done her best to reach as many as she could through the wire pens, using her sister's Dragon idol to free the captives from their debilitating collars.

In the crush that followed, Mal lost sight of her. She was consumed by the crowd of Dragon Kings still eager to have their gifts returned to them. He needed to trust that she would claw her way free of any danger. He'd seen her do it before.

A few brutes who refused to go along with Mal's plan of rebellion were subdued by Indranan. The telepaths held each in a state of immobility, trapped within their own minds, until they could be restrained by collars and manacles. The sight was sickening—immobilizing his own people—but Mal couldn't have dissenters as they took on the greatest battle in the modern history of the Dragon Kings.

At least he'd kept his temper when those dissenters fought back. He was the Giva. He was, on occasion, called on to become judge, jury, and executioner. But there was relief in knowing they could quickly find a way to subdue foes within their own ranks without needing to inflict the ultimate punishment.

Among those freed, only a few scrounged up Dragon-forged swords. The human cartels possessed no more than a dozen of the rare weapons between them, assembling them for the Grievance and reusing them for each new match. This would be a matter of skill, suppression, and crowd control, not the metal forged in the fires of the Dragon's high Chasm in the Himalayas. Their human opponents could die in so many different ways.

Together, Mal led the way up a sloping ramp that lifted up and up toward the shouts of an eager crowd. They were approaching the arena floor. The conflict should be an easy one. They were fifty strong. A hundred times that many humans would be no match for the combined purpose of so many Dragon Kings.

He burst into the arena, feeling more assured and in the moment than he ever had before. Not even when lying with Avyi had he been this much *himself*.

Yet those around him began to scream. Some dropped to their knees, clutching their heads.

Mal groaned as pain slammed through his brain and down his spine. He fell to his knees, although he never let go of his sword. That precious weapon might as well be welded to his palm. He looked to his left, where Cadmin's eyes bulged and her face contorted. Her eyes pleaded for answers.

"Let the games begin," came a booming voice.

The voice of Old Man Aster. He was laughing with a sick rattle in his throat. Mal had only met the man once, when he'd observed his first Grievance, when he'd thought so foolishly that the cartels could be reasoned with. Tricksters at work, although the Old Man was even more skilled in that respect.

"The entire arena is wired to cause this agony. You will fight one another. *Fight*. No conception as your prize this time, you beasts. Just the right to crawl back into our service. If you kill another Dragon King, you will have your collar returned to you and your place within each cartel restored. The collars will end the agony you feel now." He laughed again. "Why take one fight at a time when we can watch four dozen of these beasts fight to the death. Do you agree?"

The crowd cheered with wild screams. Some of the Garnis and even a few Pendray cried out when the powerful shouts hit their heightened senses. Indranan rolled into tight balls, elbows clutched over their ears, screaming. To be on the receiving end of that much hostility must be crippling. That left the Sath, the Tigony, and a few more resilient Pendray who'd already worked themselves into berserker furies. Already they were confronting each other for possession of the few Dragon-forged swords.

That meant they all still retained their powers. They needed to fight the pain, not one another.

Mal was heartsick. He'd led his people with such authority—into what? A trap. A fiendish plot by the cartels. Avyi might have been right in that this looked to be the last Grievance. How many Dragon Kings would remain when the bloodshed ended?

He battled the split-ax feeling in his mind and staggered to his feet. Never had he fought a stronger foe. The pain was beyond comprehension, beyond limits. Yet his reflexes remained, if he concentrated past the temptation to black out. He swung his sword in time to stop a Pendray from cutting his way through a huddled trio of shrieking, defenseless Indranan. He cut the Pendray's arm clean off, but he swore, as he looked into the crazed man's animalistic eyes, that he would not kill one of his own kind. The cartels would not force the Giva to stoop to their sick games.

He would only do what he could to stem the tide of violence.

Which didn't feel like much as he stumbled back two steps and briefly surveyed the arena.

A cheer went up when a Tigony—older than Mal, who would've participated in the secret ritual at Bakkhos—beheaded a young Sath woman. Her features so resembled Orla's that for a moment, Mal's veins iced over. But it wasn't Orla. That barely dimmed Mal's fury, especially when his clansman strode toward an awaiting human at the far side of the arena. The human must've been from the Kawashima cartel, because his finery was distinctly Far Eastern, with so many colors and, to Mal's sickened mind, ironically covered in embroidered dragons.

The Tigony man was collared by a nearby guard. Relief washed over his face. The absence of pain. Mal envied that relief, but his fury was even greater.

The man's powers had been stripped. He'd voluntarily become a slave again.

Heedless of sense, Mal raced toward the smirking murderer. They clashed swords. Mal battled the burning anguish that threatened to split his skull in two. How he managed to keep fighting was beyond his ability to comprehend. It was as if his body knew what some distant part of his mind desperately believed: that this was a desperate fight against more than a single member of Clan Tigony. This was a fight to save their entire race.

If others saw this man rewarded for killing—in a sick, roundabout way—they would follow. The cartels would have the bloodbath they craved.

Mal swung to the left, spun, and brought the pommel of the sword down on the Tigony man's nose. Blood erupted from his broken face. He dropped his own sword to cover the scarlet injury. Mal jumped on him, straddled him, and shouted past the pain. "Who did you kill in Bakkhos? Your lover or the virgin you were privileged with defiling?"

"The virgin," the man snarled. "She begged for more, until she begged for her life. You have been the worst of our clan for decades, and you're the worst of our people."

Mal slammed the pommel down again, breaking fingers, busting teeth. "You shame the Dragon."

For the first time, he meant it. He believed in the Dragon, completely, and knew this Tigony bastard represented everything cruel and wrong about their evolution as a race. Perhaps they were dying out for a reason. They profaned the Dragon. They turned their back on the creature that had given them life and extraordinary gifts.

What had Avyi said? She'd said it so often . . .

The Chasm isn't fixed.

"Malnefoley!"

He jerked his head toward the sound of a determined female voice.

Cadmin stood only a few dozen meters away. She held the bow and quiver he and Avyi had journeyed so far to bring to this young warrior. She'd drawn an arrow, no matter that her face was bloody and she held most of her weight on her right foot. The left arm holding the bow shook from where the bone had been crushed.

She aimed into the crowd, directly at the thrice-cursed Indranan witch named Ulia.

§ CHAPTER §
TWENTY-FIVE

The more often Avyi was right in her predictions, the more fearful she became. It shouldn't be that way. It should've been an affirmation of years of doubt and blind faith. It should've been her gift flying in the face of all that was natural or expected or within the realm of belief.

That wasn't the case now. As Cadmin fulfilled the vision Avyi had seen for the entirety of the young warrior's life, fear was all Avyi felt. Bow lifted, Cadmin fired an arrow straight into the crowd. The first pegged a human in the thigh. Only then did Avyi see Cadmin's target.

Ulia.

The old crone had the arena entirely encased in crippling agony.

She was practically another of Dr. Aster's pets, a former Cage warrior who'd lost a leg and retired to a comfortable life as a thrice-cursed Indranan. She'd murdered her brother and sister, in the sick tradition of the Indranan, in order to take their gifts into her own body. She was the most powerful telepath Avyi had ever met, with the ability to twist minds—and, it seemed, to focus her sick gift on dozens of Dragon Kings at a time.

Avyi had long feared that Ulia would see into her

thoughts and discover the secrets she harbored against Dr. Aster on behalf of the unborn and the tortured. Ulia never did. Avyi's only reasoning was that she had played the part so well, down to the basics of every thought, that she never registered as a threat. It was nauseating now to think she had been that able to subdue the best parts of herself.

She blinked once, then again, through the dust kicked up by the fighting. Her gut snapped taut in fear. By the old woman's side, Dr. Aster grinned his sick, knowing grin . . . directly at Avyi.

Ulia trained her sight-beyond-sight on Malnefoley. He collapsed onto the ground, writhing, shouting in the ancient language of the Tigony.

She raced to Mal. He looked up at her with an utter lack of recognition. Avyi flinched and jumped back. She didn't know the Tigony language, but what he spouted made his words feel like needles. His blue eyes were not his. They were owned by someone—some*thing*—else, namely a one-legged demon who did the bidding of Avyi's former master.

She tried one more time to reach the man she loved. Yet he was a vessel for some other being. He was the personification of rage and selfish hatred. Was this what he'd been that day at Bakkhos? Were those the memories Ulia was exploiting to turn Mal into something bestial and unthinking?

"Cadmin! Please! Try again, my young one. Try again. Save our Giva!"

The warrior's face was warped with so much pain, from the shock waves of anguish that radiated over the floor of the arena, and from the injuries she'd sustained at the hands of her own cartel's fighters. But she held the bow steady, with more determination on her face than Avyi had ever seen.

But she *had* seen it. This was the moment when Cadmin fired an arrow into the crowd at the person who had orchestrated the attempts on Mal's life. At the Asters' bidding, Ulia would've been able to track Mal across the world. He never would've been safe, and neither would the leadership of the Dragon Kings. The Asters had predicted exactly what method to use when it came to bringing the whole of free Dragon King society crumbling down.

In this case, Avyi's predictions were far more accurate.

Cadmin incapacitated Ulia with a sure, pure shot through the witch's throat. The old woman gagged and clutched. Those around her, even Dr. Aster, backed away. Some screamed, knowing now that the Dragon Kings could come after them.

This was no longer an entertaining bit of blood sport. This was death on the prowl.

The Dragon Kings, driven to near-madness by the pain Ulia had inflicted, looked dazed when they came back into themselves. Skirmishes slowed, then stopped, as they realized there was no longer a need to fight—not for survival, not for glory, and certainly not for the cartels. Some fled the arena floor in favor of the stands, where human spectators ran in screaming hordes.

Avyi could not watch the bloodshed. She understood her people's wrath, and how greatly some of the humans assembled there in Battersea deserved to die, yet she was unable to take any pleasure in vengeance. Her goals had always been more complicated, whereas her loves and hates had always been so simple.

One such love was Cadmin. She fell to her knees. Instead of running to comfort her, Avyi landed a round-house kick to the face of the nearest human guard. His armor meant the impact of the kick reverberated up Avyi's leg, but she spun at the waist and, with ambidex-trous skill, hit him from the other direction. She swept his calf and jabbed her switchblade in the exposed places where the armor latched but didn't completely protect: the wrist, the back of the knee, the leather of his boot's upper padding, and finally, when the man doubled over, she stabbed the back of his neck.

She snatched up the damping collar he held and raced back to Cadmin. "Your injuries are already bad enough," she said. "Wear this."

"What about my powers?"

"They'll be taken from you. Your choice, my young one."

"I'm not a Dragon King without my gift. This is the first time I've felt my fury gathering. It's pure. I want it, even if it means pain, too."

Avyi bent swiftly and kissed her first babe's forehead. "I knew you would be strong. I never knew you would be *this* strong."

Cadmin touched Avyi's cheek. "Mother before my mother. Save our Giva?"

"Now that you've done your part, absolutely."

She turned to find a sight out of her deepest, most terrifying nightmares. Dr. Aster. Standing over Malne-foley. He held the Dragon-forged sword.

All she could count as a blessing was that Ulia's incapacitation had allowed Mal to return to himself, with his blue eyes clear and full of the shining intelligence and canny skill she'd come to respect so dearly. But was it a blessing? To see her lover returned just in time to have his head wrenched back by the one man in the world she hated the most?

Yes. A blessing. Because with her gaze alone, she told Mal what she could not with words.

We both knew this was coming.

Roughly fifty years old, but still sickeningly handsome with a smile made of distilled charisma, he locked eyes with Avyi. "My Pet in a duel to the death. I imagine you've waited for this for years."

"No." A part of her heart ripped in two. But only a part of it—a single vulnerable edge where old memories of this man still lived. "I waited for years for you to change. I didn't want this." She nodded toward the grip the doctor had on Malnefoley's scalp, the sword poised over his vulnerable neck. The doctor was within cutting distance of killing the man who had helped make Avyi into a woman. Who had made her *Avyi*. "I didn't want to face you, until you threatened this man's life. It's always been inevitable. Only now, I'll enjoy it."

"Is this love, my Pet? For your selfish, useless Giva?"

"Not the kind of love you expected from me."

"Then, my dearest prophet, you've probably seen this, too."

He angled the Dragon-forged sword down and across. Avyi screamed and lunged. Blood covered her shirt. She was temporarily blinded with the sight of it, such a brilliant scarlet, so terribly, terribly red. The doctor's mirthless laugh rang out around them.

Her hands were slippery when she grabbed the hilt of the sword and pulled it free of Dr. Aster's weaker grip. She swung her right hand, connecting brass to jaw. He grunted. Bone on bone made a grating sound. She hit him again and again, as years of rage welled up in her like a never-ending spring and came bubbling out in a flailing geyser.

When she stopped, breathless, she looked down at the fallen form of her former master. His face was devastated. What she hadn't expected was the crushed-open cavity of his chest and the compound fractures along his thighs. For a moment, she'd become like a Pendray in the throes of a berserker fury. No memory of the violence. Just the possession of it and being possessed by it.

Aster stared up at her with eyes that barely held life. He grinned, toothless and bloody, and laughed until he coughed. Avyi adjusted her grip on the sword and swung in a clean, downward arc. The doctor's head rolled across the arena's sandy ground.

"Av . . . yi . . ."

"Mal!"

She screamed his name again, dropping to her knees as if in prayer. His throat was cut. So deeply. Oh, Dragon be, he had come within mere inches of death, and there was no certainty that death had loosed its final hold.

Three prophecies in succession. Cadmin. Her fight with the doctor. The attempt on Mal's life. They were coming faster, faster. Her stomach was a twist of acid as the copper scent of blood filled her nostrils, like a noxious poison intended to drive her mad.

A shout in the ancient, shared language of the

Dragon Kings rang out from the amplifier Old Man Aster had used.

She looked up and saw a familiar figure high atop one of Battersea's four smokestacks.

Tallis, of Clan Pendray. The Heretic.

Dragon Kings who had finished their grim work in the stands had either fled into the night or gathered on the arena floor. A flood of familiar faces were among them. Leto of Garnis waded through the warriors with astonishing speed and agility, divesting everyone of deadly swords.

But the fact that Malnefoley gagged beneath the pressure of her hands was all that mattered. With damage to his neck so severe—nearly beheaded by the doctor—would there be any saving him now?

She cursed the Dragon. She threw every word in every language to the sky, furious that the being she had trusted and believed in when others abandoned their faith had forsaken her now. He had given her a gift unique to their people, and that gift had shown her three visions yet to come.

One was Mal burning.

One was the shadow of the dragon over Battersea.

And one was she and Mal in love.

It seemed none would come true, as his blood flowed between her fingers and his mouth went slack.

All around Malnefoley was red. Red everywhere. He tried to find Avyi, with her night-black hair and eyes as gold as a cat's. He wanted to find her bewitching smile-that-wasn't-a-smile and the resilient way she moved forward with each step, knowing each step could lead her to a dismal future.

He wanted her.

"Mal," she cried, from such a distance.

At least the pain in his head had subsided. The red wasn't a physical color so much as a picture of himself from very high above. He was outside of his body, as if he'd suddenly assumed an Indranan's telepathic powers and could see the damage the doctor had wrought.

He was going to die.

There was no way to survive a cut as deep as the one that slashed across his throat.

Avyi was there. He could see her from as far away as he could hear her distant, desperate voice.

"You can't leave yet." Her hands were pressed tight around his gash, but wouldn't stop the inevitable. "Do you hear me? I have three visions left, Malnefoley of Tigony, and two of them involve you. Neither reveals you dying by that bastard's slice. So you hold on. Hold on!"

She called to other Dragon Kings, whose names rattled through Mal's brain like marbles rolling across hardwood floors. He was losing it, losing himself.

Losing Avyi.

No.

He concentrated on how she held him in her lap, and how her hands grasped him with the strength of a desperate woman. She was trembling. Or was that him? Maybe they trembled together, as the future lapped at their heels. Only this wasn't a gentle tide. This was an oncoming storm, sent to sweep them away too soon.

He wasn't ready.

"What . . . visions . . . ?"

She leaned nearer. "Don't talk. Don't you dare. Here, you, help me." Another woman joined them, kneeling in a swirl of golden silks. "What's your name?"

"Kavya," she said.

Avyi stilled. "The Sun?"

"That's right," came another familiar voice. Mal was having trouble piecing voices to faces to memories. But this one was unmistakable.

"Heretic," Mal rasped.

"I said shut up!" Avyi squeezed harder, as if to emphasize her point. "You're an Indranan, yes? Tallis, can she be trusted?"

Tallis of Pendray laughed tightly. "The Pet is asking me? The irony is thick in this place."

Mal tried to find a sword with his free hand. "Name's . . . Avyi."

"What this Dragon-damned fool is trying to say is that I'm no longer the Pet. My name is Avyi, and I need your help. Both of you." Mal felt more hands tighten around his neck. "Is Nynn here? Can you find her?"

"She's here," Kavya said. Mal liked *the Sun* better, because she glowed with the radiance of the sun he would never see again. "But what you're thinking . . . Why not just use another Tigony?"

"There are things about their clan that can't be trusted."

"That's rich," the Heretic snorted. "The mighty, vaunted Tigony? With ghosts in their closets? I never would've guessed."

"He's not thinking very kind thoughts about you right now, Tallis, dear. Do be quiet."

"Here, hold his hands in place." That from Avyi. Another woman's hands laced fingers with his and applied more pressure. "Kavya, I need you to do what you can to enter his mind. Can you do that? Are you willing?"

"Yes."

"With my help before, he used his gift to cauterize a wound in his own shoulder. I need more precision than that. I need . . ." She gasped and inhaled two quick breaths. "I need a miracle."

"I'll try," said Kavya.

Mal tried to focus on her face, but she was shining. He squinted.

Nynn arrived. Mal could smell her. Strange that his senses were more acute, even as pain obliterated physical sensation and muddled his thoughts. He couldn't remember why he and his cousin had fallen out, why he hadn't ever met her late husband or her son, Jack. It seemed another reason why dying right then, in Avyi's arms, was to shortchange a life.

No, more than one life. He found a tickling trail of reason. If he died . . . if they had assassinated him . . . there would be repercussions.

There would not be another Giva. No one would send their precious, rare children. The entirety of the Dragon King culture would collapse without a leader, even a leader as flawed as he had been. As flawed as he would continue to be. All he could do was make decisions and hope for the best possible outcomes.

He'd chosen to trust Avyi. He'd chosen to make love

to her. He'd chosen so many skewed paths in order to stay with her. Long enough to fall in love with her.

"Nynn, you need to help him," Avyi said. "I don't know if he has enough strength or control, even with Kavya to guide him."

"Dragon be, we need a sword and someone to say his funeral rites." Nynn was blunt, but tears clogged her throat.

Avyi lunged for the woman. "I won't give up on him! You need to help me. Help me fix the Chasm. It starts here with Mal!"

"Get off of me, you freak," Nynn growled. "The last time I saw you, you were Aster's latex-clad footstool."

The women tussled until Nynn was unceremoniously hauled up, onto her feet. "Enough," came the rough command of her partner, Leto. "The Chasm isn't fixed. She's said it. Others we've met have heard it in dreams. If this isn't a moment to trust in each other and the Dragon, there never will be."

Nynn sank to her knees. She joined with Avyi, their hands around his neck. Kavya's slipped into his mind.

Concentrate, Giva. We need you to live.

What were her visions? Ask her.

Avyi asked, "Ready?"

"Wait." Kavya spoke up. "He wants to know what your visions are."

Avyi shook her head. She was wild and frantic now, when Mal wanted to reassure her . . . of what, he couldn't say. "We don't have time."

"I get the feeling he won't cooperate until he hears them."

"No, I won't say." She slid her hands up to hold his

cheeks. Mal struggled to open his eyes. He found her green-on-gold waiting for him, with that raven-dark hair haloed by the bright lights circling Battersea. "I won't tell you a thing until you come back to me. That means paying attention to other people, for once, and doing your job. That means using your Dragon-damned gift to save yourself!"

Kavya slipped into his mind again. She found him like a child and held his hand, until he was able to actually see himself from above. It wasn't imagination. He could see through her eyes. He understood that through her, he was to communicate where to place their fingers—and his.

Mal cried out as the powerful women converged on him. Nynn's firecracker electric shock slid into the base of his brain like a knife, but Kavya was there to defend conscious thought from the pain. He smelled the sizzle of his flesh. He felt the tremble of his legs. There was no controlling this. He was as helpless as a baby being born, pulled through into the unknown, shrieking as the comforts of his old life were ripped away, one by one.

He lost Kavya. Her reassuring calm slipped away until he was left with his own panicking thoughts. Avyi screamed and pressed harder, but her fingers slipped in the blood. Kavya wrapped bloody hands around her head in obvious pain. "He's going. I can't stay with him. I'm sorry."

"You can't go, you stubborn *lonayíp* bastard," Avyi shouted, her lips brushing his with humid sweetness. "I've seen us in love. Do you know that? That's why it wasn't right before. We were lovers, but we weren't in love. I love you, and you're not leaving me until you can say it back and *stay* with me."

Across what must've been a hundred miles, he found his cousin's face. "Light it up, firecracker. I want to go out in a blaze . . . like our creator."

❦ CHAPTER ❦
TWENTY-SIX

Avyi had never felt anything like the power Nynn could summon. She and Mal had to be the two most powerful Dragon Kings on the planet.

Only, Avyi hated Nynn in that moment, when the woman began to conjure a ball of kinetic fireworks between her hands. Her partner, Leto, held her by the waist. Whether it was to ground Nynn for what was to come, or to protect her from Avyi's mounting anger—who knew?

But the hatred in Avyi's heart was as real as any gift, and so much more real than the Dragon that had failed her so completely. What manner of creature tempted her with a life beyond pain and torture, only to let her feel Mal's lifeblood flowing like a river between her fingers? Even their combined efforts hadn't been enough to repair severed bone, arteries, veins, and delicate nerves. Tallis wrenched Avyi's hands away from Mal's increasingly cold skin. She cried out, thrashing, swinging her brass-encased knuckles, trying everything to get back to his side.

She was practically useless when held captive by a Pendray and his Indranan lover. Tallis's arms, crisscrossed around her torso, were like bands of the thickest, most immutable steel. Kavya touched her mind, so subtly, trying to calm Avyi with a feeling of sunshine and hope.

She pushed past Kavya's ministrations. Her anguish overflowed. She was insensate with grief like she'd never known. Even seeing the painful destinies of the unborn she helped bring into the world couldn't compare. She couldn't take her eyes off Mal's mangled throat and, worse still, his expression that so resembled peace that she almost believed he was destined to be accepted back into the Great Dragon's fold, a soul forgiven no matter its sins. But that was the expression of a man who'd stopped fighting. He was her warrior, her Giva, her only love.

He couldn't stop fighting, and neither did she when she snarled and kicked Tallis. A few of her desperate swings connected with skin and bone. He grunted, cursing as ferociously as she did—a different kind of comfort than what Kavya offered.

Every Dragon King who remained in that crumbling power station was mourning. They all knew what Mal's death would mean.

She was heartsick as Nynn's bubble of energy grew and grew. For the first time, Avyi knew one of her surest predictions was not going to come true. It was betrayal upon betrayal. Her heart was cracking open for more than the death of Malnefoley. What would become of their people?

And who would she be after he was gone? There was nothing about herself she could ever trust again. She'd be a madwoman possessed by visions she couldn't trust.

They might as well throw her in a fathomless pit and seal it with a metal lid to block out the sun. There, she wouldn't be able to spread her poisonous hope to anyone else.

Slowly, as Nynn began to lose reality in favor of a trancelike swaying, the others backed away from Mal's motionless body.

Tallis pulled Kavya to a distant corner, holding her with his chin tucked against her crown. The other rebels and the freed Dragon Kings took shelter.

With the lethargy of a nightmare, Avyi stood and walked around Malnefoley. She touched two fingers to her lips and reached them toward his forehead, as if she could press that kiss to his sheet-white flesh. From there she walked to where the Dragon-forged sword had fallen during their contest against Dr. Aster. She gripped it with sticky fingers, the color of which turned her stomach to acid. Mal's blood.

He wanted to go out in a blaze, burned like the Great Dragon after it had given birth to the Five Clans before diving back into the fiery Chasm of its own birth. But fire wouldn't kill Mal. He was still a Dragon King, after all. Only beheading him—charred and bloodless—would finish the job. Only beheading him would put him out of abject misery.

Avyi would be the one to do it.

Nynn moaned. Leto waved Avyi away. "Go! You can't survive this!"

"And you?"

He kissed Nynn's neck and whispered something in her ear, something Avyi would never know. Nynn's eyes rolled shut. Leto let her go, then grabbed Avyi's free hand. He pulled her into a crevice along the arena wall. "I hated you once," he said roughly. "And I sure as fuck didn't trust you. Now . . . I'm sorry. This is an end for us. But you can't believe it's *the end*. None of us can, or we might as well drop to the ground and wait for time or the humans to take us. I won't believe that. I won't let that happen to me or Nynn or our baby."

"Baby?" Avyi whispered, chilled to her marrow.

"Nynn is expecting." Whatever joy he possessed was tempered by the solemnity of the moment. "I don't know . . ." He swallowed thickly. He smelled of sweat and blood—that of the Cage warrior he'd been raised from birth to become, only to be freed by Nynn's love and devotion. "I don't know what this will do to her or the babe. But she's doing it for him. Any of us would if we could."

The light surrounding Nynn was overwhelming, until the women disappeared in the glaze of their gifts. Nynn screamed in release as the bubble burst with a blaze of blinding color. She obliterated what remained of the deeply recessed arena. Leto used his armor to protect Avyi, but she refused the arm that he tried to use to cover her eyes. She was not missing a second of this, no matter how it burned her eyes.

The Dragon.

The dragon from her prophecy.

The heat of the explosion Nynn conjured paled compared to the spectacle. Great wings pushed a wash of steaming flame into the arena. It circled like a whirlwind above the power station. Fire ripped across the makeshift bleachers until they were hewn of sparks and cinders. Massive teeth bared in a grimace that looked like a parody of a smile. A snakelike tongue lolled just before an unearthly roar mixed with a banshee's screech split Avyi's ears. Leto collapsed at her feet, holding his ears and moaning, his senses overloaded.

Avyi had nearly forgotten that particular vision, where the Grievance wouldn't simply be the last ever held, where Cadmin needed her bow and arrows, and where a dragon flew across the night sky and breathed the fire of legend.

On his knees, Leto murmured something in the ancient language of the Dragon Kings, the language that predated what had developed uniquely among each of the Five Clans. In human myths, it would be their language before the fall of Babel. Only, Avyi heard the words and knew, deep in her heart, what Leto said.

"The Great Dragon. It is risen. It lives."

Avyi watched in fascinated horror as the dragon assumed the five shapes known to the clans. It circled the power station with another magnificent screech of bone-shaking ferocity. Dragon Kings dropped in reverence when, finally, it assumed its true form. Elements of each of the Five Clans' interpretations could be seen. It had a forked tongue that jutted out from a sharp, angular face that was lined with overlapping scales. Each scale shimmered with color that moved and bent depending on the glint of the light.

Four powerful wings gave its flight a staggering grace. It could've been swimming rather than flying, so easily did it move through the skies.

Awed, Avyi stepped past Leto and walked to where Nynn lay dazed on her back. Leto joined them both within seconds. Together they pulled the woman out of harm's way, although instinctively, Avyi knew none of them would be harmed by the Great Dragon—because, oh, it truly was the Great Dragon risen.

She still held the sword that she'd intended to use on Malnefoley, to put his body and mind out of the prolonged misery that would hold a Dragon King until he or she was beheaded. But her eyes were playing tricks on her. Her mind was failing her. Because as the Dragon flew overhead, she looked for Mal's body.

He should've been a charred mass of writhing flesh, bloodless now, and waiting for death.

Instead, his body was gone.

Avyi looked up. Her head spun with promises of prophecy.

The man she loved circled Battersea with a glorious flick of his three-pronged tail and serpentine body. The man she loved had become the most powerful being in all creation.

He raged and twisted and burned.

He breathed out and felt the stinging delight of fire ripping free of his mouth.

And apparently, he had chores to attend to.

Watching Mal fly free was the most excruciatingly beautiful thing she'd ever see. He was the elements and eternity. With another twist, he spun over the makeshift arena.

Swooping down, he grazed the topmost edge of the seating reserved for the audience. Avyi scanned the line of seating and with an amazing clarity of sight, saw Mal's target. The Old Man. She would know that grizzled face anywhere, with evil that shone from unrepentant eyes. An easy, gorgeous flap of wings made flicking shadows of the bright arena lights, but then there were no more shadows. With a gusting exhalation, fire and smoke burst from between bared teeth. Old Man Aster shrieked, but his was nothing to the screaming anger of the Dragon.

"What's happening?" shouted Orla, the woman once known as Silence. Now she had the strongest voice among the dozens assembled. "Avyi!"

"I don't know!"

She had cursed her gift as often as she'd valued it. Only now did she realize how much she had depended on its presence in her life. This moment was unprecedented. She genuinely didn't know what was going on, which was made all the more terrifying because Mal was at the heart of the confusion.

The Heretic, Tallis of Pendray, appeared at her side. His expression was stony. Only his eyes moved, following the skyward path of the dragon. "The Dragon is supposed to die in the fires of the Chasm. He has a long way to fly to reach Nepal."

A shiver wracked Avyi's body. The Chasm wasn't fixed, and perhaps it wouldn't be until the most powerful Giva in centuries asserted the full extent of his strength and leadership. Nestled high in the Himalayas, the Chasm was thousands of miles away. She could imagine this beautiful creature strong enough to make such a journey—and die upon its completion. Was that what their people needed? Did they need Mal to die in order for their kind to endure?

Her stomach pinched.

The Dragon roared. Rippling grace surged through his muscled, serpentine body. Three forked tails balanced through every banking turn as he sailed through the air. He breathed out another gust of fire.

Mal circled higher and higher in a spiraling arc above Battersea. Fires in the arena glinted off his iridescent scales—the only way Avyi could see him as he flew up into the night.

Tallis shook his head. Kavya appeared equally troubled. "He may be right," she said. "What if he's not coming back?"

Avyi shook her head, at a loss for words. Not only were her predictions gone—or outright wrong—she couldn't even order her thoughts. This wasn't happening. She'd seen so much of the impossible, but those impossible things had never threatened such a heart-wrenching love.

Orla reached out with her free hand. Avyi took it, gratefully, and watched as others joined them in a loose circle.

Hark was standing gingerly at Orla's side, balancing on his injured leg. "You know how the Sath have secrets? We're gossip pack rats, keeping them like treasures."

"Do we need your chatter?" Leto glared from the other side of the circle, where Nynn leaned heavily against him, with her arm wrapped around his middle.

Orla took up her partner's tale, speaking in monotone. "A powerful Giva is destined to rise in times of crisis, standing tall, to end the squabbling and renew our people. When the wrongs are righted, he returns home as he has a dozen times before. It's a cycle. What's that old saying? What was once will happen again. Then the Chasm is fixed."

"And," Hark added, "it just so happens that the ancient Sath word for *dragon* is *Giva*."

Tallis practically snarled. "My ass."

Hark shrugged, but his expression was clear and intent. "I never gave it much credence. But whispers among the Leadership make a lot more sense when Malnefoley is flying over London."

"No!" Avyi found her voice with a vengeance. She broke free of comforting hands and stared up where, she hoped, a glittering dragon circled far overhead. "We are the Children of the Dragon. We are those young voices on the edge of the Chasm, calling out to choose our Giva. He belongs with us. He belongs with *me*."

A glint of green, then blue, then red shimmered and grew larger as it swooped earthward. Avyi's pulse leapt. Suddenly he was upon them, flying dangerously low. He shrieked. Bricks shook loose from the power station. Dragon Kings ran for cover.

"Stay!" She lunged and caught Kavya's arm. "Two from every clan. He needs us all. *Please!*"

Dragon Kings emerged from the shadows. No . . . the ones who volunteered didn't creep. They *strode*. They were not ready to give up on this life or on their Giva. They were not afraid.

Avyi joined the others in a circle. Until . . .

A circle of ten. Fires surrounded them and wove between them. They were implacable amid a roaring inferno that rivaled the Chasm itself.

She dropped to her knees. "Malnefoley of Tigony! We choose you!"

Love and groundless hope fueled her words until shout after shout rubbed her throat raw. The other nine in their circle joined her in the chant. It was unearthly. It was ancient and terrifying. She couldn't breathe or think, and when she chanced on the memory of how she and Mal had moved together when making love, she used it to shout even louder.

Avyi was unafraid of the beast who circled with such grace and shimmering life. But in her heart, she traded one truth for another. She had been right all her life in believing in the Great Dragon. All the myths were true. Her gift had not led her astray . . . except for one prediction that would haunt her for the rest of her days.

She would never be given the chance to live her life with Malnefoley of Tigony.

Her Giva.

Mal.

Perhaps she'd been wrong, all those endless hours ago, when they'd been tangled together in the utter, untouchable peace that followed their joining. Perhaps that was all the time they would be allowed.

She'd simply wanted more.

Now she would be a woman without a partner. She would not be buried for life, half mad, untrusted and feared and hated. She would simply be a woman who mourned what had briefly, so briefly, been hers.

Still, she chanted with all of her voice and every beat of her heart. Former enemies who had become friends—even an odd sort of family—did the same.

The Dragon faltered. His tails tangled. His wings flapped without rhythm. His great head lolled from side to side with a scream of what sounded like pain. A shot of flame was only a puff against the darkness, not like the ten-meter gusts of flame that had left the heads of the cartels in piles of dust. He spasmed and hunched, rolling into the massive banners of the various cartels. Tangled in those banners, he crashed through walls, steam stacks, seats, and charred concrete, until he was simply . . .

Falling.

✤ CHAPTER ✤
TWENTY-SEVEN

There was no Chasm to catch his body. There were only the dying fires that charred the arena floor.

Avyi screamed her lover's name.

The others scattered as the giant body fell and fell. They gasped as it disappeared into the flames. The greatest being on earth hit the ground with a thud that made Avyi scream again. A gust of smoke obliterated the fires, leaving a small crater at the center of Battersea. The concussive force of the impact tossed the Dragon Kings to the ground.

The others dragged themselves upright, looking dazed and worn. On her knees, Avyi found Mal's sword and pulled it behind her, fearing that after all he'd undergone, she would still need to swing that deadly blade—be it against a man or a dragon. Without the Chasm, how would the Dragon die? Or had this been its final act?

Heart pounding a jumbled rhythm in her throat, she climbed down into the smoking crater. Knees unsteady, eyes filling with tears that had nothing to do with the swirling cinders, she pulled back the white banner that concealed what she knew would be a bloody splatter.

Instead, she found Malnefoley. His body steamed in the cool night air.

She edged closer. "Mal?"

Avyi didn't dare believe, but the nearer she crept, and as more of the steam cleared away from his skin, she saw the truth she didn't dare believe.

He was alive.

Whole.

Unbroken.

Sprawled in a tangle of white banners, but otherwise nude.

She threw the sword aside and practically pounced. She examined his neck. Completely healed. He shimmered, as the Dragon had, but his skin was that of a man. He was her Malnefoley returned to her. Unless . . . .

"Mal?"

As when she'd hesitated so often—with Cadmin's arrows and her bow, and with Orla's Dragon idol—she couldn't force her hands to touch his body. There would be no pulse. No life. Not even a Dragon King could survive what he'd just endured.

Could he?

Knowing she owed it to him, and to herself, and to the unlikely love that had grown between them under the most trying circumstances, she forced herself to reach out. She touched the base of his throat. Only a few minutes before, that same throat had gushed with Mal's lifeblood. She still bore the stains in deep red arcs around her fingernails and in the crevices of her knuckles.

She gasped in surprise, cried out in relief and delight, and cast out the last thoughts of disbelief.

He was alive.

More than that, he radiated the intensity of a man in his prime. His heartbeat was vigorous and strong. Now that the steam had cleared, she could see every sign of life, where pulse points throbbed with the pump of blood. His bare, broad, muscled chest took in deep breaths and expelled them with equal force.

She threw herself down on his body, holding him, crying. She'd thought she had nothing left to give, but that had been the thought of a woman preparing for the worst—a poor and ineffective try at self-defense. Now she gave him her tears and sobs, her soft words and her angered ones. Mostly she gave him her touch, with unsteady fingertips and a mouth that wanted to taste every bit of him, just to add more certainty to what her senses told her.

"Mal," she said, ignoring the begging tone in her voice. "Malnefoley, you've come back to me. Please, my love. Open your eyes. My Giva, don't leave me now. Not after so much."

The familiar touch of his hand against the back of her head made her flinch, then shiver. Arms that were not that of a dying man but of a man reborn encircled her shaking body. "Do you see it now?" he asked.

He'd spoken. *Spoken.* But what did he mean?

"Tell me," she said. "What do I need to see?"

"Your vision. You and I together, tangled together in white. In love." He kissed her forehead. "Because I do love you, Avyi."

She looked down at where their legs intertwined. Of all things, the white banner of the Aster cartel was their sheet. She'd been right all along, but her interpretation had been skewed. Because, really, who could've read her vision this way? Who, even with her experience and faith, would've seen an image of them wound together as lovers and assume anything other than a bed, comfort, satisfaction?

Now she had the peace of knowing the last of her prophecies had been fulfilled.

"You love me?" she asked tentatively. So strange to be tentative now, but fear still triumphed. She was simply too stunned. She was barely used to living in the present, let alone one so astonishing as this.

"Of course I love you." He dipped his lips lower to kiss her mouth.

"You taste of . . ." She framed his face, the face of a man born to rule, but who'd never been more of a leader than when he lay there wrapped in the white banner of their mutual enemies. "You taste of smoke and fire."

"I've been busy. Now kiss me again."

She did, with all the love and emotion pent up in her chest. The taste of fire on his tongue was intoxicating. She had him back, not just as a man, but as a man who'd enacted and survived a miracle. She wanted more of that power until it filled her blood and washed her clean of fear.

"You were the Great Dragon," she whispered. "Do you remember it?"

"I was. I do." He shuddered and tried to sit up. Avyi pushed him down with an entreaty to rest. "I . . . Avyi, I fought him."

"How do you mean?"

"It was like—" He swallowed and gasped for a breath. She petted his chest and arms until he calmed.

"I was drunk on what it felt like to be this astonishing being. I was angry. I was greedy for more. But I wouldn't let it overtake me." Brushing loose hair from her temples and cheeks, he looked into her eyes. The stunning blue Avyi saw was clear and crisp and wholly Malnefoley. "I saw you standing here in the arena, unafraid. It was the first moment when I knew I could fight the temptation. And then the others . . ."

"I didn't know what else to do," she said. "It was all I could think of to bring you back to us. To me."

"It worked. I saw the circle—but it wasn't like the rigid traditions. Nynn, Leto, you—crossbred from the Five Clans. It was a coming together. Powerful. But . . ." This time he did sit up. His upper body appeared even stronger and more defined, with sharp ridges of muscle and unbreakable bones. "But mostly, I wanted to come home to you."

Malnefoley was able to stand, with Avyi's help, but then his body took over. He felt superhuman. No, that was the wrong term. He felt even more powerful than the strongest Dragon King that had ever lived.

"This has happened before, my Avyi," he said against her temple. She was wrapping the banner around his body.

"How do you mean?"

"I saw it all."

Others from the circle were gathering around, although Mal wanted them gone. He wanted Avyi to himself. He wanted time to process the mush the last hour had made of his head. But he could have neither . . . yet. He was the leader of the Dragon Kings, and they needed to know what he had experienced. As much of it, at least, as he could put into words.

"I saw Givas of old. Dragons of old. Each time our people became too decadent and too fractured, with the Five Clans as contentious as rabid animals, there has been a resurrection like . . ." He shook his head, almost unable to admit what had happened. "A resurrection like this."

"The Dragon has always been one of us?" asked Kavya. Mal could feel the quiet tapping of her mind inside his, as if looking for proof of what she'd witnessed— or proof that he was actually the same man returned to them.

That wasn't the case at all. He would never be the same man.

"I don't know about always," he said carefully. "There's always a start. But there are downward cycles, too. And there are, apparently, moments of rebirth."

"Told you," Hark said, grinning tiredly.

"But nothing has changed." Leto held Nynn, who still looked dazed. "You destroyed the cartel leaders, but that doesn't mean other human opponents won't spring up in their place. And who's to believe the tales that come out of this place?"

"We rebels are but fifty-odd," Orla added. "Leto is right. Of the few hundred of us left on the planet, who will believe what we witnessed here?"

Avyi's expression was distant. "I dreamed for decades of a time when I would no longer be plagued by visions of the future."

"And now?" Mal asked, his words intent.

"No more static and overlapping predictions." She

sounded so relieved that Mal smiled. He embraced her, holding tight, as emotion overwhelmed them both. They were free to be together without specters of distant fears to leave them wondering at the future, always around the corner.

"What does this have to do with making everyone else believe?" Tallis asked.

"Because I have a new vision for the future now. Only one."

Avyi gave Mal's hand a gentle squeeze before letting go. She walked to face Nynn, who eyed her warily. "I understand your hesitancy, just as I hope you can accept my apology. For . . . for so much."

Nynn nodded, her arm looped through Leto's— perhaps for support, but Mal doubted it was because she needed physical strength. "Will you . . . ?" She shook her head as if she couldn't believe her own thoughts. "Will you tell us about our baby?"

A collective gasp lifted from those gathered at the center of the arena. Even Mal felt his heartbeat speeding. Avyi looked unsurprised.

"I would be honored," she said softly.

Kneeling slowly, she lifted her hands toward the low slope of Nynn's stomach. Nynn's eyes widened until the whites were visible around pools of liquid aquamarine. The woman warrior was clad in soft leather lined with silk. With shaking hands, she lifted the front portion of her armor, which revealed a slim stretch of skin. She curved her free hand around her womb, so gently rounded, and nodded her encouragement. It was enough for Avyi. She slipped her fingers along that bare skin and closed her eyes.

Mal waited. Everyone did.

"She will fly," Avyi whispered. "That's what I see. Oh, Dragon be, she will be born healthy . . . and she will fly."

"What does that mean?" Leto's voice revealed just how close he was to losing his temper. Had he been in the same situation, Mal imagined he would react the same way. His woman and his child and their future, all unknown.

Avyi swayed on her heels. Mal caught her beneath the arms and once again pulled her into his embrace. She had always been a slight woman, but the energy still surging through his body made her featherlight. He held on even tighter.

"I saw her," she said. "I saw her flying in the company of other dragons."

Leto cursed under his breath. Then his gaze sharpened, pinned to Avyi's open, awed features. "But she will live? She will be born healthy?"

"Yes."

Leto rubbed his face in agitation. "That Nynn is pregnant at all is miracle enough."

Avyi smiled with the sleek, playful grace Mal remembered from their private moments together, there in the labyrinth on Crete. "As you say."

"It's time. Our people deserve more," Mal said firmly, taking control of the emotional scene. "That means relearning what it is to be Dragon Kings."

A sarcastic voice piped up. "You fucking Tricksters."

Mal turned to find another familiar smile. Hark, with his arm around Orla's shoulders, was grinning.

"We thought it was because of your silver-tongued way with human beings. But it's because you can fly around as the Great Dragon *and* pull off wearing a toga like it's come back in style . . . after a two-thousand-year absence from the haute couture runways."

Mal looked down. The way Avyi had wrapped the Aster banner around his naked body indeed resembled the white togas of ancient Greeks and Romans. A shiver snaked down his back, but he only returned the sarcastic bastard's smile. "You're jealous."

"Totally."

"Then." Kavya looked at the assembled faces. "What now? Nynn has had a child before. Maybe she's the only one."

"Or maybe . . . ." Avyi lifted her head to the sky, where smoke and ash obscured the lights of London. "Maybe she's just the first of many. Each of the Five Clans need their progeny. Imagine a sky full of our people, flying as high as the clouds. What was once will happen again . . ."

Mal took Avyi in his arms, face to face. They were so close that he could see every black lash and the way her nose turned up ever so slightly at the end. Her eyes shone more gold than green. "Did you see any of this?"

"Your neck slit. You burning." She wiped away a tear. "I lost my faith for those few minutes when you were dying. How could we love one another if I lost you?"

"Doubting yourself? That doesn't sound like you at all."

She tucked into his arms, nuzzling the flesh of his shoulder where they'd worked together to heal ravaged skin. Even that scar was gone. "Maybe I doubted because what I wanted was too overwhelming. I couldn't trust that my desires weren't obscuring my gift."

"Now you know better. And tell me, what do you want? What are your desires?"

She smiled almost shyly. "Simple, my Giva. My Malnefoley. Just you. For the rest of the time the Great Dragon grants us. As long as you believe in it now. That's absolutely mandatory."

"Of course I do. I'm still him."

Sobering, he kissed her with remarkable passion, as if they were alone rather than surrounded by fixed gazes. Then, just when Avyi was breathless for him and he was breathless for her, he stepped out of her firm, possessive hold. "I didn't transform back into a human and leave it behind. I'm something new. The Dragon didn't dive into the Chasm. He lives inside me. I think it's happened this way for thousands of years—moments of renewal."

Another few gasps gathered in Mal's ears. He wanted to shake off the truth, but it was as real as the love he felt for Avyi, this stubborn and undeniable half of his soul. "Come," he said to her, his hands out.

As brave as ever, she stepped into his embrace. Mal closed his eyes. Just before he released a modicum of control, he whispered against her mouth, "I love you, Avyi. That will never change. Do you know that now?"

"Yes."

Mal gripped her to his chest, then picked her up, his arms supporting her back and the bend beneath her knees. He expected pain as wings grew and tails shook loose, flicking in the night air. But no pain came. He moved easily from one form into another, as easily as inhaling the smell of Avyi's soft skin. Before he shed one body and gave himself up to another, he rasped against the mouth of the woman he adored, the woman who hadn't just made him into a better man but into a creature who could be man and dragon. Both. The true savior of their people.

"And you trust me?"

"Always, Malnefoley."

He smiled against her temple. "Then it's time for me to show you what it's like to fly."

CAGED WARRIOR

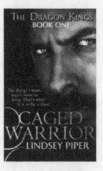

**Once worshipped as earthly gods, they now face extinction.
They fight underground in the Cages for the twisted pleasure of
humans, desperate to earn the chance to mate.**

Welcome to the brutal, erotic world of
The Dragon Kings . . .

Banished for falling in love with a human, Nynn of Clan
Tigony has been living quietly as a wife and mother. But when she
and her son are kidnapped and Nynn is sent to the Cages, she must
face her true warrior nature – and the magical birthright
she has tried to ignore . . .

Leto of Clan Garnis is a Cage warrior, using his superhuman speed
and reflexes to destroy all challengers. Within the Cages, he has had
no equal . . . until he is forced to train Nynn.

Nynn sees proud Leto as no better than a slave, whereas he
considers her a traitor. Forced to be allies, tormented by lust, the
sparks between them threaten to explode as they learn the high
price of honour in their violent underground domain.

BLOOD WARRIOR

The Dragon Kings were once worshipped as earthly gods. Centuries later and facing extinction, a brutal, tortured warrior and the woman who caused his downfall may be their only hope.

Tallis of Pendray's dreams are not his own. For decades he has suffered visions of a stunningly beautiful woman who uses his helpless desire for her body to force him into fulfilling her violent needs. His desperate craving has destroyed his family, his free will, and almost his sanity. When he finally tracks her down, he has one desire only: revenge.

To her followers, Kavya of Indranan is a peaceful saviour. When Tallis steals her, he throws her clan, and the whole future of the Dragon Kings, into lethal disarray. In truth, Kavya shares little but a name in common with his avowed enemy, and with her bloodthirsty, lethally powerful brother out for their blood, time is running out for them – and for their species.

There is one chance left. Suspicious, tortured Tallis must learn to trust Kavya – he must give everything, including his heart, to protect her – otherwise a war will come that will destroy them, and their kind, forever . . .

SILENT WARRIOR

**An exciting, emotionally charged prequel novella to the
Dragon Kings trilogy featuring warriors fighting for their lives
in violent cage matches to guarantee their clans' survival –
available exclusively as an ebook!**

A silent woman ashamed of her criminal background becomes a
Cage warrior to seek redemption.

An unrepentant fortune hunter will do anything to escape his
mounting debts.

Although rivals on the streets of Hong Kong, they find common
ground when seeking their clan's stolen idol, but for vastly different
reasons. Neither one suspects that love will begin when he becomes
the first man in five years to hear her speak.

*'The romance was brilliant; I swooned all over the place. I
thought they were amazing together, the chemistry was explosive
in and out of the bedroom.'* **Amazon US**

*'It has a Black Dagger Brotherhood by Ward feel to it. Rough,
handsome and hard Dragon Warriors with a lot of attitude and a
boat load of trouble following them around.'* **Amazon US**

*Need it? Want it? Buy it here:
http://www.piatkusentice.co.uk/ebooks/silent-warrior/*

Do you love fiction with a supernatural twist?

Want the chance to hear news about your favourite authors (and the chance to win free books)?

Keri Arthur
Kristen Callihan
P.C. Cast
Christine Feehan
Jacquelyn Frank
Larissa Ione
Darynda Jones
Sherrilyn Kenyon
Jayne Ann Krentz and Jayne Castle
Lucy March
Martin Millar
Tim O'Rourke
Lindsey Piper
Christopher Rice
J.R. Ward
Laura Wright

Then visit the Piatkus website and blog
www.piatkus.co.uk | www.piatkusbooks.net

And follow us on Facebook and Twitter
www.facebook.com/piatkusfiction | www.twitter.com/piatkusbooks

piatkus